TIME PURGE

Jeff –
Fuck Geoffs.

Visit the author's website at www.martina-fetzer.com.

Cover by okdoodle.net. Edited by Ellen Campbell.

If you purchased this book without a cover, be aware that your book is ugly and it is going to fall apart.

TIME PURGE

**

MARTINA FETZER

TABLE OF CONTENTS

CONTENT NOTE

This series is meant to be funny. Many of the characters have traumatic backgrounds and gruesome events sometimes happen, but none of these are described very graphically. That being said, content warnings for each book in the series are available at the author's website: martina-fetzer.com.

For reasons

RECAP

This is the second book in a series. If you haven't read *Time Binge* yet, go do that. I don't know what you were thinking buying a book with a 2 on the spine, but you've made a huge mistake. If you have read *Time Binge* and need a refresher, look no further...

Hudson Marrow was born immortal. He also invented a time machine. As it happens, using said time machine bestowed that immortality on others. Others like Edward Smith. Smith and his (work and life) partner Arturo Brooks work for a paranormal research organization called the Reticent. It purports to be a medical research firm, and the public doesn't question the name or what they do because nobody cares. They were promoted to President and CEO, respectively, after just about everyone else with seniority died thanks to a Reticent experiment gone awry (i.e., a giant tear in time and space over Manhattan). Brooks and Smith died too, but they got better. Now Brooks is a cyborg and Smith, in addition to being immortal, already lived all the way to the year 2090 before returning to their present. He's not particularly happy about that.

Also immortal are Patience Cloyce and Lemon Jones. Patience is a Puritan from Salem, Massachusetts circa 1692 whose neighbors hanged her for witchcraft. She survived, traveled to the present, and had no desire to return to Salem, for obvious reasons. Lemon is a hipster from Luna circa 2202. She never died; she just stayed in the past for the culture. Both girls live with Brooks and Smith in Brooklyn.

tl;dr: time travel happened and now there's a hodgepodge family of time orphans.

PROLOGUE

The last time Arturo Brooks used a time machine on a whim it didn't end well. That is to say it ended in his being stabbed to death in the past before having his corpse dragged back to the present and turned into a cyborg, traumatizing the love of his life in the process. But that was then, this was now. Knowing that said adventure had left Edward Smith somewhere between 'glum' and 'despondent' on the Ayn Rand Scale of Misery, Brooks resolved to make their upcoming eight-year anniversary a memorable one.

This venture led him to meet with Hudson Marrow, the immortal inventor of time travel and part-time rock fraud analyst. Because Hudson lived on Staten Island and going there was against Brooks's (and indeed anyone's) best interests, the two met at a coffee shop near the Battery. It was cramped, as Manhattan coffee shops tend to be, and the two leaned in so adjacent tables wouldn't hear their conversation.

"So you want to use the time machine," Hudson said. He picked up his cup and blew into it, trying to cool his drink.

"Yeah," Brooks said.

"You know I buried it—"

"Underneath a Chipotle. Yeah, I know."

Hudson continued. "And we all agreed not to use it..."

"Yeah, I know," Brooks said.

After everyone who had experienced time travel decided that it was annoying and convoluted, they had agreed never to use the time machine again. At least not until the year 2202, when the Moon would be in peril and they had already used it.*

Hudson set his coffee down. "So it's urgent, then?"

---

* The verb tenses associated with time travel are complicated.

Brooks scrunched his face in a way that indicated it was not.

Hudson sighed. "What do you need?"

"Listen," said Brooks. "Eddie's still kind of down about the whole 'living seventy-some years as an immortal' thing. I want to do something that will cheer him up."

"You want to take a time vacation?" Hudson asked. "If so, I don't recommend the 1400s..."

Brooks laughed. "No. Nothing like that. I just want to... get him a present from the past?"

Hudson put a hand to his chin, in thought. "Hmm..."

Lost in an earlier paragraph was the fact that Hudson's time machine was a device capable of immortality transference. Hudson was born immortal and objects that traveled through the machine with him sometimes stole that ability and rubbed it off on others. That's how Edward Smith had done 'the whole living seventy-some years as an immortal thing.' It was how a group of hell-bent Puritans had spent three hundred years formulating a plot to remake the world in God's righteous image, a plot that culminated in the destruction of a significant chunk of Manhattan. It was also the main reason the time machine was now buried under a Chipotle in west Texas. Making people immortal at random was dangerous.

"I know," Brooks said. "I know. But it's a present for Eddie, so we don't have to worry about accidentally making someone immortal. He already has that going for him."

"That assumes no one else ever touches it," Hudson said.

"Well, it's not like he has friends."

"What did you want to bring back?" Hudson asked.

"Something from the set of the original *Star Trek*. I thought you might have some ideas."

"I'm a *Star Wars* fan," Hudson corrected.

"Whatever. It's all the same," Brooks said.

"It's not remotely the same," Hudson said.

Brooks stared at him and pleaded. "Help me?"

Despite his offense at the *Star*-title mix-up, Hudson agreed. A mid-fifties divorcé, he didn't have anything better to do with his time, and the fact that Brooks was his boss made the decision a lot easier. A few days and a quick jaunt to the 1960s later, Brooks was in possession of a mint-condition type-3 phaser. He was going to make 2015 a good year, one way or another.

1 / A BIG REVEAL

Entrepreneurity Hour was the kind of show people watch at an airport bar. It's hard to imagine anyone intentionally switching channels to see Jerald Finkel drone on about stock futures and NASDAQ trends at two o'clock in the morning. He had the appearance and charisma of a city bus driver, with the caveat that there was nothing even the slightest bit offensive about him. Were he an actual bus driver, he would never have the nerve to kick someone off his bus, not even for boldly urinating in the rubbish bin. Finkel just sort of *existed,* and that had been enough to keep him employed with Financial News Network for over forty years.

Like they did many things, Brooks and Smith were about to ruin that. As CEO and President of the Reticent, respectively, they were the world's biggest names in biomedical research. This made them perfect interview fodder for Finkel, who had no idea the organization actually researched paranormal threats. Both men came overdressed in black suits, the mandatory Reticent attire. Brooks met the qualifications for tall, dark, and handsome, while Smith batted .333 at tall, pasty, and passable. They sat on a grey couch across from Finkel, next to a tasteful, modest-sized fern.

Finkel leaned in, his sweater vest stretching to capacity. "How do you respond to people who call you the business world's biggest power couple?"

"I don't," Smith said. He hated interviews, and he was hungry.

Brooks nudged him. "It's flattering."

"Oh, yeah," Smith said. "It is."

As Brooks droned on about commitments or something, Smith couldn't help but inspect the handful of reflective buttons speckled across Finkel's outfit. They weren't in normal places for buttons. There were a few down each arm, two on his chest, even a crotch button. Looking a bit closer, Smith noticed that some of the buttons weren't on his clothing at all. There was one on Finkel's forehead, tucked under an obvious wig. There was one on each ear, disguised by the man's hearing aids. If Smith didn't know better, he'd have sworn the host was suited up for motion capture.

Finkel continued with his questions, this one directed at Smith. "How do you balance running the Reticent with raising a family? I understand you have two girls..."

It was the first time in recorded history that a man had been asked about work-life balance, and Brooks and Smith shared a perplexed look.

"Well, they're teenagers, so they reject being raised," Smith said.

Finkel and Brooks shared a laugh.

Brooks added, "Really. It's not that hard. We're in charge of the Reticent, so we just make everybody else do all the work."

Finkel laughed another restrained, middle-aged laugh. As he did, Brooks stared at the camera. In its lens, he saw his own reflection next to Smith's. But where Finkel sat there were only reflective dots. He gave his eyes a subtle shift, just strong enough that his partner would notice. Smith eyed the lens, then Finkel, then the lens again.

"We'll have more after a few words from our sponsors," Finkel said.

Smith cupped his hand to cover his mouth and whispered. "So he's a vampire."

"I was just about to say," Brooks said.

"What do you want to—"

Brooks was too distressed to make a decision. "They're CGing his body in real time? I don't get it. He's not charismatic or anything. Why bother? Do you know how expensive CGI is?"

"I'm with you, but what do you want to do about it?" Smith asked. He nudged his face in the direction of his pocket. "I have a stake."

"No, that's not a good idea," Brooks said.

"Are you saying it would be a—"

"Don't do it," Brooks muttered.

"—mis-stake?"

Brooks was exasperated. "*¿Te doy un aventón al metro?*" he asked, rubbing his temples.

Smith knew that was rude. That's why it had been said in a language he didn't understand. He let out a monolingual "pfft."

Finkel took the reins again. "We're back with Arturo Brooks and Edward Smith, who have been praised for their efforts to rebuild and rebrand the Reticent following last year's tragic incident, during which their headquarters was destroyed. How do you think—"

Smith wasn't listening. He was too busy considering the consequences of staking an obvious vampire. They could lose their jobs, sure, but they couldn't lose their lives. And it wasn't like either of them particularly liked running a company. The girls would be fine. The house was paid for. Brooks wouldn't be *that* mad about it.

Thrill-seeking won out. Without warning, Smith reached into his jacket, grabbed his wooden stake, and—with a dramatic leap—thrust it into Finkel's heart. The vampire exploded into a wispy cloud of grey dust. For viewers at home, the experience wasn't dissimilar. As the mocap buttons shot out into different directions, the CGI version of Finkel split apart before the dust cloud appeared.

Brooks put his hands to the sides of his face in horror. "What did you do?"

"A damn good job," Smith said, smiling. It was the cleanest staking he'd ever made. He turned to face the camera directly. "Vampires are real."

And just like that, the world was on the cusp of a paranormal revelation.

2 / A GREY MATTER

Godwin Zane was ahead of the game in recognizing that the world was changing. Unfortunately, he was so caught up in the idea of being a superhero that he never noticed how utterly miserable the 64,372 employees of Zane Industries were. That was a misery rate of 99.99%. It would have been 100%, but he was actually his own 64,373rd employee, thanks to a surprisingly uncomplicated tax scheme. He himself was not miserable, on account of all the money.

As he gazed at lower Manhattan from the eighty-second floor of Zane Tower, he couldn't help but smile at the six block radius where dozens of construction cranes were busy rebuilding everything from the third floor up. The Six Block Disaster, though terrible for human life, had been great for business. Property owners, worried that another mysterious void in time and space would consume their investments (an event not covered under most insurance policies), had sold pretty much the entire area to Zane for cheap. The one exception—Reticent headquarters—bothered him immensely.

There was a certain aesthetic he was going for in rebuilding the area: a sleek, modern style he called the 'monochromatic motif.' Reticent headquarters, previously an eighteenth century brick abomination, was being rebuilt into a gaudy skyscraper that was going to ruin everything even more than the original design, and his own designer's suggestion that they block the view with trees was contemptible. Zane wanted that damned property, he was going to get it, and he lacked the self-awareness to recognize that this was not superheroesque behavior.

Not much about him was superheroesque. In black jeans and a black turtleneck, he looked like either the CEO of a tech startup or a beat poet. And though he wore a grey cape over his outfit at all times, it was a mere gimmick. *Look at Me!* was how Godwin Zane had made most of his fortune. Prior to the series of stunt films he had been wealthy, but not buy-ing-six-blocks-of-Manhattan wealthy. It turns out what peo-ple love—more than advances in science and technology, more than any invention—is watching grown men in capes take nut punches and try to see who can fill an outhouse the quickest.

Having spent ten minutes sitting in silence counting the fifty-seven advertisements on the back of his cape, Abigail Waters piped up. "Did you call me here to watch you brood over a building?"

He turned and spoke frankly. "No. I called you here be-cause your breasts are fantastic."

Zane's appearance was sickening enough without his atti-tude. He was thin with grey skin, beady black eyes, and white hair that fell to his chin in a messy way that screamed 'eccen-tric billionaire.' His nose was warped from a lost battle—not with a supervillain but with a particularly disgruntled home-less man who'd been offended at being thrown a penny—and his chin made Quentin Tarantino's chin look like a per-fectly reasonable chin. His heroic alias, Monochrome, de-rived from this appearance. His attitude came from one or a combination of the money, the superpowers, and the fame.

"Okay. I'm out," Abigail said. The reporter stood up, straightened her skirt, and headed for the door. She hadn't heard much from the billionaire, but it had been more than enough.

To his credit, Zane knew he'd been an asshole.

"Wait. No. That's not what I meant," he said.

Against his credit, he doubled up on his original response. "No, that's a lie. I meant it."

When she didn't turn back toward him, he blurted some-thing he was sure would make her stay. "I know what hap-pened last year."

She turned. "The Six Block Disaster?"

"Yep."

Abigail sat back down and pulled out her tablet, appalled but ready to listen.

3 / STEERING AWAY

There was a major problem brewing in the Brooks-Smith household: Patience had developed a taste for country music. It had started innocently enough—a poppy Taylor Swift song here, a crowd-pleasing Garth Brooks number there— but had reached the point that she was listening to Trev Cracklin's "Drinkin' Beers and Draggin' Queers" on a daily basis. Following an explanation of the song's lyrics, Patience switched to "Drinkin' Beers and Ropin' Steers (Radio Edit)" but it was almost as unbearable. For the third time that morning, the song's opening chords twanged throughout the kitchen.

"I wake up in the back of my truck," Trev sang. "Feelin' kinda ornery, don't give a—"

The sound of a cow mooing censored the next word.

Edward Smith failed to censor himself. "Why is that cocking song on again?"

Just above the kitchen table was a framed cross-stitch that read:

> *HOUSE RULES:*
> *1. No F bombs*
> *2. No time travel*
> *3. No spoilers*

Smith's efforts to comply with the first rule and remove the F word from his vocabulary had garnered mixed results. He looked across the table to Brooks for a nod of approval, but received a quiet headshake instead.

"I think what he's trying to say—" Brooks started.

"Is we all hate country music," Lemon finished, descending the stairs.

Patience tapped the pause button on her phone. "Really?"

"Yes," Brooks said.

"But it hearkens to a simpler time," Patience said.

"It makes me wish I could die," Lemon added, rifling through a cabinet. She couldn't. None of them could. It was a long story.*

"What I don't get is why you can't just use headphones," Smith said.

The thought made Patience uneasy. "I don't like them," she said. "With music in my ears it becomes impossible to hear anything else."

"Yeah, that's the point," Smith said. "What else do you need to hear?"

"All things," she answered. The twenty-first century was a noisy place, and Patience was often on edge. There had been no bicycles in Salem, let alone subway trains, and the Puritans had shunned all of their beggars out of the village. New York City was a completely different animal that required her utmost attention. She'd even stopped wearing her bonnet—letting her red hair flow freely and committing a minor sin in the process—in order to improve her hearing.

Brooks made a let-it-go gesture at Smith and looked directly at the young Puritan. "Enough Cracklin for now, okay?"

Patience nodded, and resumed eating cereal in silence.

"Whoa-whoa-whoa!" Brooks shouted, turning his attention to Lemon.

She looked up from a well-worn box of Pop-Tarts, confused. "What?"

"What are you holding?"

A raise of her hand revealed that it held two pastry packets. "Pop-Tarts?" She said the brand name with a sigh, longing for the music of Pop Tart & the Activation Energy, a band

---

* Called *Time Binge*. It's not actually that long.

that didn't exist yet. It was one of only two complaints she had about the year 2015; the other was institutional police racism.

"Two packs?" Brooks asked.

"Yes?" Lemon set them on the counter. "What's your deal?"

Brooks sighed. He weighed the pros and cons of honesty for a moment before declaring: "We're broke."

Smith tossed his own two Pop-Tart wrappers into the trash and coughed a little as a distraction. "I thought we were going to have this talk later?"

"We might as well get it over with," Brooks said.

"Wait. I thought you guys were *blasting poms*," Lemon said.

Brooks cast a pointed look as he translated her twenty-third century euphemism. "We *were* making bank until *somebody* decided that an interview with the *Entrepreneurity Hour* was the place to reveal to the world that vampires are real—oh and stake one who wasn't doing anything wrong, by the way, *because of reasons*."

"The host was a vampire, so he needed to die. That's not my fault. And I can't help that I have a pathological need to tell people about weird shit," Smith said.

Brooks lowered his voice. "And yet—"

Smith knew exactly what was coming next, and he scowled.

"—you couldn't tell me how I was going to die?" Brooks finished.

When they argued, Smith had a tendency to count facts. "One: *You* knew you were going to die. Two: I gave you every possible hint that it was the damn time machine. Three: I thought if I told you it would literally destroy the universe. My mistake. Four: You got better anyway. I'm the one who got to live a wacky seven decades thinking you were dead."

As their voices became louder, Patience dropped her spoon into her bowl and covered her ears for the one thing she didn't want to hear. In some ways, she thought being back in Salem would have been preferable to hearing her adoptive fathers argue. The people in Salem never raised their voices, after all. On the other hand, they did press people to death, so she reckoned it was a wash.

Lemon interrupted the bickering, arms crossed. "Is there a point to this?"

"Yes," Brooks said, putting a stop to the argument. "Now that Eddie went and Snowden'd the Reticent, it's being investigated by every possible government entity, including some I didn't even know existed."

"That doesn't mean you don't get paid, though?" Lemon asked.

"No, it doesn't," Brooks said. "The fact that we've been let go by the board does."

"On the bright side, they didn't mindwipe us," Smith said through a half-smile.

Seeing the half-smile, Patience uncovered her ears.

"Am I still having a graduation party?" Lemon asked, always concerned about the things that really mattered. She had *perfected* the playlist and couldn't bear the thought that her friends might not get to hear it.

"Yes," Brooks said, rolling his eyes.

Lemon motioned a little fist bump. Her deep cuts would not go unheard.

"You may want to get a job, though," Smith said.

"Why?" Lemon asked.

"Because college is on you." He turned to Patience. "You too."

Patience found it confusing that women were allowed to pursue higher education. Lemon found it confusing that college wasn't free yet. They each pondered those thoughts as Brooks headed toward the living room and motioned for Smith to follow him.

Smith obliged, whispering "go ahead and take two" to Lemon as he passed. She was one step ahead of him, grabbing the Lemon Special: one packet of strawberry and one packet of brown sugar. Patience offered a disapproving glance.

"What?" Smith asked when they were out of the girls' earshot.

Brooks stared at him, pleading. "It's Wednesday."

Wednesday was new comic book day, and Smith responded with that in mind. "I know we're broke. I have my pull list on hold until we get new jobs."

"What?" Brooks kept staring. "That's not what I—"

Smith groaned. "I *know* what you meant. The answer is no."

"Please."

"No."

Brooks had tried everything he could think of to get Smith to tag along to see his therapist. He'd tried positive reinforcement*, negative reinforcement†, and even neutral reinforcement‡. Nothing had worked, so he resorted to begging.

"Please," he said again.

"No." Smith paused before returning the politeness. "Thank you." He was quite proud of his efforts to act like an upstanding citizen for the girls' sakes.

Brooks sighed.

"I told you," Smith said. "I went to a therapist once. Once. I'm not doing it again. I'm fine."

Brooks blinked. "You tried to strangle me in my sleep."

"Well, you can't die, so it's fine."

"You actually don't know that," Brooks said.

When the Reticent made Brooks into a cyborg, they didn't

---

* Bribes

† Threats

‡ Developed by early 21st century hipsters, neutral reinforcement involves not mentioning the desired action at all and, if someone else mentions it, pretending it is passé. This serves to make the desired action more appealing to a disagreeable person.

exactly hand him an instruction manual. If one ever existed, it had burned in the fire they'd started to destroy the building and stop a rift from consuming the universe. If one had survived that fire, it had been soaked when some poor construction planning flooded all twenty-six of the building's subfloors. For all Brooks knew, his parts would degrade eventually. For all he knew, he had a bomb in his chest. For all he knew, he had secret Russian programming that would activate at the sight of a playing card. He didn't, but he didn't know that.

He continued his rant. "And that's your answer to everything now, isn't it? No reason to worry! You've got night terrors? That's fine! We don't have jobs? That's fine!"

"It *is* fine," Smith said. "Nobody in this house can starve. We're not going back to—We're not gonna be on the streets giving handjobs for handouts."

Brooks puffed air through his teeth. "I'm really having trouble stopping myself from hitting you right now."

"You can if you want to—" Smith started.

"So help me, if you say 'it's fine—'"

Smith shrugged. "It is, though."

Brooks headed for the door, skipping any departing pleasantries.

"It's fine!" Smith shouted after him as the door shut.

From the kitchen, Trev Cracklin began to wail.

4 / LEMON PARTY

There was no sign of Trev Cracklin at Lemon's graduation party. The only thing reminiscent of country music was the bejeweled cowboy hat her friend Tilor wore ironically.

In some ways, Lemon didn't think it fair that she had earned a party for displaying the barest minimum knowledge that a 21st century high school education required. Every year of public school had been easy, but her last had been the easiest by far, notwithstanding the incident where she forgot that the 28th and 29th Amendments hadn't been written yet*.

In the 22nd century, Lemon had been an outcast who kept to herself. In the 21st century, she was a mingler, and it showed. Her obsession with early 21st century culture came across to people of the day as an appealing lust for life. What Brooks and Smith had assumed would be an intimate gathering turned out to be a raucous shindig. No fewer than seventy teenagers swarmed their brownstone—chattering about Instagram and vaping and whatever else teenagers talked about—and neither man was particularly happy about it.

Patience wasn't happy about it either. She quarantined herself in her room, where she could sit and read in peace. Relative peace, anyway. Since she refused to use headphones, she had no choice but to listen to the unpleasant wailing of Sigur Rós as her eyes scanned the book she'd taken from Smith's office. She was certain she'd never seen him read a book that didn't have pictures in it, so he wouldn't miss this one. Still, she felt guilty. She glanced up at the blond-haired, blue-eyed Jesus on her wall and shook her head. A sudden

---

* The 29th Amendment regarded states' rights to claim territory on the Moon. The 28th expressly forbade anyone with the surname Trump from ever running for President again.

knock at the door led her to toss the book under her bed before unleashing a meek "Come in."

Lemon stood in the doorway, arms crossed. "What are you doing?"

"Reading," Patience said.

Lemon looked around for a book and rolled her eyes. "Come on. Everybody wants to meet you."

That made Patience uncomfortable. The last time a large group of people wanted to see her, they hanged her to death.

"Why?" she asked.

"For all intents and porpoises,* you're my sister, so..."

Patience was not interested, but Lemon persisted. "Come on. You might even meet a guy."

"I am acquainted with several men," Patience noted.

"You know what I mean."

Patience did. It had come up more times than she cared for. "No, thank you. I'm not interested."

"Duke has a sister named Duchess, if that's more—"

Patience frowned. All she wanted was to explore books, ideas and places... on her own. Lemon's attempts to engage her were well-intentioned, but unnecessary.

"Please let me be," she pleaded.

"Come onnnn—" Lemon started.

"What are you doing up here?" a voice interrupted. This time, the cross-armed figure in the doorway was Brooks. He unfurled them for the purpose of making air quotes. "Someone named 'Luxx' is fighting with someone named 'Adler' about a 'Netflix and Chill' gone wrong, and I might actually burn this place to the ground again to avoid having to listen to them for one more second."

"Oh no," Lemon said. "Luxx wasn't supposed to show up until later—" She pushed past her father and rushed downstairs to calm her guests.

---

* Lunan for "all intents and purposes."

"Come downstairs," he said to Patience in a way that made clear it was a request, not a demand.

"I don't like any of those people," Patience said, feeling guilty for saying it. Blond-haired Jesus's blue eyes seemed to be locked on her.

"I don't care for them either, but—" Brooks took a seat next to her. "It's important to her, and it's only one day."

"Therapy is important to you and it's only one day, but you don't make Edward go."

She didn't realize how much her statement stung.

"He has issues," Brooks tried to explain.

"I have issues as well!" Patience chirped, hoping this would get her out of going downstairs.

"I'm sure you do," Brooks said. "Really." He put a hand on her shoulder. "I'd like it if you came downstairs, though. Eddie and Lemon would like it too."

Guilt tripping was the foundation on which Puritanism had been built. As such, it worked exceptionally well on Patience. She acquiesced and followed Brooks downstairs.

Already downstairs, Lemon had a sneaking suspicion. Having settled the feud between Luxx and Adler by sending Luxx to get more veggie chips, she settled in the kitchen for a breather. In the corner, Smith spoke to Erin Burroughs, his former work partner, and there was an undeniable chemistry between them. Lemon perched herself on the kitchen table and glared at them. Smith chuckled. Lemon glared. Burroughs chuckled. Lemon glared harder. Smith chuckled again. Lemon glared her hardest. Apparently he saw the last glare, as he made a 'one second' gesture at Burroughs and made his way to the table.

"Did I do something?" he asked.

Lemon huffed. "I don't know. You tell me."

Smith wasn't playing that game. "You're a legal adult now. You can either tell me or you can get over it."

She snorted. "Fine. I have a problem with you flirting with

Agent Burroughs."

"Yeah?" Smith asked, smirking.

"I mean it. My bedroom is right next to yours and I hear *everything*." And the fact of the matter was that she hadn't heard anything but bickering in a long time. "You're going to pretend I didn't just see what I saw?"

"I *was* flirting," Smith said, this time with a full smile.

"I knew it!" Lemon hopped off the table and poked at his chest with a pointed finger, ready to unleash a lengthy diatribe. Flirting with the woman who once stabbed Brooks to death (albeit under orders) was unconscionable. "I can't believe—"

He was unmoved and cut her off. "Did you also know that when there's a crowd—like the one in this house—people instinctively look away from couples engaging in public displays of affection? Kissing, touching, flirting..."

She didn't see the point. "So?"

"This is *your* graduation party, right?"

"Yeah?"

"You want the attention to be on *you*, right?"

"Yeah?"

As if on cue, a miss Jen Wei scurried over to where Lemon and Smith were conversing. "Excuse me," she said, butting in. "Are you the vampire guy?"

"I don't know what you're talking about," Smith said, nonchalant.

Jen's head bobbed back and forth for a moment as she sized him up. "Yeah you are. I saw you staking that guy on YouTube."

It hit Lemon that Smith had been trying to do her a favor, and her jaw dropped.

"You never told me your dad was the vampire guy," Jen said.

"Uh—" Lemon wasn't sure what she could say to save her party.

"Hey!" Jen shouted at a group across the room. "Check it out! Lemon's dad is the vampire guy!"

Smith narrowed his eyes and mouthed a snippy "thanks" at Lemon. She stood helpless as her friends circled him, more interested in tales of the supernatural than the PJ Harvey track she'd taken six hours to select. This, she reflected, was bullshit.

"What's going on?" Brooks asked, joining the commotion with Patience at his side.

"Apparently the *Entrepreneurity Hour* is on YouTube," Lemon said, kicking at the floor.

Brooks took some amount of satisfaction in watching Smith endure a barrage of questions, such as "What do vampires wear?" and "Have you ever, like, seen a vampire vape?" That question was followed by "What would happen if you vaped garlic at one?"*

Lemon noted her father's satisfaction and made a conscious decision to ruin it. She blurted, "Are you guys breaking up?"

"What? No," Brooks said. "Why would you ask that?"

"Seems like it. Patience thinks so too," Lemon said. If she couldn't be the star of the evening, she could at least have some fun tormenting the rest of her family.

Patience had leaned against a wall and was lost in glancing around the room when she heard her name. "Pardon me?"

"Do you think Eddie and I are breaking up?" Brooks asked.

"Hmm?" She wondered. "Oh, no. What God has joined together no man can separate."

After processing that and translating it to modern English, Brooks replied. "We're not married."

"You're not?" Patience asked in genuine confusion.

"Why would you assume that?" Brooks asked.

---

* Nothing. Nothing would happen.

Patience had difficulty tracking cultural mores, but she was fairly certain on this one. "That's acceptable now, is it not?"

"Yeah, but not all gay couples are married."

"You live together, so I had assumed—" Just when she thought she was beginning to understand the future, Patience found out about unwed cohabitation.

As Brooks began explaining to Patience the myriad reasons Smith wasn't the marrying type, Lemon burst out laughing. When she was satisfied, she walked across the room and parked herself on the couch between Duke and Duchess.

"Not interested in the vampire stories?" she asked.

The siblings let out a simultaneous "meh."

"Obvious CGI," Duchess said.

Duke nodded. Even if they were real (and he had his doubts), the world had known about vampires for *weeks* now.

"Vampires are played out," he said.

"And cable news isn't?" Lemon asked. She pushed a braid out of her eye for a better look at what the siblings were watching (on closed captioning, of course, so as not to drown out the music).

Duke rolled his eyes in his sister's general direction. "We were flipping through and she saw *Monochrome*."

"Okay. He's awesome," Duchess said.

Duchess was but one of many Monochrome fangirls. Despite his appearance, the superhero had a certain charm about him. Nearly everything he said was appalling, but the way he said it—with a confidence only several billion dollars can buy—was incredible.

"He's a corporate tool," Duke corrected.

"You just hate him 'cause you ain't him," snapped Duchess.

"You got me. I really wish I were a grey-skinned pervert."

"—With superpowers!" Duchess flailed.

Duke raised his eyebrows and lowered his voice in disdain. "You don't actually think he has superpowers?"

"You've seen his movies," Duchess said.

"*Unfortunately.*"

"If he didn't have superpowers, he wouldn't survive that stuff."

'That stuff' included being locked in a trash compactor, being locked in a port-a-potty, being locked in a safe, and being locked in a giant lock. There was a theme.

Duke continued to complain. "*If* he has superpowers, he doesn't *do* anything with them. He could single-handedly stop crime and he just makes those stupid movies and occasionally gets a cat out of a tree. He's a fraud."

"He's not a fraud!"

"Lemon?" Duke asked.

"He's fine, I guess? I don't really think about him, to be honest." She wasn't being completely truthful. Pop Tart & the Activation Energy once recorded a scathing song about Monochrome, and she thought about their music all the time.

"That's my girl," Duke said. He meant it, but like everything else he said, it sounded cynical.

In the distance, there was a shout of "He's a cyborg!" and the crowd of teens abandoned Smith to swarm Brooks. Moments later, Burroughs and Smith joined Lemon, Duke, and Duchess.

Smith sat and let out a sigh of relief. "Well, that takes care of—" He stopped mid-gloat when he realized what the grey-scale superhuman on TV was saying.

The closed captioning read:

> And so, after thorogh research I can definitively stay that the Reticent were behind teh Six Block Disaster. There research into parallel dimensions cost all of us deer lee.

"Oh, shit," Smith said.

"Oh, shit," Burroughs repeated.

Smith gave his position a second thought. "Actually, we might be able to use this."

5 / BURROUGHS

Erin Burroughs had flown under the radar since 1997. That was the year LL Cool J released *Phenomenon*, and it was the year she joined the Reticent. Due to illegal dumping of questionable substances, the dumpster outside her Queens apartment had grown a new, sentient species. Quidrils were gooey green creatures that liked to crawl into people's skulls through the ear and eat their brains. As grey matter was removed, it was replaced with green matter. Signs a person had been infected included addiction to purchasing reusable shopping totes, the urge to vote for unelectable third party Presidential candidates, and a willingness to try vegan hot dogs. Burroughs discovered and named the species, and determined how to kill them*. Then she settled into a comfortable life as a completely average agent. She liked it that way.

Unfortunately, recent events had left the agency more than a little short on staff. Some died in the rift, some quit on account of the rift, some were fired by Brooks and Smith for their involvement in creating the rift, some quit because they were outraged that Brooks and Smith had fired perfectly good agents, some were outraged that Brooks and Smith themselves had been fired, and so on. Others insisted they were still working but just sat at home collecting paychecks while the building was being rebuilt. The effects cascaded. At forty-one, Burroughs was among the most senior surviving agents, so she found herself promoted to the board as head of Security.

The other board members were:

Travis Marsh, head of Undead Studies. He was murdered once. As happens sometimes, he got better. He also got

---

* Fire. It's always fire.

promoted, thanks to his newfound expertise in zombieism.

Zephyr, head of Prophecies. Most agents didn't believe in prophecies, but the risk of firing Zephyr and finding out she was in touch with powerful black magic was greater than the risk inherent in paying her $45,000 annually to remain on staff.

Henrique Wiles, British Guy. He was also the head of Inventions and Gadgets. He was also the person who had insisted that the division name include the word 'Gadgets.' He was a fan of rugby, tea, and driving on the left-hand side of the road.

Knut Knutsson, head of Research and Investigation. This was by far the Reticent's largest division, and he was exactly the kind of slick corporate tool who could be trusted with an entity's largest division. On appearance alone, he could have starred in a sequel to *American Psycho*.*

Diamond Trebly, Public Relations. Too perky demeanor. She was the kind of person who listened to TED talks all day while working. Her efforts to make everyone like her meant that nobody liked her.

The Weber triplets (Brandon, Abandon, and Sarandon). Like most sets of triplets, the Webers were unsettling. They were a pale, bald, emaciated group and each one had a different form of heterochromia. When lined up in alphabetical order, their eyes made a smooth transition from blue to green to brown and back to blue. They were in charge of various small groups, most notably Human Resources, and they tended to juggle responsibilities amongst themselves. No one was sure whether they were brothers, sisters, a combination, or space aliens. Each bore a striking resemblance to Benedict Cumberbatch.

The nine members of the board had gathered in the agency's temporary home—a tent in the unfinished first

---

* It's a good thing nobody ever made a sequel to *American Psycho*.

floor of what was to be their enormous skyscraper—to select a new CEO and President, but an argument had erupted on the subject of how to handle Godwin Zane's public accusation. Travis Marsh felt that throwing Brooks and Smith under the bus was not merely justified, but ideal. When the others objected to literally throwing them under a city bus, he settled on arguing for a metaphorical bus.

"They have it coming," he said. "Plus it acts as a lesson to new agents. If you tell people about the supernatural, you lose your job and worse."

"You can't blame them for Six Blocks," Burroughs said. "If they hadn't shut that portal down, millions would have died instead of thousands."

"Brrraaaaaains—er, Brrrrooks and Smith can't die. Whatever public shame they'll endure won't brrraaa—break them. They're the perfect fall guys."

"We shouldn't have fired them in the first place," Burroughs argued. "You're just mad because you died."

Marsh crossed his rotting arms. "I have the right."

"And we all know why you stand up for them," Zephyr said, waving her hands around all woo-woo like. She always gave the impression that she knew more than everyone else, probably on account of the prophecies.

"Do you?" Burroughs asked. "Did you see that in your crystal ball?"

Zephyr leaned in toward the table, and the sixteen pendants hanging from her neck clanked together. "Time is but an illusion and the veil of mystery that surrounds—"

"Maybe you could have foreseen that the experiment Parallel Universes was working on would *eat a portion of lower Manhattan*," Burroughs said.

Zephyr was aghast. "Are you insinuating that the event was my fault?"

Burroughs shook her head. "No. It was nobody's fault. They didn't realize what their experiment was doing and we had poor oversight. That's all we need to say. Owning up to it is the mature thing to do."

The group considered that for a moment.

"No. We need somebody to blame," Wiles said.

Marsh and Zephyr nodded.

Knutsson, Trebly, and the Weber triplets agreed.

6 / INTERVIEW WITH A QUAGMIRE

Brooks stood in a Zane Tower bathroom, clutching a folder that contained his one-page résumé and the fourteen-page personality questionnaire required as part of the application package for all Zane Industries positions. He set the paperwork down next to the sink and stared into the mirror for a moment.

"*Estás bien pendejo,*" he muttered at no one, certain that he'd botched the last test.

It wasn't a job seeker's market, and it showed. Five rounds of interviews—during which there had been a lie detector test, a twelve-person round table discussion, an official MBTI type evaluation, and both a swimsuit and talent competition—and he still wasn't done. All of this for a lowly Lead Researcher position that paid enough to rent one eighth of an apartment in Manhattan. Brooks splashed some water at his face because that's what people do in movies, but all it did was make him wet in addition to annoyed.

He patted his face with a paper towel and stepped back out into the sixtieth floor lobby.

"I'm sorry," the human resources representative said, greeting him with a sympathetic gaze. "The group has decided not to refer you on to Round Six."

Smith was referred to Round Six.

Godwin Zane had enough quirks to fill a room, and he had enough money that they could be considered mere quirks and not clinical insanity. He insisted on speaking with every single person his company intended to hire. Sometimes it lasted one minute and he asked a simple question like

"What's your favorite color?" Any answer but green meant the person could join his staff. Sometimes he played a co-op video game with them. As long as their team won, the person was hired.

Other times, when he didn't like the cut of someone's jib, he would ask an obscure trivia question, something like "Name all past and present members of Depeche Mode," to which the interviewee would respond "Depeche Mode is still a band?" and promptly be dismissed. Nobody disrespected Depeche Mode on Zane's watch.

Still other times, Zane would end up having a lengthy conversation with the prospective employee. That was the case on this day. Smith sat facing Zane's desk, but not the man himself. The thirty-two-year-old President of Zane Industries liked to dramatically turn mid-conversation, revealing himself when his interviewee would least expect it. Smith had thus far only seen Zane's face via the eight-by-twelve foot *Look at Me!* movie poster that adorned the wall behind the man himself. On it, the billionaire stood on a rooftop, hands at his hips and cape blowing in the wind.

They had gone over the basics: who Smith was (an asshole) and why he felt qualified to take on the position of Lead Researcher (because the only skill necessary was Google, and he was an expert at finding obscure shit in the depths of the internet). It was time for the weird stuff.

"You're driving down a road," Zane said.

"Where?" Smith asked.

Zane paused. "It doesn't matter."

"It sort of does. Am I in the city, am I even in the United States? If I'm driving in England, I'm on the other side of the road—"

Zane was unprepared for backtalk. "Shut up. You're driving down a road. You see three people stranded: an old woman who is going to die any moment, an old friend who saved your life once, and someone you don't know who will turn out to be the love of your life. You can take one passenger. Who do you pick up?"

Since Zane wasn't looking at him, Smith mouthed "what the fuck" before proceeding to his answer: "None of them. I don't know why they're out there or what they're doing. I don't have old friends, I already know the love of my life so I'm not missing anything there, and I definitely can't tell whether some old lady's gonna croak just by looking at her. The whole thing is none of my business."

Zane found his disregard for the elderly appealing.

"How do you feel about aesthetics?" Zane asked, dramatically turning mid-question.

Smith blinked. "What?"

"Aesthetics. The principles behind beauty."

It was an odd question coming from a man who was grey. It wasn't even a nice grey like he appeared on television. In real life, it was a washed out grey. Smith had learned that it was possible for grey to appear washed out.

"I know what aesthetics are," he said. "I don't understand the question."

Zane squinted, sizing Smith up. He couldn't get a good read on the man's emotions because they were buried under decades' worth of garbage, so he tried to provoke some.

"Did you know I'm rebuilding Manhattan?" he asked.

"The Six Block Disaster zone?" Smith nodded. "Yeah. I saw that."

"Did you know there's one building I haven't been able to acquire?" Zane asked.

"No?" Smith wondered.

Zane jumped up and slammed his fist onto his desk. "You're a liar! I've been trying to buy the Reticent building and you're going to tell me their President didn't know anything about that?"

"How long have you been trying?" Smith asked, staring at the spot where Zane's fist hit the desk. There was a small crack in the wood that seemed to be both glowing and growing.

"Two weeks," Zane admitted. He sat back down and shook his fist as if to cool it off.

"Yeah, I may have lied on my resume. They fired me a month ago." At this point the desk appeared to be melting, and Smith had no choice but to bring it up. "Is that normal?"

"It's fine," Zane said. He pressed a button on his desk phone and a cheery voice asked how it could help him. "I need some liquid nitrogen in here. Again."

"You do have superpowers," Smith said quietly.

"Yeah," Zane said, shaking his fist and blowing at it.

It's worth noting that Monochrome's superpower, if it could be called one, was that magma flowed through his body. Nobody understood how it worked because anyone who tried to understand it met the business end of some magma.* On occasions when Zane became overly excited or agitated, it had the tendency to leak. This obviously did not do wonders for him in the bedroom, which in turn did wonders for how often he turned conversations perverse out of sheer sexual frustration. The Zane Industries Human Resources department had its work cut out for it.

"So you didn't know about the building, then..." Zane trailed off.

"Uh, no," Smith said.

"But you *were* the President when your company created a rift in the universe that killed sixteen thousand people."

Smith shifted in his seat. "Not exactly. My partner and I sort of... stopped that and killed the people responsible. That's why I'm here."

Zane didn't follow. He made a 'go on' gesture with his hand.

---

* If you're worried about the scientific plausibility of this, I have some bad news about time travel...

"I don't want Arturo Brooks or myself to be implicated in whatever you're going to tell the world, and I'll do whatever you need me to do to make sure that doesn't happen."

"You'll give me a blowie?" Zane asked, unaware of how uncomfortable that question could make a person.

Smith scratched his head. "I, uh..."

"I'm kidding," Zane said. "Geez."

He stood up and Smith copied him. They shook hands.

"Welcome to the team, Mr. Smith."

Smith didn't understand the formality, but he rolled with it. "Thanks, Mr. Zane."

Zane waved dismissively. "Please. Call me God."

Smith suppressed the urge to quit right then and there.

"So what am I going to be researching?" he asked.

Zane grinned. "The afterlife."

7 / THE GOD ALLUSION

Patience was from 1692, and somewhere along a line that included being hanged for witchcraft, dying from said hanging, resurrecting, traveling through time a few times, being tortured, and enrolling at P.S. 45, she'd had a crisis of faith that blond-haired, blue-eyed Jesus couldn't solve. While it was natural, she supposed, for God's plan to be incomprehensible to humans, it was not acceptable for the plan to be... whatever this was. While Lemon was out with Duke and Brooks was out interviewing for a bartender position at Flaming Saddles, she made what she was certain would be a bad decision and decided to talk to Smith about her troubles.

She knocked at his office door, but her weak taps were no match for the sounds of Kitten Orgy, a thrash metal band out of Cleveland.* Patience debated going in for exactly twelve minutes and sixteen seconds, per her phone's stopwatch. At that point, Smith threw open the door and nearly ran into her.

"What are you doing?" he asked, coming to a halt.

"I wanted to talk to you, sir—uh—" No matter how many times she'd been told that honorifics weren't necessary, she kept using them.

Smith had given up trying to correct her. "So you decided to stand outside the door...?"

"I didn't wish to interrupt."

"Hang on." He popped back into the room and silenced Kitten Orgy. "Go ahead and sit down. I'll be right back."

Patience complied. Smith returned to the room with a bottle of cooking brandy. He dished out a small pour for himself then tucked the bottle under his desk.

---

* Do not google "Kitten Orgy."

"Are you supposed to be drinking that?" she asked.

"Nope, but what Brooksy doesn't know won't hurt him."

That didn't sound right to Patience, but she didn't think it her place to argue. Still, her reproving blinks compelled him to offer further explanation.

"I've earned it," he said. "Zane hired me today."

"That's welcome news," Patience said, somewhat bewildered by his defensiveness.

Smith changed subjects. "What do you need?"

It again occurred to Patience that this was a bad idea, but she had already come this far, so she asked what was on her mind: "Do you believe in God?"

Smith laughed a hearty laugh.

"I fail to see the humor," Patience said. It was a phrase she repeated often enough that she could have trademarked it, if she understood what a trademark was.

"You're the one who stole my copy of *The God Delusion*," Smith declared. It was an atheist screed, purchased when he'd been more angry at life than beaten down and disappointed.

Patience's eyes grew wide. Whatever punishment awaited was sure to be—

"Yes, I noticed. No, I don't care. No, you shouldn't take Dawkins's word for it. That guy's an asshole. Trust me, I'd know."

"So... you do believe in God then?"

Smith didn't think about his answer for even a millisecond. "No," he said.

Patience had thought that maybe there would be more to it than that. She sat in uncomfortable silence until Smith realized she wanted more.

"I used to," he finally offered.

She leaned forward. "What changed your mind?"

"Doesn't matter," Smith said.

"Please," Patience said. "I wish to know."

Smith had intended to take a sip of his drink but ended up downing the whole glass. He scowled at himself, grabbed the bottle from under the desk and poured a little more. Did he regret it? A little, but he wasn't about to continue this particular conversation without assistance. As Patience stared at him in anticipation, Smith sighed, sipped, and got on with his story.

"My parents," he said, then corrected, "My *birth* parents— took me to church every Sunday. So every week I got to hear about fire and brimstone and how God punishes the wicked."

Patience nodded. This bit was familiar.

Smith took another sip. "I believed it. I was a rowdy kid. All kids are rowdy kids. So when my parents beat me, I knew it was my fault. When they were too hopped up on drugs to buy groceries and I starved, I knew it was my fault. When they shot my dog in front of me because she was barking, I knew it was my fault." He lost himself in thought for a moment, debating whether those things were still his fault. They weren't, obviously, but they still kind of... were. "I did everything I could to be the perfect child. I did everything adults told me to do. I stopped talking back. I stopped talking at all, really."

"What happened then?" Patience asked.

"My parents blew up our house trying to make meth." He seemed satisfied. "They died. I survived because they'd locked me outside so I wouldn't bother them."

Patience's voice took a cheery note. "So you were saved?"

He stared at nothing in particular until his phone's vibration interrupted him. A text from Brooks.

Just got off the train.

Smith looked back up at Patience. "That's what I thought at the time. My parents had been punished and I had been saved." He scoffed at himself again.

"But you changed your mind?"

"After a few years in the foster system?" Smith shot her a pointed look before realizing that she wouldn't get the point. "Yeah. I changed my mind." He downed the rest of his drink. "I found myself with people who were a lot worse than my parents."

"Worse?" Patience frowned.

Smith nodded. "Worse. And I kept thinking it was my fault, that there was something inherently bad about me. I had to have done *something*."

Patience perked up. "You don't think there's something wrong with you now?" There was hope. If he had gotten over the same feeling she'd been having, she could too.

Smith laughed. "There's *a lot* wrong with me, kiddo, but no... I don't think the bad things that happen to me are some God's fault."

"Why not?" Patience asked.

Smith sipped at his empty glass, realized it was empty, and frowned. He looked down at his phone, noted that Brooks would be home any minute, and decided against pouring any more. He popped a Listerine strip into his mouth and looked around for something else to keep himself occupied. He settled on the stress ball Brooks had insisted would help. He took it into his hands and resumed stressing.

"I did everything I was supposed to. Even living in two homes a month, I was good. I did everything adults told me to do." His squeezing the stress ball had turned into sort of punching it from one hand to the next. He spoke through his teeth. "I ended up living with this..." He considered censoring his words but didn't have a good alternative. "...this fucking pervert. He was rich as hell, and all I had to do, he said, was not tell anyone wh—" He couldn't finish that sentence, so he switched to another. "Long story short, I found myself living with someone who was wildly successful, beloved by everyone in the community. He abused me every night and it was obvious he wasn't being punished. So I decided to do it myself."

"What did you do?" she asked.

Smith again considered softening his words but blanked on polite terms. "I bit his dick off."

Patience's eyes went wider than when she'd been caught stealing. Those weren't words a normal person would say in this situation. This was not a normal situation.

Smith relieved her of any expectation that she would speak by continuing. "I realized that God wasn't helping or punishing anyone. It's all just people. Mostly shitty, sometimes okay... people."

"Is that when you decided to do the work you do?" Patience wondered. "To help others?"

Smith laughed. "What? No. I started drinking, stopped giving a shit, and dropped out of school."

Patience wondered whether she too should drop out of school. It seemed to have worked out for Smith, and her remedial classes were painfully dull.

"I was turning tricks in an alley when I joined the Reticent—"

Patience immediately decided against dropping out of school. She didn't want to end up performing magic tricks, as that was a surefire way to end up in Hell.

Smith continued his story. "Some vampires attacked. They killed my client. I killed them, and Burroughs recruited me on the spot."

Patience wasn't sure any of that helped her with her predicament.

Brooks, who had been listening to the last bit from just outside the door, opened it and pretended he hadn't been.

"Hey. There you are," he said.

Smith wiped the misery off his face along with some sweat.

"Hey," he said.

Patience wasted no time, and questioned her other father. "Do you believe in God?"

Brooks took off his jacket and tossed it over a chair. "Hi. Nice to see you too." He paused for a moment, pondering her question. "Uh... yes?" His voice betrayed his lack of confidence. "To be honest, I'm not sure. I want to." He sighed, taking a seat at the desk's edge. He shot a look at the spot of brandy he'd unknowingly seated himself atop. "If you had asked me a year ago, I'd have said 'yes' without a doubt."

"What changed?" Patience asked.

"I died," Brooks said.

Patience could relate.

He continued. "I died and nothing happened. I never really believed God intervenes day to day because—hey, way to go—but I had to believe in some sort of afterlife. Then I was just... dead." He cheered himself up. "Maybe I can't remember what happened because it's a different plane of existence or something. I don't know..."

"I don't know what to believe," Patience admitted.

"Well, that's normal," Brooks said. "You're sixteen. You still think Trev Cracklin has talent."

"He's quite talented—"

"Seriously," Smith said. "This is normal even for people who haven't traveled through time. Just take it one day at a time and don't worry about it."

"You'll figure it out eventually," Brooks added. "Or you won't. It's nobody's business but yours."

Patience nodded. She left the room feeling a tiny bit better than when she'd entered it.

When she was gone, Brooks moved to the edge of Smith's chair and looked into his partner's eyes.

"You were drinking," he said.

"Yeah," Smith said.

There was no point denying it. Three glasses of brandy had cheered him up about as much as the Type-3 phaser he'd received for their anniversary (that is, not at all).

"Do you need to talk?" Brooks asked.

"Not about that," Smith said. "I have some good news, though."

8 / CREEPING

2045 was a bustling restaurant, so much so that no one at the table heard what Patience said. She dutifully repeated herself over the sounds of clanking silverware and emphatic conversation.

"I had nine siblings, I fear dolls, and my favorite Trev Cracklin song is 'In the Back of the Truck.'" Patience eyed the rest of the table nervously, wondering whether she had properly followed the conventions of Two Truths and One Lie.

She had, and Smith hazarded a guess. "You're lying about the song. It's that one about dragging steers or roping queers or whatever."

Patience smiled. "No."

"So the dolls then," Lemon said, grabbing a piece of bread.

"No." Having stumped her adoptive family, Patience beamed. "I only had eight siblings." When nobody was impressed, she added, "It was most unusual for the time."

Smith looked to Brooks, then to Lemon, then back to Brooks. "Fine, if nobody else is going to say it... Who the hell is afraid of dolls?"

"I am," Patience said. "As I just told you."

His face met his palms. "But *why*?"

"Because they're imbued with cast-out spirits."

Smith had no response but a rapid blink.

"*Obviously*," Brooks said, poking his partner with an accusing finger. "Don't you know anything?"

Smith, as he was wont to do, offered a glare and a snide comment. "I know how to ace an interview."

That's what they were celebrating. The Brooks-Smith impoverishment had lasted only a month, and it was miraculously thanks to Smith.

"Yeah, you do." Brooks smiled. "A toast!"

"We're all drinking water," Lemon noted. She looked at Patience with disgust. "...or milk."

"We can toast water," Brooks said, trying to hide his own disgust. "...or milk."

They raised their glasses and made a few clinks.

"To Eddie," Brooks said.

"To not being broke," Lemon added. "And not paying for college."

American Puritans had outlawed drinking toasts in 1639, so Patience had nothing to add but a forced smile. She set her glass of milk down as soon as was socially acceptable.

That he wasn't allowed to drink at a celebration of his own accomplishment didn't sit right with Smith, so he excused himself to the restroom. On the way, he ducked around a corner, grabbed an unfinished glass of merlot from an empty table, and downed it in one swift movement. Then he coughed a little. Then he coughed a lot. Then he coughed out a two-carat halo-cut engagement ring.

"Yikes," he said to himself. He set the ring on the table, certain that someone in a very bad mood would return to retrieve it later. Then, in a rare moment of empathy, Smith imagined himself in the position of the rejected proposer and gave a little shudder before proceeding to the next abandoned table with a few drops of wine remaining.

It wasn't entirely a booze ruse. He did need to use the restroom, so he made his way there. After a short visit with a luxury self-flushing urinal, complete with a hibiscus-infused urinal cake, Smith found himself staring into the mirror above the sink. While the muzak version of Phil Collins's "Against All Odds" filled the room, Smith's mind filled with disdain. Eyeing up his dark circles and scowl, he wondered whether everyone else could see what he could. Then he thought about having a mental crisis to the sounds of Phil Collins and resented himself even more. He closed his eyes for a long minute, wishing away any signs of distress.

Some people have motivational phrases they say to themselves in situations like this. Things to the effect of "Hang in there" or "You can do it." Smith had no such thing.

"Fuck me," he muttered to himself.

When he opened his eyes, he held his chin up, faked a smile, and headed for the bathroom door—

Right into a bathroom attendant.

"Christ," Smith said. "Why do you people still exist?"

"Hot towel?" the mustachioed man offered.

"No. Goddamn." Smith shrugged it off and murmured "creep" on his way out of the room.

As he re-approached his family's table, he noticed a problem. While Patience happily ate her pasta, Brooks and Lemon both looked up in bewilderment at a man in a suit who had confronted them. He was obviously the restaurant's manager, what with the engraved gold tone nametag that read 'Nitish Mitra: Manager' pinned to his chest.

"I'm afraid I'm going to have to ask you to leave," Nitish said.

"Why?" Brooks asked.

Smith butted in, assuming that this—like most things—was his fault. "Is this because I called the bathroom attendant a creep?"

"They are creeps," Brooks agreed.

Lemon also agreed. "Totally. You can't fault him for that."

The manager's response was vague. "I'm just not comfortable serving you two." There was a beat. "And we don't have bathroom attendants." He hurried away from the table to call the police.

*
**

Outside, the group shuffled down the sidewalk at a pace slow enough to allow Patience to continue eating from her to-go container.

Lemon wondered out loud. "That was weird, right?"

"Yeah," Smith said. "That was about as close to 'we don't serve your kind here' as you can get."

Brooks could smell the expensive wine on his partner's breath, and he was furious. But the fury could wait until they were home, where the girls would experience the sounds of muffled argument rather than full-on verbal combat.

Now that they weren't 'at the dinner table' where it was 'rude,' Lemon pulled out her cell phone and noticed that there were over seventy unread texts.

"Damn," she said, pulling one up.

OMG is this 4 real? youtube.com/watch?v=NtRlyALnk

As she tapped the link, an oncoming pedestrian slowed as he neared the group. He was an older gentleman who thought his eyes deceived him. He stopped and squinted, focusing on the faces of the men approaching. His eyes were not deceiving him, he decided, so when Brooks and Smith were right in front of him, he sneered, leaned forward, and hocked a ping pong ball-sized loogie smack dab in the middle of Brooks's left cheek.

"Aaaagh... WHAT THE HELL!?" Brooks swatted the phlegm from his face and scowled at the old man.

Patience frowned at her pasta, which had been caught in the crossfire. She shuffled to a nearby garbage can and tossed it.

The old man shook a wrinkled fist. "If I were thirty years younger, I'd give you better than that."

"Is this a gay thing?" Smith asked. "Did we walk through a portal into the 1950s or something? Because... that could have actually happened." It wouldn't have been a first.

In old movies, people always find out information by walking past a store window that just happens to contain a dozen tube TVs airing the nightly news. The modern equivalent of that was Lemon holding out her phone so the others could gather around it to watch a video.

"Uh..." Lemon hesitated. "It's a lot worse than that."

In fact, her discovery was in no way worse than living in the 1950s, but the show *Happy Days*, broadcast in reruns to this day, was encoded to make people think back on that decade fondly.

"Turn the sound up," Brooks said, noting that his and Smith's faces were plastered in the upper left hand corner of the screen above some newscaster.

"It's up all the way," Lemon said.

"Damn ambient city noise," Smith said as he, Brooks, and Patience all leaned in as close as possible so their ears were practically touching. The old man who'd spat on Brooks tried to form another spitball. Fortunately for the group, his mouth had gone dry, and he walked away harrumphing.

The newscaster spoke. "The Reticent's new CEO and President Danny Guerrera stated..." HONK HONK. "Responsible for the Six Block Disaster were initiated by Agents Arturo Brooks and Ed..." HONK. "Viewers may know from their appearance on the *Entrepreneurity Hour*. While others in the organization tried to stop the dangerous experiments..." HONK HONK HONK. "Insisted upon proceeding and the result was thousands of lives lost."

"That's not good, is it?" Patience asked.

"No," Brooks said. "That's really, really not good."

9 / DOTH PROTEST TOO MUCH

One sign read 'Justice for Six Blocks.' Another read 'Make Them Pay.' Still another asked 'Who Is Responsible?' The last sign—because there always seems to be one—read 'God Hates Fags,' and all the other protestors made a point of staying away from *that guy*. The stairs in front of the brownstone acted as a dividing line, with a few dozen outraged citizens on one side and one tone-deaf curmudgeon on the other.

They may not have been homophobic, but the protestors on the opposite side weren't much nicer than the old coot. When Patience arrived home from summer school, one of them tripped her. The clay mug she'd made in art class was a casualty, and it tumbled into their three-by-four foot patch of lawn, right underneath the protesters. She dared not attempt to retrieve it, lest she cause a scene.

Inside, Smith tended to Patience's cuts and scrapes while Brooks argued on the phone with an assortment of journalists, government officials, and people who'd seen his contact information on 4chan.

"My mom's already dead, thanks," Brooks said to the brave internet warrior on the other end of the line before hanging up in exasperation. "What are we going to do?"

Smith looked up from Patience's knee. "Well, the good news is none of us can die, so—"

Lemon looked up from Twitter to halt the incoming argument. "Seriously, though. We should move, right?"

As she said that, a bottle smashed through the living room window, shattering glass everywhere and indicating that the answer to her question was most likely yes.

"There's not a person in the country who doesn't know what we look like," Brooks noted.

Suddenly, it occurred to Brooks what Smith had been

doing for the last three minutes. He stared at Smith, then at Patience's leg, then at the First Aid kit on the floor, then back at Smith.

Smith caught on, looked up, and tilted his head. "What the hell am I doing?" He turned to Patience. "Why aren't you healing?"

"I don't know, sir."

"Why didn't I notice?" he asked.

"I don't know, sir."

"Why do you keep calling me sir?"

"I don't—"

Brooks interrupted. "This isn't good."

"This is great," Smith said simultaneously. A little bit of danger was just what he needed.

They glowered at each other.

Smith stood and scampered to the pile of shattered glass where the bottle had landed. Someone outside saw his silhouette in the window and began shouting. He jumped to the side to dodge another airborne object. Patience's tasteful, russet-colored mug flew past his head and shattered as well. That was followed by the PSSSHT! sound of the NYPD officer on scene calling for backup and shouting at the crowd to disperse. Smith picked up the biggest glass shard he could find.

"PBR," he said. "Of course."

"I'm just surprised someone had a bottle rather than a can," Brooks said.

"Save the cap," Lemon insisted. Her custom-made bottle-cap guitar picks were a big hit on Etsy.

Smith took the shard in his right hand and with a quick slash made a shallow cut to the side of his left arm.

"Fuck," he said. It hurt.

"I don't know what you expected," Brooks said. "It would have hurt whether it heals or not."

It didn't heal, and Brooks was next to him in seconds,

dressing the wound.

"Huh," Smith said. This was promising.

"We need to get out of here," Brooks said.

"Yes, please," Lemon said. In a less dramatic fashion, she had poked just the tip of her finger with the scissors from the First Aid kit and found that she too had failed to heal.

Brooks turned to Smith with a plea. "Look, I know you have zero desire to go back to Indiana. I mean, nobody does. But—"

"*No.*"

"Who do we know who would take us in? I've got two tías in Flatbush and a handful of cousins I'd rather not associate with. We need to leave the city."

"No, we don't. I, for one, am starting a new job next week."

Patience offered a suggestion, and she could practically taste the microwaved popcorn as she did. "Mr. Marrow would likely allow us to stay with him."

As far as suggestions went, it wasn't a bad one. Staten Island was far enough from anything useful that protestors weren't likely to follow them there. And the residents of Staten Island were so inured to misery that the damage caused by Six Blocks didn't faze them.

Still, Brooks declined. "No. I don't think that's a good idea."

"Why?" Lemon asked. Despite hailing from the future, she was still a teenager, and insensitivity came with the territory. "Are you still afraid of Staten Island?"

"I'm not afraid of it," Brooks said. It wasn't a lie; his feelings toward Staten Island went well beyond fear. Since 'I watched my whole family be murdered there and then I died' was a played out excuse, he made up a better reason. "Hudson still works for the Reticent. I don't think we should be staying anywhere associated with them, given that they just threw us under the bus."

"We're safer here than we would be anywhere else," Smith said. "Where else are we going to have police surveillance 24/7? Just stay away from the windows and we'll be fine."

"Until someone throws a Molotov and sets everything on fire," Brooks said. "You're not healing." He gestured toward the two teens. "They're not healing." He faced the very real possibility of losing his entire family. Again.

Smith pondered for a moment. "Okay, let's go. You and me. We'll leave them here. The cops will stay, but the people will disperse."

"Cops aren't people?" Brooks wondered.

"No. Shut up."

"I don't like that plan," Lemon said.

Patience shook her head. "Nor do I."

Brooks patted Patience on the shoulder. "We won't do anything that puts you in danger."

He looked at Smith and gestured toward the stairs.

"A moment?" he asked.

When he and Smith were out of earshot, he changed his tune. "I'm with you."

"Yeah, I know," Smith said. "Eight years, give or take a few decades."

"... not what I meant. Your plan."

Smith's plans weren't always the best plans, but they were at least plans. This one, Smith reckoned, would keep the girls safe and give him and his partner some much-needed alone time. Brooks didn't have any better ideas, so he and Smith packed two small bags before relaying their strategy to the girls. The packing had to come first, or they'd have more time to guilt trip their fathers into staying.

When the bags were packed, the girls tried to guilt trip them into staying.

"You're going to abandon us?" Patience asked.

Brooks shook his head. "No, not abandon. Lemon will keep you safe for now."

"I will?" Lemon asked.

Brooks nudged her.

"Yeah, I will," Lemon said, playing it cool.

The NYPD assured them that their building would be surveilled for the foreseeable future. They, in turn, assured the NYPD that they would go nowhere near their home, giving the protestors no reason to return to the brownstone. Brooks and Smith would stay on the move.

"We'll contact you later tonight," Brooks said. "And every night after until this blows over."

Smith, in a cheery mood now that life was dangerous again, chuckled "blows." He received a death stare.

10 / CHECKERS

Brooks and Smith didn't check in overnight. At 5:50 AM, Patience made sure Lemon was aware of that fact. When a few rounds of gentle tapping at the bedroom door didn't work, Patience offered a soft apology to no one in particular and walked right into the room.

She let out a meek, "Lemon?"

She tried the same thing a few times with no change in result.

Re-strategizing, Patience opened the curtains wide, and Lemon hissed from her bed. Outside, it was clear that Smith's idea had worked. Having seen the perpetrators of the Six Block Disaster leave, the crowd had dispersed. A lone police cruiser marked that anything had ever been amiss.

"What time is it?" Lemon groaned. When she checked her phone, she was not pleased. She had just gone to sleep three hours earlier after a long Tangl* session with Duke and Duchess.

"It's past sunrise," Patience said, as if that made her wake-up call reasonable. "Misters Brooks and Smith should have contacted us by now."

"They probably got busy looking for a place to stay," Lemon said. "Or getting busy."

"When have they misled us before?"

Lemon sat up and propped her pillow behind her. "Let's see. Every time Eddie says he's not drinking, that's a lie. Every time they pretend they're not fighting, lie. Just yesterday, when Turo said he's not afraid of Staten Island... mega

---

* Tangl is an app developed in Austin, TX used for multi-person video chat. Why it was developed is not clear, as there are thousands of apps that do the exact same thing.

lie. That spot on the basement floor—"

A loud crash downstairs interrupted her recounting of Brooks and Smith's lies. Patience hopped backward in fright and Lemon grabbed the baseball bat that hung above her bed.

"Shall we hide?" Patience asked.

"No," Lemon said. "Come on."

They crept into the hallway, the unarmed Puritan tucked behind the armed Lunan. As they descended the stairs, there was no further sound from the first floor. Only a gentle creaking of the steps, one by one until they reached the bottom.

"Who's there?" Lemon called out.

There was no response.

"H-hello?" Patience offered. "We would have words?"

Still no response.

They turned the blind corner at the bottom of the stairs. A pair of arms rushed Lemon from the side, and her bat tumbled to the floor as she shrieked. Patience fled back up the stairs, stumbling on her frumpy, hand-sewn frock.

Lemon's scream turned quickly from horror to laughter as she realized the identity of the hands' owner. Her older brother, Tangelo, let her go and chuckled. She jumped and hugged him, then let him go again.

He eyed her up and down. In just under a year, she had grown two inches.

"You're tall now," he said.

Lemon shrugged. Everyone on the Moon was tall.

An NYPD officer pounded at the front door. "Is everything all right in there?"

"Yeah!" Lemon said. "I just saw a spider!"

She was fairly certain she heard the officer mutter something explicit as he walked away, but it didn't matter. She turned to Tangelo. "What are you doing here?"

"You sent a letter about your graduation party," he said.

Lemon eyed the familiar time machine in the living room: a seven-foot-tall hunk of metal shaped like a cartoon space-ship with a diner booth inside. "You overshot it a little. It was over a week ago." She looked up. "Patience, it's fine! Come back!"

Patience peeked downstairs. "We're not in danger?"

Lemon pulled Tangelo into Patience's line of sight and she sighed in relief.

Tangelo was disappointed. "I missed the party?"

"Don't worry about it. It was super lame. Everyone just talked about Eddie's vampire thing."

Tangelo blinked. "Should I—" He gestured toward the time machine. "I can go back a few more days."

"No. Seriously. You didn't miss anything. I'm glad you came now. You'd hate my friends."

"You have friends now?" Tangelo teased.

Patience willed herself to interrupt. "Would you help us find Misters Brooks and Smith?"

Lemon rolled her eyes. "They're not missing."

"Where are they?" Tangelo asked.

"We don't know," Lemon admitted.

He shot a critical look. "I'm not going home if you're not safe."

Lemon rolled her eyes again. "I don't need to live with par-anormal detectives to be safe. I'm eighteen *and* immortal."

Patience leaned forward like she was gathering the mental fortitude to interrupt and correct the second part of that statement, so Lemon raised a finger slightly to warn her. Patience stepped back and didn't say a word.

"Is there anything I can do to help?" Tangelo asked.

"No. Seriously. She's just tremtacular*."

Tangelo seemed to accept that. "Well, I brought you some-thing."

---

* Lunan for 'paranoid.'

He handed her a gift wrapped in moonpaper reconstituted from moondust. It was obvious from the moony texture, and Lemon ran her fingers across it for a moment, recalling her home world before daring to open the gift. When she did, she found a staple of her wardrobe: a black t-shirt. On the back, it said nothing. On the front, it was adorned with white Helvetica text that read:

Trevor&
Lin&
Jaxx&
Miranda&
Lemon.

"I don't understand," Patience said.

"Nobody will!" Lemon hugged her brother tight. "I love it!"

In order to ease Patience's confusion, Lemon explained. "It's the members of Pop Tart & the Activation Energy. My mom named me after one of them. They don't exist yet." Her wistfulness made her tear up a little. "This is perfect. Nobody will understand and I'll be able to tell them it's about a band they've never heard of!"

"I thought you were named after the citrus fruit," Patience said.

"Both," Lemon and Tangelo said at once. Their parents had been the rare combination of farmer and hipster.

"And—" Tangelo started.

"There's more?"

He kept the suspense for a moment before answering. "It's a Thinkwayve shirt."

Lemon's eyes went wide. "No way."

She rushed to put the shirt on over her other black t-shirt and thought *Staten Island Dumpster.*

In her head, the song began to play.

"It works!" she said. "I'm jamming!"

Staten, Staten Island, sitting bumper to bumper
See a homeless man staring into a dumpster
It's just not right
It's just not right
Got my stomach pumped on a Saturday night

Before Lemon even got to the chorus, Patience abandoned the conversation. She shuffled across the room and seated herself, perplexed.

"I'll let you try it on later," Lemon said. She hugged her brother again. "You're the best."

"Oh, now I'm the best. Used to be I was 'suffocating you.'"

"You were," Lemon said. "And you will be again if you insist on babysitting us."

"Lemon—"

"We'll find Eddie and Turo. Don't worry about it." Ignoring the spoiler policy on the wall, she added, "I'll send a letter to the future if I'm wrong."

Tangelo considered arguing with her but decided against it. "I trust you." He looked at the Puritan. "Nice seeing you again, Patience."

Patience looked up, having fretted the top layer of skin from her lips. Her goodbye for Tangelo was a weak raising of one hand. She coped with being alone in the 1690s. She coped with her new family in the 2010s. She didn't, however, believe she could deal with having no adult guidance in what was still very much the future to her. Internally, she panicked. Externally, she shuffled a bit in her seat while Lemon and Tangelo said their goodbyes.

With her brother gone, Lemon noticed. "What's wrong?"

"I believe we would have been served well by additional help," Patience said. "There is also the matter of the time machine."

"Relax," Lemon said. "We don't need a time machine. We know exactly how to find them."

"We do?"

Lemon nodded.

11 / SNIP

Brooks and Smith awoke in a room no bigger than a jail cell, but without such luxurious amenities as a toilet, cot, or the ability to leave and spend eight hours making license plates for two dollars. There was, by some odd circumstance, a lone beanbag chair in the corner, its orange and pink tie-dyed print faded from overexposure to the sun in its previous resting place. It was on that chair that Brooks regained consciousness, and it was on a brown and mustard retro print linoleum floor that Smith did the same.

Arising from his unexpected floor rest, Smith groaned. "I don't want to be immortal, but I don't want to deal with back pain either." He eyed the floor and beanbag, then his partner, who appeared to be in an equal funk. "How did we get here?" he asked, knowing Brooks wouldn't know.

"I don't know," Brooks said.

Smith stood and rattled the handle of a metal door: the room's only exit. It was locked.

"Already tried," Brooks said. "You want to share the bag?"

"You want to double-team it?"

Brooks rolled his eyes.

Smith shrugged and nestled himself in an awkward position, such that his ass was planted on the floor and his top half was on the beanbag between Brooks's legs. The beans made a repeating SHRRRK CRRRRP sound as he got settled. "So I guess we've been kidnapped."

"Sure seems like it," Brooks said.

"Is it just me or does your head hurt too?"

"It's just you," Brooks assured him. The lack of a toilet had made him particularly irritable, so he added, "probably going through withdrawal."

"Oh, stop." Smith rubbed the side of his head. "Seriously...

we don't know where we are. They could have implanted something in my head."

"Do you want me to cut it open and check?"

Smith made a sassy "rawr" sound and leaned to the side so he was facing his partner. "What did I do?"

Brooks exhaled a half-laugh. "What *didn't* you do, Eddie? We were on top of the world and you blew it for us. You didn't talk to me before telling everybody in the world about vampires. You're not even remotely concerned that you and the girls are in danger now. You've fully descended into the drunk detective trope, and you're not even doing it ironically. I can't figure you out."

Smith began recounting facts. "One: I don't understand irony. Two: We both know you were tired of running the Reticent anyway. Three: Being normal isn't the same thing as being in danger, and you know it. Three—"

"You're on four."

"—Four: You don't need to figure me out. The only thing we need to figure out right now is how to get out of this Brady Bunch nightmare."

As Smith finished his sentence, a bit of convenient timing led a man to open the door to their room. He was an average guy of average height and weight who probably had average hobbies like fishing or putting together puzzles. He wore the Average Guy Starter Outfit—a pair of khaki shorts, sandals, and a maroon polo shirt—and carried a picnic basket with two bottles of store-brand water poking out of the top.

Brooks was confused. "You're guarding us?" His disbelief went beyond the man's averageness. Via his HUD, Brooks could see that the man was in fact below average, given his high blood pressure and pulse.

"Yep!" the man said cheerfully.

Brooks eyed the basket. "And that is..."

"Oh, you guys are gonna love it. I've got some Natural Sunshine granola bars, all-natural cashews, and fruit leather!"

Brooks's eyes shot at Smith, whose eyes returned fire. They scouted the average man and, after a silent count to three, jumped him. The guard was not a strong person, and he surrendered. Knocking people unconscious is dangerous and not advised, so Smith held the man in a bear hug while Brooks pulled the bean bag open and ripped its fabric into strips. Once the man's hands and legs were tied together, they dropped him onto the pile of loose beans with a CRRRRP. Smith grabbed a strip of fruit leather, and they headed for the door.

Theirs was a short imprisonment. Brooks and Smith casually walked out the door into a wood-paneled hallway. As they stepped, their feet sank several inches into mustard-colored shag carpeting. It appeared to be stained but a closer inspection revealed that, no, that was just the pattern.

"Ugh, it's terrible," Smith said. All fruit leather is, and he tossed the barely nibbled strip to the floor, where it was absorbed into the off-putting carpet. He added to his complaint, "It smells like Tareytons and Dippity-Do. Really takes me back to my childhood."

"Sorry," Brooks said, aware that was unfortunate.

Smith theorized that they might be in an abandoned roller rink or shopping mall in the suburbs, and sought confirmation from his partner. "Can you tell—"

"My GPS isn't working," Brooks noted. "Actually, nothing's working now." He tried to read his partner's vitals and came up with nothing but a Blue Screen of Death.

Smith hated Brooks's dead expression when he was doing cyborg stuff, but since Brooks was touchy about said cyborg stuff, he didn't mention it. "Well, at least—"

Before Smith could finish that thought, Brooks did another cyborg thing and shut down completely. His eyes closed and his body went stiff and tipped so that he was leaned against the wall.

"Brooksy?" Smith snapped a finger in front of his face.

Theirs was a short liberation. From nowhere, a black bag covered Smith's head and blinded him. The next thing he knew, he was flailing, struggling in vain against being hauled away.

12 / NO BS

Patience and Lemon only knew two people who worked for the Reticent: Hudson Marrow, the inventor of time travel and proven adultery enthusiast, and Erin Burroughs, head of Security and part-time Smith flirtee. When they went to check Hudson's apartment, they found that it was no longer Hudson's. When they visited Reticent headquarters, the woman manning the front tent informed them that there was no one in the company who went by his name. So they made a mental note to investigate *his* disappearance later and headed for the Queens apartment of Erin Burroughs, an unknown entity.

Lemon was still convinced that something untoward was happening between Burroughs and Smith. When the girls arrived at Burroughs's doorstep, she made that clear with the most potent of stink eyes, even as she pleaded. "We need your help."

"Come in," Burroughs said, unaffected by Lemon's attitude.

The apartment was surprisingly tidy considering the number of laptops, tablets, routers, old video game consoles, and robots of questionable usefulness. All of the electronics were piled in neat stacks and reined in with color-coded cable management systems. It was beautiful, if you're into that sort of thing.

Burroughs offered the girls some water and seats at her dining room table.

"Do you have any milk?" Patience asked.

Burroughs stared at her. "No."

After a brief moment of Lemon convincing Patience that the water in Queens was potable, they accepted Burroughs's offer. Lemon explained their dilemma as the drinks were poured.

"Eddie and Turo are missing," she said. "I didn't think it was a big deal two days ago, or yesterday even, but they were supposed to check in every day and it's been fifty two hours and counting."

"That sounds like Eddie," Burroughs said, setting down two glasses of water.

Lemon shot her another glare.

Burroughs rolled her eyes. "I'm not sleeping with your dad," she said. "I wish I could say I'd never do that, but... I did do that."

"I knew it!" Lemon gritted her teeth.

"Ten years ago," Burroughs said. "It was before he and Brooks were partnered up. A *lot* of things were different back then. Relax."

Lemon wasn't satisfied. "Did you love him?"

Burroughs broke into a cackle. "Ha! No. God help the poor fool who does. This was purely a sex thing."

Patience's cheeks turned the color of her hair. She fought through her embarrassment at hearing the word 'sex' and piped up, "Lemon believes that Mr. Smith is being unfaithful to Mr. Brooks. She brings it up in conversation most days. It's quite taxing."

"It's not taxing," Lemon insisted.

"It's not really relevant to their being missing," Burroughs said, "but I doubt it."

"Why?" Lemon asked.

"Eddie's a bastard in a lot of ways—a *lot* of ways—but he adores Arturo." She paused. "Tell you what. I'll help you figure out what's going on after we find them."

Lemon nodded. "Okay."

"Now where did you last see them?" Burroughs asked.

Lemon relayed every bit of information she had: Brooks and Smith's plan, the dispersed protestors, Smith's new job that he would soon lose, and Hudson Marrow's sudden, hopefully unrelated disappearance.

"Let me check the police call logs," Burroughs said, grabbing one of many laptops. In theory, the officer who had been stationed outside the Brooks-Smith brownstone may have alerted other officers to which direction the two men headed. Burroughs worked some computer magic that is far too tedious to describe, and within fifteen minutes the group found itself listening to relevant conversations. They discovered that Brooks and Smith had headed east. It was information, but not useful information given that there were a lot of places a person could head on Long Island.

"I have a photograph of those who gathered outside our home," Patience said, handing over her phone.

"I thought you hated pictures," Lemon said.

"Only if I'm forced to be in them," Patience said. "I had hoped the fear of being photographed would drive the protestors away."

"Why would—" Lemon gave up trying to understand Patience's views on technology, and continued. "Everyone wants them dead. A picture won't narrow it down at all."

The sepia-filtered shot taken from Patience's bedroom window didn't help, at first. But when Burroughs took a closer look, she noticed that something was off. Two protest signs in the back of the shot appeared to float in mid-air. There were no human beings holding them up, and no wooden posts securing them to the ground. She zoomed in on the photo, but the words didn't become any clearer. She squinted, trying to make them out.

'Vampire Lives Matter' said one. 'Fangs = Friends' said the other. Burroughs read the words aloud as she deciphered them.

"That's tacky," Lemon said.

"Tacky? Yes. Suspicious? Also yes," Burroughs said. "There's probably nobody more pissed off at Eddie and Arturo than vampires, and we have proof they were scouting your house."

"Well, how do we find vampires?" Lemon asked.

"Should we confront such creatures?" Patience asked.

"No you shouldn't," Burroughs said. "But they're not hard to find."

She turned her laptop to face them. On screen was an embarrassing, out-of-date website with the URL aava-usa.angel-fire.com. It was the first Google result for 'Vampire Lives Matter' and it read: Association for the Advancement of Vampire Americans (AAVA). On the left side of the page, visitors were informed that a list of events was 'coming soon.' On the right side of the page, just under a broken GIF of a dog running back and forth, was the organization's address.

"We're going," Lemon said, tugging Patience.

Patience made a short peep noise in fear.

"Don't do that," Burroughs said. "Seriously. You two may not have experience with how dangerous these creatures can be, but trust me—"

Lemon had already made her way to the exit, dragging Patience by the arm behind her.

"You're not going to listen," Burroughs said, resigned and to no one in particular. Everyone always had to learn their lesson about supernatural beings the hard way. She had learned it the hard way, Smith had learned it the hard way, and Brooks had learned it the really, really hard way. She stood up, grabbed her bag of hunting supplies, and chased after the girls.

13 / DO CYBORGS SCREAM FOR ICE CREAM?

Brooks had found a nickel on the floor and kept flipping it into the air. It had landed on heads twenty-three of twenty-four times now and the incongruent statistic bothered him. On the twenty-fifth flip, he dropped it, and the gentle clinking sound of the coin coming to rest on concrete made Smith groan as he came to, again on a floor.

"Are you okay?" Brooks asked.

Smith rubbed at his temples. "It's like you're shoving nickels down my eye sockets."

"It's really not that loud... what did it land on?"

Smith picked up the coin. "Heads."

"*Hijo de puta*," Brooks said. The math made no sense.

This room was smaller than the last, but just as shoddily floored. The concrete was once coated with a sealant, but it had worn in places, leaving errant light grey areas all over the dark grey floor. It was cold, almost like a walk-in freezer, and the lone decor was a wire shelf stacked with empty milk crates.

Smith realized that he had awoken on the floor of a walk-in freezer. Brooks sat nearby, atop a milk crate.

Smith sat up. "This makes me wonder... can you freeze?"

Brooks tilted his head. "I don't see why not. My cells are just as organic as yours. There's just a computer inside my head or whatever." He really wished he had an instruction manual.

"Would you burn or melt?" Smith wondered.

"Oh my God, Eddie. Can you not give me an existential crisis right now?"

"Sorry." Smith stood. "One more."

"*What?*"

"Do you... dream of electric sheep?"

Brooks groaned. "I'm not an android, and how long have you been waiting to ask that?"

"Pretty long." Smith took two steps toward the door to inspect it. Having once spent four months working at The Meat Pantry, he knew just where to look for an escape.

Brooks had already done that. "The safety latch has been tampered with."

"Well." Smith turned around, grabbed a milk crate, and seated himself next to Brooks. "What *do* you dream of?"

"What?"

"Philip Dick notwithstanding. What do you dream about?"

"You don't want to know," Brooks said.

"I kind of do?"

"No. You don't."

Smith dropped it. "So... any theories?"

"You were thinking old mall. Now I'm thinking old grocery store."

Proving itself old, the freezer made a loud buzzing noise, and both the blowers and the fluorescent lighting shut off. On the bright side, it was instantly warmer. On the dark side, it was dark.

"It does that," Brooks said, unaffected. "Comes on for ten minutes, goes off for thirty." His HUD was still down, but he was one of few people who still wore a watch. That was good enough.

"Wait. How long have I been unconscious?" Smith asked.

Brooks glanced down at his wrist. "Three hours since I woke up."

That was unusual. They'd been knocked or drugged unconscious more than a few times in their years with the Reticent, and Smith had always awoken first. It was a source of pride, in fact. This made two times in one day when that hadn't been the case. Smith chalked it up to the cyborg thing.

"They don't want us dead," Brooks said. "Whoever they are. They sent that guy to feed us once, and they'll do it again. Probably with better security."

"Better than one guy with a picnic basket?" Smith scoffed. "But how?"

Brooks shrugged, then realized his partner couldn't see the shrug. He grunted.

Smith put a hand on Brooks's shoulder. "You know what would be hilarious? If they came to get us and—"

Brooks cut him off. "No."

"You didn't even let me finish."

"You were going to say 'if they came to get us and we were banging.'"

Smith shrugged. "Yeah. I was. So?"

"We've already done that one."

"That was 'trapped in an elevator.' We've never done 'trapped in a freezer' before," Smith noted. "And I'm pretty sure the best way to fight hypothermia is to get naked."

"That doesn't sound right," Brooks said. "And the cold is off at the moment..."

Smith stood up and began unbuttoning his shirt.

"What are you doing?"

"You have night vision. Figure it out."

"I'm still bluescreened," Brooks complained. "I can't see a damn thing."

"Well, I'm stripping down. It's extremely erotic."

"Is it?" Brooks asked with no emotion.

"*Extremely.*"

Three sounds followed: the awkward shuffle of a man taking his shoes off, the rustling of a belt being removed, and the loud THUD of a human body hitting concrete.

***

When Smith awoke again, his pants were around his ankles and there was a gun pressed against his head. All in all, not the worst thing that had ever happened to him, but not a promising position to be in. The freezer lights and blower had come back on, and the same average guy from before had replaced his cheer with testiness. With his right hand armed, he used his left to place another picnic basket on the freezer floor.

"Don't do anything," the man said. "I just want to leave this here."

Smith wiggled his head a little so he could see Brooks. "Did he knock me out?"

"No. I'm pretty sure you *tripped* trying to get your pants off."

"I'm going to back away," the kidnapper said. "Just stay there and—"

Catching the emphasis on 'tripped' in his partner's sentence, Smith kicked the man's feet out from under him. Brooks leapt from his crate, grabbed the gun, and pointed it right back at their kidnapper.

Smith stood up and belted his pants. "I love you."

Brooks demanded an answer from the average guy. "Who are you?"

Their kidnapper dusted himself off and stood tall. "I am mujahid Urwah Saleem."

The claim was suspect. "You're white and... ginger." Brooks added, "You're wearing khakis."

"I am engaged in jihad against the—"

"You were just doling out granola bars and now you're a terrorist?" Brooks asked.

"I am engaged in jihad against the—"

"Is he reading from a script?" Smith asked.

"I am not. I am engaged in jihad against the—"

"Ask him something weird," Brooks said.

"Why do I always have to come up with the weird stuff?"

"Because you're weird," Brooks said.

Smith stared into the kidnapper's eyes. "How big is your dick?"

"See?" Brooks said.

Their kidnapper stuttered. "Uh... um... this matters not. I will, uh, destroy you and—"

"He's flustered," Brooks said.

"Yeah, okay. Script." Smith punched the man in the face, sending him to the floor bleeding and holding his jaw. He didn't feel bad, on account of the racist impersonation and terrorist threats. "Let's go."

They stepped out of the freezer into an abandoned industrial kitchen. Brooks's weapon remained drawn. He expected a fight. He expected dozens of armed men to swarm them. He expected an extended action sequence. He expected something dramatic. Instead, both men became lightheaded and fell to the floor, their escape attempt once again foiled.

14 / VAMP IRE

Halloween was months away, but the AAVA was ready. Their office on the fifth floor of a building that also housed an Italian market was marked by a black sign with dripping red letters. The window was framed in black and orange tinsel and there were dozens of black bat decals festooned to it. A trickle of machine-made fog seeped into the hall from under the door. Patience coughed in its wake.

"I thought they were against stereotyping," Burroughs said, flicking a plastic bat.

"Same." Lemon reached out to knock on the door.

"Wait," Burroughs said. "Are you sure you're ready?"

Patience shook her head and Lemon nudged her.

"Yes," Patience said.

On the way over, they'd received a crash course in vampire staking, one that Burroughs hoped wouldn't be necessary. Vampires savored their hunts, and walking straight into their lair wouldn't make the three women challenging kills, which would keep them safe. In theory. Still, Burroughs armed Patience and Lemon with a stake each, just in case.

Lemon tapped at the door. Just when it seemed like it was taking a bit too long for someone to respond, the door creaked open a few inches and a rushed voice emerged. "Quickly! Enter!"

Burroughs went first, followed by Lemon and Patience. When the Puritan left the door cracked behind her, the same voice hissed, "Shut the door! They're working with garlic downstairs!"

She obliged, and a spooky motion-sensor bat flew forward and hissed at her. Patience ducked behind Lemon.

They couldn't see a thing in the pitch-black room. Not until the vampire attending to them lit a few candles on a mantel. Then they were able to absorb the scenery: dusty shelves lined with dusty books, dusty velvet chairs lined with dusty blankets, and a few dusty coffins lined with nothing but dust. Not normal, modern coffins, but splinter-laden wood coffins that looked straight out of an Old West cartoon. The windows were painted black and covered with black velvet curtains. Cobwebs—mostly artificial but some spider-woven—littered the area. It was ghastly, but not in the way the vampires intended.

"And how may I help you?" the vampire asked. In the soft light, it became apparent that his face was caked with white costume makeup and he wore a green velour cloak, its budget threads coming undone around the hood. His black, slicked-back hair contained white streaks at the temples that appeared to have been spray painted on.

When the vampire reached up and adjusted his teeth, Burroughs couldn't stop herself from laughing. "Are you people serious?" she asked.

"Do *not* disrespect us by calling us people!"

"But you're not vampires." Burroughs tucked her stake back into the waist of her pants.

"*WHAT*!?" shouted a muffled voice from within a coffin.

"If we aren't vampires, why is he sleeping in a coffin?" the standing vampire asked.

The coffin creaked open, and the coffined vampire coughed a few times. He used an inhaler to take a deep breath and recover from the excitement.

Burroughs buried her head in her hands and removed it only once she'd collected herself.

"I've seen vampires," she said. "I've staked vampires. You're not vampires."

"We are so."

She refused to play along. "I do want to know how you disappeared in photos, though."

"Because we're vampires!" the vampire said.

"Special effects, then?" Burroughs didn't care enough to interrogate them further. She nudged Lemon and Patience toward the door. "Come on." She added, "Also, garlic doesn't even affect them."

The original vampire blocked their path. "Did you come here just to mock us?"

"No, we came here for information, but you obviously had nothing to do with it." There was no way Brooks and Smith had been taken by a group of vampire cosplayers. They could and did make stupid decisions, sure, but they were a *smidge* more talented than that.

"Nothing to do with what?" the vampire asked, re-tying his cloak.

"You had protestors at our house," Lemon said. "They were there the day Edward Smith and Arturo Brooks disappeared."

"The guys who staked one of our kind for all the world to see are missing?" the vampire asked. "Good riddance."

Lemon puffed her chest and stomped at the wannabe creature of the night. "Shut your mouth. You aren't even a vampire!"

"Please, sir. We wish to have our guardians back," Patience said.

"They're not—" Lemon started.

"I like the way she speaks," the vampire said. "It's elegant."

"Thank you, sir," Patience said.

"Still, that's no reason to help you."

The asthmatic vampire disagreed. He stumbled out of his coffin and approached his friend. "Frank," he said. "If we're trying to prove that vampires are good, we can't encourage kidnapping."

"We didn't do it," Frank said. "We're not encouraging it."

"No, but we saw who did."

"You saw who took them?" Lemon asked.

The non-Frank vampire nodded. "They didn't get very far

from the house. We followed them for a little bit so we could throw some rubber bats and hiss at them."

"Naturally," Burroughs said.

Frank crossed his arms and glowered at the other vampire as he ratted them out.

"A few blocks away, a white van rolled up next to them. A couple of guys jumped out and nabbed them."

"Did you get the license plate number?" Burroughs asked.

"No," the vampire said. "Who does that?"

"Nobody," Burroughs sighed. Her years as a detective would have been much easier if people were the least bit observant.

"But," he said, "we did get a good look at the guys."

"Do you know who they were?" Lemon asked.

The vampire shook his head. "I'd help if I could, but—"

"You can," Burroughs said, formulating an idea. She motioned toward the door. "Come with us."

"Are you crazy? It's daylight!"

She looked the vampire in the eyes and refused to blink for a solid thirty seconds. "You. Are. Not. A. Vampire."

The vampire, unaccustomed to conflict, dragged his feet a bit, but acquiesced. "Fine." He pulled the hood of his cloak over his head and grabbed a nearby umbrella. "This will protect me for a short time."

With that, they set out into the sun.

15 / IN ZANE

It was not sunny inside Godwin Zane's mind, and it was about to have even more cloud cover. One of the best and worst parts of being a celebrity was that reporters asked for Zane's opinion on everything. Inquiries into his thoughts on subjects ranging from green living (he didn't care) to the latest conflict in Turkey (he didn't care) made him feel important, but the last thing Zane needed was a greater sense of self-importance.

The second-to-last thing he needed was to be interrupted. His mind was deep in thought as he made his way from Bumpin' Grind to his office building. That's why he needed the coffee. Zane Tower had three coffee shops, but he'd stocked them with cost-cutting brew for his miserable employees. So he began every morning three blocks away with toasted coconut aeropress garnished with a pat of grass-fed butter.

Thirty-two hours without sleep and he hadn't fully formulated a plan. He needed Reticent headquarters, but the organization had publicly severed its ties to the only potential 'in' he had when it renounced Smith. And now a pack of hungry reporters blocked him from entering his own building. He almost ran into one.

"Is there any truth to the rumor that your company recently hired Edward Smith?" the reporter asked.

Zane sighed. On a normal day, he'd love playing the PR game, but he was trying to scheme.

"I don't do our hiring," he lied, pushing his way through. "I couldn't tell you."

"Do you not still vet every employee?" It was something Zane was famous for.

"No," he lied again, in hopes that bluntness would make

them leave him alone.

Zane nudged a few more people out of the way, but another reporter blocked his path. "In your opinion, what should happen to Edward Smith and Arturo Brooks?"

Zane considered that for a moment. Somewhere deep in his brain, a gear had been nudged. It wasn't spinning yet, but the beginnings of a plan were coming together.

"Nothing," he said. "There's no proof they were involved in Six Blocks. All we know is that the Reticent were, and they should continue to be investigated."

A different, more belligerent journalist chimed in. "You really think that's enough?"

"What would *you* do?" Zane asked. "Tar and feather them in the streets?" He lost his train of thought and made a mental note to find out what tarring and feathering entailed.

The reporter continued. "If rumors can be believed, they've gone missing. It's not unthinkable that some of the victims have sought their own justice."

"It's not unthinkable," Zane said, "but there's a reason I don't go out and act like a vigilante."

Reasons Zane didn't go out and act like a vigilante included interest in maintaining the mystery of whether or not he had superpowers and disinterest in putting his life on the line. But Six Blocks and now the vampire situation had changed things. No one had ever taken such an accusatory tone with him before, and years of being softballed by the media left him unsure how to respond to what came next.

"In light of everything that's happened, there are some people who think you should do more. That is, assuming you can do what you say you can."

"Assuming?" Zane raised an eyebrow.

"Assuming you have powers," the reporter repeated, "why don't you help people?"

"Oh, I have powers," Zane said, distracted. "I have the best powers. It's just not safe to use them."

Two reporters looked at each other and shrugged.

"I have powers," Zane insisted.

He pushed his way into the building, but his mental planning session had come to an end. From the second the reporter's question had ended, it was all he could think about. Well, it was all he could think about other than sex, aesthetics, and how to fit another three ads on the back of his cape. It occupied sixty percent of his thoughts, give or take.

Why don't I help people?

16 / BACK TO BLACK

The police station was abuzz with activity: phones ringing, fingers tapping at keyboards, officers coughing in response to stagnant office air, walkie-talkies making that PSSHT sound they make, soda machines dropping 20 oz. obesity enhancers, and so on. They weren't all productive sounds.

When Burroughs, Patience, Lemon, and Alan (the non-Frank cosplay vampire) arrived, the officer manning the front desk was dutifully ordering a pizza. Not rattled by the all-too-common appearance of a cloaked being at the precinct and not seeing any immediate injuries among them, he put up his index finger in a 'one moment' gesture.

One moment passed.

Then another.

Then another.

Then there was a dispute over whether a coupon granting free breadsticks was still valid. It was labeled with an expiration date of January 1st, but it didn't specify which January 1st. A manager was summoned to assist.

The officer moved his mouth away from the phone and whispered "sorry."

Another moment passed. Once the free breadsticks were granted, the group of visitors was able to make its request. Alan, they explained, had seen the men who kidnapped Brooks and Smith, but he didn't get a picture and he was a terrible artist. They were there to report the kidnapping and see what a police sketch artist could come up with to release to the media.

Brooks and Smith weren't the most popular men in New York (in fact, they were the second least popular behind Andy Dick), but a missing person was a missing person. It wasn't long before the quartet sat in front of Officer

Christine Garrison—about twenty minutes. When her BFA in Studio Art from NYU left her with eighty thousand dollars in student debt and no job prospects, Garrison tested into the NYPD. Her job mostly involved regular police filings, but once or twice a month she was asked to act as a forensic artist. Those moments were bright spots, and she immediately made time for them. She jotted down the information about their case in a hurry: Brooks and Smith had been missing for seventy-one hours, abducted by three men in a car, scribble scribble. That part wasn't of particular interest. She wanted to get to the drawing. When the filing was done, a huge smile came across her face as she struck pencil to paper.

Unfortunately, she wasn't a very good artist. With Lemon, Burroughs, and Patience looking on, Garrison took her time and savored the attention. The strokes were deliberate and the group was hopeful. When she finished, Garrison picked up her sketch and presented it with pride.

The party shared puzzled glances.

Burroughs offered an accurate assessment, "That looks like Samuel L. Jackson."

"Too old?" Garrison asked. "I can make him younger."

"Well," Alan said. "None of them were bald… or black. Maybe I didn't do a very good job describing them. The first guy was pretty tan—but not black—and he had a beard. He kinda looked like that guy in System of a Down?"

"Mmhmm. I think I understand," Garrison said.

The artist crumpled and tossed Samuel L. Jackson, then got to work on a new sheet of paper. Lemon tried to sneak a glance at her work in progress, but Officer Garrison shielded her pad from view. This drawing was going to take a bit longer.

"Where do we go from here?" Patience asked Burroughs as they waited.

Burroughs had no faith in the sketch artist. "Assuming this turns out to be the bust it looks like it's going to be, I'm not sure."

When her pencil stopped moving, Garrison held up yet another sketch. It was very different from the last, and it did have a beard, but something still wasn't quite right.

"That's Ice Cube," Lemon said.

"Was he not in System of a Down?" the officer asked.

"N.W.A.," Burroughs corrected.

"I told you the guy wasn't black," Alan said.

"Not. Black." Lemon said, tapping her fingers.

"Shoot. You're right. Sorry. I'll get it right this time."

Lemon folded her arms and grunted as Garrison went back to the drawing board.

The next two drawings were of Idris Elba and Chiwetel Ejiofor, respectively. By the time Garrison presented the last one—a spitting image of Jamie Foxx—Burroughs had to escort Lemon from the room before she could get into a rightful shouting match with the officer. When they were all safe outside the building (except for Alan, who tucked away in a bathroom waiting for sunset), Patience again inquired about their plan.

"How are we to find Misters Brooks and Smith now?" she asked.

"We're not," Lemon said. "The wanted posters are going to be for Idris Elba! What are we supposed to do, personally find every guy in the city who looks like Serj Tankian?"

Burroughs made the cause seem even more hopeless. "Actually, we don't even know that he was from the area, so... really, it could be a worldwide search."

"Are you sure you don't want Mr. Tangelo's help?" Patience asked.

"No," Lemon said, finding both her courage and stubbornness. "We can do this."

"What will become of us?" Patience asked. Though she wasn't sure who Serj Tankian was, she had begun to settle into life in the twenty-first century and now faced a complete upheaval.

"Hard to say. The good news is they're on the record as missing. That means we have a lot of eyes on the lookout." She glanced at Patience. "The bad news is you're under eighteen so as soon as Officer Garrison stops drawing black actors and realizes that, they're going to need to figure out who your legal guardian is. That might also mean some scrutiny of your paperwork. That might mean I end up in prison since I falsified the hell out of those documents."

"Should we go missing too?" Lemon asked.

"No," Burroughs said. "Don't be dramatic. I would have told those idiots not to do it either, but here we are." She patted both of the girls on the shoulder. "For now, you can stay with me. We'll figure something out."

17 / CHAINED MELODY

When Smith came to again, there were shackles on his ankles and wrists keeping him against a cement wall on an equally cement floor. His first thought was that the chains were a bit overkill. His second was that, wherever they were, at least it wasn't freezing. His third was *shit shit shit.* He wiggled to the left and realized his range in that direction was only about two feet. He wiggled to the right and found the same. He leaned forward and—sure enough—he had about two feet of clearance. Someone, somewhere wanted him to remain stuck against this cement wall. Wiggling backward through the wall was impossible because physics is a thing, and when Smith realized that, panic set in.

Brooks was in a similar predicament, minus the extreme fear of being bound. He observed the abundance of cement along with the rickety wooden staircase leading out of the room and decided they were probably in someone's basement. From his own chains, he saw his partner struggling and set his grievances aside.

"Shit," Smith said, sweat forming at his brow. "Shiiiiiit," he repeated, drawing the word out as he attempted to pull his wrist out of its cuff. He normally kept a pin in his sleeve for such an occasion, but having forgotten many things in their rush to escape Brooklyn, he was unprepared. He tugged and tugged until his wrist was red.

"Hey," Brooks said.

Smith ignored him and continued pulling, his motions becoming more and more frantic. *"Come on."* The chains clinked and clanked, but they wouldn't budge. He paused for a moment, then used his right arm to twist and yank at his left. There was a slight popping sound followed by a not-so-slight shout. Smith had dislocated his shoulder, and he was still trapped. "That was stupid. Shit!"

Brooks tried to get his attention again. "*Hey.*"

Smith was too busy trying and failing to control his rapid breathing. He put his arms around his knees and leaned forward, eyes shut. If he couldn't see that he was trapped, he thought, it wouldn't bother him. Then his thoughts slipped out from under him. He thought about what would happen if he never escaped and was trapped there forever. His memories assaulted his brain: memories of what felt like decades trapped at the Reticent being experimented on, memories of his time living with Tristan Gounaris, memories of his parents' closet in their godforsaken trailer. He thought about everything and opened his eyes, only to find them hazy and unfocused. "Shit."

"Hey!" Brooks repeated with force. He clapped his hands together and the sound echoed throughout the room.

Smith turned his head toward his partner, just barely.

"Look at me," Brooks said. When nothing happened, he made his instructions clearer. "Don't look down. Look up. Look at my face."

Smith's head swayed back and forth as he obliged. "Okay..."

Brooks had no idea what he was doing, but like any good Reticent agent he was well-versed in post-traumatic stress of his own. He felt that he had to try something. It would be worse, he thought, if Smith believed that he didn't care. "Uh..." He aimed for distraction. "What do you see?"

"What?" Smith asked in a low mumble. Then he snipped, "A basement."

Brooks gestured at himself, chains clanking. "Look at me. What do you see?"

Smith blinked a few times. "Uh... a hot Hispanic twunk?"

It was a strange answer, but Brooks went with it.

"What else?" he asked.

"Uh... a really good detective? Six-foot-one? Male? I don't

know what you want here."

"Just keep talking." Anything to keep Smith distracted would do.

"You're... I don't know... You have bad taste in movies."

"Sure," Brooks said.

Lies, Brooks thought.

"And music," Smith added.

A fan of Kitten Orgy had no right to say that to anyone, but Brooks held his tongue. "What else?"

When his eyes stopped shifting and stayed with his partner's, Smith blurted what came to mind. "And men."

Brooks tilted his head. "Why would you say that?"

"You're too good for me, that's for damn sure."

On one hand, Brooks had successfully distracted his partner. On the other, he had somehow managed to draw out Smith's deep, unfaltering hatred of himself. That was bad.

Smith's voice was softer than usual, but honest. "I'm some chubby asshole who tries to strangle you in your sleep. I really don't know why you put up with me."

"I don't 'put up' with you. I love you. I want—"

His heartfelt attempt was cut short as Smith kept talking. "I thought this would be better..." Smith looked back down at his chains and jerked himself back up, breathing heavily. He leaned back against the wall and closed his eyes, trying again to forget that he was trapped.

"What?" Brooks asked.

Smith kept his eyes shut, partly so he wouldn't see the restraints and partly so Brooks wouldn't see his eyes. The words that followed were a more effective distraction. "For ten years," Smith said, "I was miserable because I knew you were gonna die in Willowbrook Park. Because you were the bright spot in a big pile of shit, and I knew you were gonna bleed to death right in front of me and I would never see you again."

"I'm here, though," Brooks said, very much not dead.

Smith continued, "Then I escaped the Reticent and spent, what, almost eighty years alone just... wallowing in despair. Which is pathetic in its own right, but... do you know how many times I traveled back in time trying to fix it and bring you back?"

"No," Brooks said.

"Four hundred and three, give or take."

Brooks gasped. "Jesus."

"So I failed, obviously... I failed a lot. But now you're here."

"Eddie, look at me."

"No," Smith said.

"Eddie," Brooks said. "I *am* here."

Smith brought his hands to his face and circled them around his eyes. He managed to wipe away the tears, but the fact that they'd been forming was obvious. He turned to Brooks. "I know. You're here and you're great. Really. It's just... I'm not."

"What?" Brooks asked.

"It's not circumstances. It's me. I should be the happiest motherfucker who ever time traveled, and all I can think about is how *bored* I am. Finding out I can get injured again is the best thing that's happened in months."

"It's not..." Brooks thought for a second. What he was going to say was a lie, so he corrected it. "It might be you, but it doesn't mean it's your fault. That's why I keep telling y—"

Smith dismissed him. "I know. No."

"She's a really good therapist—"

"I can't do it," Smith said.

"Why?" Brooks asked. "It couldn't make you any *more* miserable."

Smith wouldn't articulate anything more. "I just can't."

"That's not good enough," Brooks said. "We've been together for eight years—"

Smith snapped. "You know that's under a tenth of my life

at this point, right? Do I have to recount every horrible thing that's ever happened to me? I said I won't do it."

Brooks was stressed. For a moment, he forgot he was trying to talk his partner down and snapped back at him. "You know what? I don't care. That's not good enough."

For a moment, Smith's scrappiness overtook his anxiety. "Oh, fuck off."

"It's not! And whatever your problem is, you don't get to talk to me like that." Brooks moved his hands forward to gesticulate, but they didn't stop two feet from the wall. There was a loud clang as the chains broke from their moorings, then a series of softer clangs as the chains settled on the floor. He sat for a moment, absorbing what had just happened. "Well."

He freed his legs and walked across the room, chains dragging. He knelt down and pulled Smith's chains from the wall.

Smith broke the silence and tension at once. "You couldn't have done that before?"

"Sorry," Brooks said. "I guess my strength didn't go with everything else. I still forget I'm not a person sometimes."

Smith was concerned. "What?"

"Nothing. Let's go."

The rickety staircase squeaked and buckled with every step, but it held up. When the two men reached the top, Brooks popped a door off its frame.

"What the hell?" Smith said as the upstairs room came into view.

18 / THE WORST VAMPIRES IN THE WORLD

If there's a creature more stubborn than a human teenager, it hasn't been discovered yet. Lemon paced in front of the bottle-made hole in the brownstone's front window, thinking about how inconvenient their situation was. She could have written her brother to figure out what happened to Brooks and Smith, but she was determined not to do so. When she decided to stay in the past, she did so to prove herself independent, and she wasn't about to ruin that. Plus, they had a 'no spoilers' policy.

"We were warned to stray from the window," Patience said.

"I can't help it," Lemon said.

They'd returned to pack some things so they could stay with Burroughs for a while. Lemon's idea of packing was two flannel-tinged outfits, a pile of indie records, her violin, and an unconventional makeup palette. Patience's idea of packing was every frock she owned and a handful of books, three of which were Bibles that varied only slightly. Their guardian would arrive any moment, but until then Patience wanted to hide.

"There's another crowd outside," Patience said, glancing out the peephole.

"They don't seem to be shouting as much," Lemon said. She squinted. "Actually, they're not shouting at all."

The new crowd was not comprised of protestors. On the contrary. One sign read 'Bring Them Home Safe.' Another read 'Innocent Until Proven Guilty.' The final read 'Vampires Care.' The angry old coot was there again, but the vampires had pushed him and his 'God Hates Vampire Fags' sign to the back of the crowd. Lemon pressed her face against a bit of glass that still remained in the window frame and squinted. Wannabe vampires made up the entire gathering, minus the old dickbag, and at the front of the group was none other than Alan from the AAVA. She moved to a glass-free spot and called out to him.

"What are you doing here?" Lemon asked.

"We're proving that vampires aren't evil," Alan said.

Another added, "We have forgiven your fathers and the world needs to see that."

The world would see that, as a group of reporters had arrived on scene.

Lemon rolled her eyes. "You. Aren't. Vampires."

The crowd forgave her remark and began singing a modified version of "We Are The World."

We are the dead, we are the vampires
We are the ones who shirk the light of day
'Cause we've stopped living
There's a choice we're making
We value every life
It's true we'll make a better day
Humans and vamps

Lemon threw herself onto the couch. "Thetans, come and take me."

"I don't know what that means," Patience admitted, taking a seat next to her.

"It doesn't matter." Lemon grabbed her phone and resumed tweeting.

A strong feeling came over the Puritan any time she felt an opinion coming on. The feeling was two parts guilt, one part fear, another part shame, and a pinch of repression. Ten months in the twenty-first century hadn't sent it away, and it existed even when speaking with someone who was, for all intents and porpoises, her equal. She took a deep gulp to overcome her anxiety and spoke.

"I am not too feeble-minded to comprehend if you would explain," she said.

"Huh?" Lemon looked up, mid-tweet.

"I know that I don't understand many things and that's why they've put me in the classroom of ill repute, but—"

"I don't think you're stupid," Lemon said, setting her phone at her side. It vibrated, but she ignored it for the moment. "It just doesn't matter. It's a stupid phrase from Scientology."

"Oh," Patience said. "What's that?"

"Some dumbass religion," Lemon said.

"That seems impolite."

"Well, it's more of a cult?"

"I'm not sure I understand the difference."

Lemon chuckled. "I know you don't."

There is some dispute on the formal definition of a cult, but suffice to say it involves a passionate belief system that is misguided, often to the point of being dangerous. Someone whose belief system called for the hanging of witches understandably found religions and cults difficult to distinguish. Making matters more confusing, Smith was always going on and on about something called *Firefly* and its cult following. Patience sighed inwardly.

"Do you believe we'll find Misters Brooks and Smith?" she asked.

"No," Lemon said. "I think they'll find us. That's what detectives do."

"But you believe they're alive and well?"

"I believe they're *alive*," Lemon said. "Well is... well, I don't know that they're ever well." She doubted that anyone who had ever worked for the Reticent could be well.

Patience rearranged herself in her seat, preparing herself for making a statement. Her discomfort made it obvious that she was about to speak, and Lemon tilted her head to the side, waiting.

"Please don't leave for school," Patience said.

Lemon tilted her head the other direction. "What? I already graduated..."

"I mean for college. I don't wish to live alone. Edward and Arthur—"

"—turo—"

"—are always—"

Lemon finished her thought. "Going through some ridiculous drama or another? Tell me about it." She scoffed and insulted them in Lunan. "Glorbdinks."

Patience had no idea what that word meant, but she nodded at the context. "You, however, are steady as a rock."

"I like that," Lemon said. She grabbed her phone and updated her Twitter profile so that it read 'Lemon Jones: I am a rock.' Lemon hadn't yet decided what she was going to do with her life, but Patience had given the older girl something new to consider. Something her brother had always considered. Something that rhymed with treeschponsibility.

19 / ECCENTRIC

Having made it out of confinement three times in a row, Brooks and Smith were fast becoming the world's foremost experts in escape artistry. They wouldn't get another chance to practice any time soon, though. The basement stairs led up into another basement. It, in turn, had stairs that led to another basement. At the top of those, finally, was what looked to be a normal suburban living room from the 1950s, complete with teal wallpaper and a wooden stand TV. The only lighting, aside from what little seeped through dusty geometric patterned curtains, was a tri-color stand lamp: red, green, and yellow.

"What the hell is going on here?" Smith wondered out loud.

"Don't be mad," a voice said.

"I think it's a little late for that," Brooks called out, mad.

From behind an old, nonfunctioning grandfather clock appeared Godwin Zane. Lit by the green portion of the lamp, his grey looked an olive drab that was even less appealing than usual. He was not remorseful, but he was a tad embarrassed. "So—"

Brooks stared at him, arms folded. Smith also stared at him, but with his left arm disabled the folding didn't convey irritation as much as it did injury. He scowled to get his point across.

"This is awkward," Zane said.

The two men asked questions at once:

"Where are we?" Brooks asked.

"Why the fuck—" Smith started.

"You're at my parents' house in Amagansett," Zane said, answering Brooks. "Well, former house. They're dead." Before Smith could continue his inquiry, Zane answered it as well. "I didn't want you two doing anything stupid while I figured out how to clear your names."

"While you *what?*" Brooks asked.

Zane pointed at Smith. "It was his idea."

Smith threw up his good hand. "No it wasn't! What part of being *kidnapped* was my idea?"

Zane pulled out a compact and dusted himself with grey powder as he answered. "You said you didn't want you two implicated in Six Blocks. Well, the Reticent implicated you before I could drag them through the mud so I'm trying to un-implicate you. I figured being kidnapped would get you some sympathy while I did my thing." He hadn't figured that his captives wouldn't give him much heart-wrenching material to leak to the press, but he could probably make Smith's latest outburst about being tied up work to their advantage.

Smith turned, pressed his forehead against the wall, and began cackling. When the laughter stopped, he turned and shouted. "You could have just told us you had a plan!"

"Well, then you wouldn't have been scared!" Zane shut his compact. As he continued explaining, he tried to make himself seem like a better person. "To be fair, I didn't know you had the weird thing about being chained up." He squinted at Brooks. "Or that you're a cyborg. That's neat."

"It's really not." Brooks stared at an overtly racist sambo figurine on a shelf. "What is with this place?"

"Have you not read my autobiography?" Zane asked, appalled at the thought.

"No," Brooks and Smith said simultaneously.

"My parents were... *eccentric,*" he said.

Smith muttered under his breath. "Imagine that."

"You were just in the fallout shelter," Zane said. "Before that, the second kitchen. Before that, the chef's quarters. You should read it. All the details are in the book."

"The chef slept on a bean bag chair?" Smith asked.

Zane shrugged. "It was the sixties."

"But—" Brooks said, eyeing an alligator skin rug.

"Oh, their taste was awful," Zane said. "I like to think I do better."

Brooks scowled. "Not at all what I was going to ask."

"Oh. What?"

"Why did the guy have to be a Muslim terrorist?" Brooks asked.

"Yeah, that part seems racist," Smith said.

Brooks nodded.

"He didn't *have* to be," Zane said, shuffling. "I tried to come up with a compelling script. I'm not racist. I'm Jewish, for crying out loud."*

"Jews can't be racist?" Brooks asked. "That's pretty racist."

Smith nodded. "*Extremely* racist."

"Stop hanging out with Millennials!" Zane shouted.

"Aren't *you* a Millennial?" Brooks asked. "I think I technically am and you're younger than me."

"No!" Zane said. "'Millennial' is a catchall for 'young people who annoy me.'"

The men smiled at their ability to fluster Godwin Zane, who in turn straightened his shirt in an effort to regain his composure and avoid an incident.

"Script wasn't very compelling either," Brooks added.

At the critique of his writing, Zane's hands began to glow. "I didn't have enough time to work on it!"

Brooks eyed the glowing hands. "Is that normal?"

"Yeah." Smith rolled his eyes.

"So he actually has powers?" Brooks asked.

"Yeah," Smith said. "If that counts."

"Stop antagonizing me," Zane said. "I'm trying to help you." He glared at Smith in particular. "I gave *you* a job."

"You kidnapped me before I could start!"

"Just," Zane gestured toward one of those weird round

---

* He wasn't.

couches with an elevated portion in the middle, "sit down. We'll talk this through. I'll be very calm, not melt anything. It'll be great."

Brooks curled his lip at the dusty pleather, but obliged. Smith noted the thick dust and opted to sit on his partner's lap instead.

"*Really?*" Brooks asked.

Smith shrugged.

Zane continued. "You guys can have this place to yourselves. I just need you gone while I work this out. The hostage videos would have been a nice PR touch, but we can do without."

"And the plan?" Brooks asked.

"Hmm?" In the two seconds since he'd last spoken, Zane's mind had already wandered.

"You have a plan?" Brooks asked.

"Oh. Yeah. I just figured it out. I think. The plan is to get the Reticent to screw up again while you're not there."

Smith's eyes darted from side to side as he formulated a thought. "Oh my nonexistent god." He tilted his head. "You're still trying to get that damn building."

"What?" Brooks asked.

Smith explained. "He wants Reticent HQ so he can make it pretty or something. It's some Lex Luthor shit."

"It's about *aesthetics*," Zane corrected. "And yes, I'm still trying to get it. You think I'd just help two random guys out of the kindness of my heart?"

"Obviously not," said Smith.

Brooks scoffed. "Why would a *superhero* ever do that?"

"It doesn't matter *why* I'm helping you," Zane said. "Just let me get you two assholes reinstated over there. Then you'll at least let me tweak your blueprints."

Brooks had a concern. "When you say you're going to get them to 'screw up again—'"

"Nothing serious," Zane said. "I assure you. I don't want

anyone dead. We're talking PR disaster, not actual disaster."

Brooks blinked. "O...kay?" He nudged Smith into facing him. "This sounds okay with me. You?"

"Generally," Smith said. "Wouldn't mind seeing *that* organization go down without us."

"We need to call the girls," Brooks said.

"Don't do that," Zane said. "They're looking for you and it's going to be a perfectly tragic news story." He added, "They're with your friend Erin Burroughs. They'll be fine."

Neither Brooks nor Smith was okay with the secrecy, but they did know Patience and Lemon would be fine in Burroughs's care. So they agreed to his scheme.

"Hurry this up, though," Smith said.

"I will," Zane said, standing. "Trust me. The sooner I get that building site, the better. They start putting up the exterior and..." He shuddered. "I don't want to think about it."

When he was gone, Brooks pushed Smith off his lap. It wasn't a gentle push.

"Hey, that was uncalled for," Smith said. He added, with soon-to-disappear sarcasm, "I'm hurt."

He was sarcasmcised when Brooks spoke. "We're not going to pretend we didn't just have the conversation we had downstairs."

"I was kinda hoping we were," Smith said. "Since it was under duress."

"That's not an excuse—" Brooks started.

"You know," Smith said, "I'd be happy to discuss this with you. How about some place a little nicer, like *Staten Island*? Willowbrook Park is lovely this time of year."

Brooks ignored the obvious attempt at goading him. "Do I have to say it again?"

"That I need help?" Smith wondered. "No. You don't. I'm not going to a damn therapist because *it won't help*."

"You don't know that."

"Can they reset my entire life? Because if not, *it won't help*."

Brooks repeated himself. "You don't know that—"

Smith gesticulated with his good hand. "You know I had access to a time machine for decades, right?"

"No, I hadn't heard that one before—"

Smith ignored that. "I've tried it all. Killing me, killing my parents... killing Hitler. That never works." He continued. "I went to the future once, saw *Star Trek 38*. Great movie. Life still sucks."

Arturo Brooks was—Staten Island notwithstanding—a courageous man. In his time with the Reticent, he had faced ghouls, quidrils, changelings, more vampires than he could count, and one particularly odd krokodil addict who thought of himself as an actual crocodile.* A year earlier, Brooks had seen his own death coming and, thinking the universe would be destroyed by paradox if he didn't, faced it in stride. The only time he had to actively convince himself to be brave was when he uttered his next words.

"Then we're done," he said. "I can't take this."

"What does that mean?" Smith asked.

Brooks stood and walked away, seeking the cleanest bedroom in the house where he could settle in for a few days or weeks. A place he could figure things out.

Smith called after him. "What does that mean?"

---

* He died trying to eat a live wild boar.

20 / TAKE A BREAK

It meant they were done, and it was an awkward situation given they were basically the only occupants of a twenty thousand square foot mansion filled with doilies, patterned sofas, and various other bad decorating decisions. Basically. The ginger-haired faux terrorist, whose real name was Mike, remained on site for surveillance and to perform basic house-keeping functions. Unbeknownst to him, he would also be forced to endure one half of the Brooks-Smith duo's incessant need to talk to someone. He and Brooks sat in the master bedroom, so untouched since 1992 that a teal and purple jazz print solo cup still sat on the nightstand. Alarmingly, the dye had not faded.

"Has he said anything to you?" Brooks asked.

Mike shifted a bit in his khakis. "No."

"Nothing?"

"No." Mike's abrupt response bordered on snippy, but he needed to pee, and he'd been listening to the former Reticent CEO prattle on about responsibility and relationships for almost an hour. He'd heard all about their time travel adventure, their brushes with death, their prevailing mental health issues, and more. They'd even covered the latest season of *Orange Is the New Black*, and Mike's ears had been talked off. What immeasurable speck of cheer he had left was ready to disappear.

Somehow, even in a labyrinthine mansion, the sounds of Kitten Orgy traveled. Brooks could feel the walls vibrating and he again took his dissatisfaction out on Mike. "It's always that same stupid music. The lyrics are garbage. The singer sounds like he's eating glass. And he complains about my music?" He rambled on. "He's probably drinking right now—"

"I wouldn't know," Mike sighed and rubbed at the bandage that stretched across his nose.

"—I've never met anyone so unwilling to accept help." Brooks paced. "I get it. I do. Bad things happen. I get that more than anybody. I mean, hello? They made me into a cyborg *after I died.*"

Mike was desperately bored. "Uh huh."

"I don't even know how my own body works. Of all the people in the world, I get it."

Mike refused to make eye contact. "Uh huh."

"So shit happens, but that's why you get help, right?"

"I guess." Mike's instructions from Zane were to serve Brooks and Smith and make sure they felt at home in the rundown estate. The more he was forced to listen, the less enticing Zane's promise that he would appear in *Look at Me! 7* seemed.

"Can you check?" Brooks asked.

"What?"

Brooks still cared, deeply. "Can you check on him?"

"Sure," Mike said. With Smith in a different wing, he would pass no fewer than four bathrooms on his way to check on the man. It was a promise of relief.

"Then again—"

Mike's heart sank in his chest. His bladder sank in his bladder region. Brooks debated back and forth with himself for another ten minutes before his humble servant was finally free to pee.

Smith, meanwhile, had made a little den for himself. It was impressive considering that he and Brooks had only been separated for ten hours. It was also impressive considering he'd just dislocated his shoulder. Apparently he was healing again. Even the annoying headache was gone. For a normal person, this would be welcome news. For Smith, it was not. Healing meant immortality, and immortality meant monotony, at best.

He had moved the most comfortable bed he could find from its original location on the first floor to a corner office upstairs, along with some other treasures: a stereo system from the 1980s, a plastic red egg chair, and the Presidential portrait of Lyndon B. Johnson. The thirty-sixth President held an expression that was just the right mix of disdain and cockiness to reflect Smith's general mood. Also like Johnson, he called his penis Jumbo, albeit never aloud.* Though embarrassing, it was still better than William Howard Taft's nickname for his penis: Ole Puddinmaker.†

"You all right in there?" a voice asked from the other side of the room's closed door. Its owner knocked as hard as he could in hopes of overpowering Kitten Orgy.

The music quieted, and a few moments later the door flew open. For a second, Smith was obviously thrilled that Brooks had come to discuss and reexamine their situation. His half-smile dissolved into a whole-scowl when he realized his visitor was not his cyborg, but Mike.

"What the hell do you want?" Smith asked.

"Your, uh, whatever asked me to check on you," Mike said.

Smith attempted to close the door. "I'm great."

Mike stopped the door with his foot. "He also asked me to see if you were drinking."

Smith folded his arms and rolled his head back. "Of course he did."

"So..."

Smith developed a mischievous grin. "What if we give you conflicting directions?"

"What do you mean?" Mike asked.

---

* This is a verified Lyndon B. Johnson fact.
† This is pure speculation.

"I mean: Zane told you to do whatever we ask you to do. What if what Brooksy wants you to do and what I want you to do are opposites?"

Mike was not being paid enough to think about this. "I... uh..." He tilted his head. "What do you want me to do?"

"I want you to leave me alone," said Smith. "So you can either do that and not get him an answer, or you can come in here and go against *my* wishes."

Mike complained, "I just want to be in *Look at Me! 7*, man. Please don't make this hard on me."

"Fair enough. Tell him I'm drunk as hell, and it's none of his goddamn business."

He kicked Mike's foot away and slammed the door.

"Okay," Mike mumbled from the other side.

That left Smith alone with his thoughts and that, he decided, was not okay. On the other hand, Mike returning to Brooks meant that Smith was without surveillance. That was better than okay.

21 / A GREEN HERRING

After she scraped her knee, Patience hemmed and hawed more than usual at opportunities for adventure. On this occasion, the hemming and hawing was done on the platform for the Staten Island Ferry, New York City's worst example of public transportation. It was eight minutes late and counting.

Never was there a more wretched hive of scum and villainy.* The platform had all the coughing and wheezing of a hospital waiting area, without the hope granted in knowing the coughs and wheezes would soon be treated. People slept on benches, not from tiredness but from mental exhaustion. The only decor was a series of city-sponsored safe sex posters, likely there to discourage Staten Island Ferry riders from breeding rather than out of any concern for their health.

The girls had moved in with Burroughs for the time being, but cable management and daytime television offered few thrills. So they stood, awaiting a ferry that was nine minutes late.

"We have to look for Hudson again," Lemon said, putting a hand on her nervous sister's shoulder.

"I don't see how that's the case," Patience said.

"You heard Burroughs. There's nothing we can do about Eddie and Turo. We can at least do something about this." Lemon's idea was simple: find Hudson, find time machine.

Patience simply hated the idea. "That was all well when we were unable to die, but—"

"Hey." Lemon knelt down to Patience's eye level. "You told me that you spent most of your evenings in Salem

---

* Not long ago. Not in galaxies far, far away. Not even at the Republican National Convention.

wandering around the forest alone."

"That's correct," Patience said.

"You could have died back then, couldn't you?"

"That's correct."

"So you were brave." Lemon pointedly poked her shoulder.

"I was also unafraid of dying then," Patience said. "Now I live as an abomination."

Her religious circumstances may have been a bit more complicated now, but the ferry situation was not. As Lemon tried to explain to the Puritan that she wasn't an abomination, the ferry grew later and later, and the crowd of passengers-to-be grew. Some fell asleep on the floor. Some fell asleep standing up. Some stayed awake just so they could complain about it.

When the boat was sixteen minutes late, Lemon confronted a transit worker. "What's going on?"

The man ignored her.

She leaned forward and stared him straight in the eyes. "Excuse me?"

He ignored her again.

"Excuse me!" Lemon bellowed.

The worker's Jersey accent was as thick as his neck. He snapped, "*What?*"

"Do you know what's going on with the ferry?" she asked.

"It's late."

"That's super helpful," Lemon said, returning to her sister.

Patience stood on her toes to get a better view than the one her 5'1" height naturally provided. "I believe it's approaching," she said.

The ferry approached, all right. It took a while for the dazed, miserable crowd to notice, but it didn't stop approaching. The ship headed for the terminal at full speed, and scattered cries of "fuck" and "ayyyy" emerged as people realized it.

"Come on!" Lemon said, grabbing Patience by the arm.

The shrieking sound of scraping metal woke most of the sleepers as the boat rammed into the dock and smashed through layers upon layers of steel and glass. The flock of pigeons that had been waiting for the ferry to dock and its passengers to discard their trash on the ground scattered.

Despite the commotion, most commuters didn't move. By the time a transit worker screamed for everyone to get out of the way, it was too late. The ferry pressed onward, unleashing more and more screams as it crushed dozens. It came to rest with its bow in the crowded waiting area, the entire thing nestled atop the corpses of once-sleepy commuters and once-furious transit workers.

Patience and Lemon made it out of the ferry's path in time, and they looked on in fright. There were bodies everywhere. Not just beneath the ferry but aboard it as well. The exterior observation deck's railing was draped with corpses, and there was something peculiar about them: they were green. It wasn't a natural, sick green. Every passenger—black, white, and everywhere in between—now had chartreuse skin. She texted Burroughs:

monsters or smthng on SI ferry, snd help

Burroughs texted back:

get out of there

"Get everyone out of here," Lemon directed, not taking the advice for herself.

They'd never covered up a paranormal event before, but the girls tried. While Patience escorted survivors out of the ferry terminal, assuring them that it was a Coast Guard exercise, Lemon searched for a compelling cover-up for why everyone on the ship had turned green. Like a desperate thirty-

something in a bar bathroom at last call, she found her answer in graffiti. She turned over the corpse of a vandal huddled in the corner and found it equipped with several cans of
spray paint.

She shook one and sprayed it on the wall. Blue.

She shook another. It was empty, and it made a sad little
'pfft.'

She shook a third can and hit the jackpot. It sprayed bright,
vibrant green.

Lemon scaled the boat and began spraying bodies, hopeful
that the NYPD's medical examiners would be as competent
as its sketch artists. Whatever had killed the ferry passengers
was no longer on board, but something disturbing was. On
the lowest level of the ship was a message, smeared in human
blood across a wall:

WHERE IS MONOCHROME NOW?

She gave the can a good shake and began retracing the
words in green.

22 / VIRTUAL FANTASY

Godwin Zane was suspended upside-down on an inversion therapy table, his cape falling sadly to the floor as the lead software developer for The Afterlife™ tried to explain to him the difficulties his team was facing. Unfortunately, the developer found his inverted boss too distracting.

"I can come back later," he said, turning to leave.

Zane shouted after him. "Come back with a working product!"

The table did not have the Zen effect he was told it would. It just made the billionaire feel like all of the magma in his body was rushing to his head, which in turn gave him a headache, which in turn made him irritable. He shimmied a bit to put himself right-side up, but the table became stuck halfway. Shaking from side to side didn't help. Suspended in midair, he called out for the person he'd just heard enter the room. The visitor approached, figured out that Zane's cape was jamming the table, and freed him, tearing an advertisement off the cape in the process.

"Damn it," Zane said. "Now I need to get that fixed before RotoTire sees." On his feet, he stared at Smith. "Your shoulder healed quickly."

"Yeah, it wasn't that bad in the first place," Smith lied.

"How did you get up here? We have three factor authentication," said Zane.

"Eh, you know." Smith shrugged. It involved a laundry chute. Nothing unusual.

Zane set the RotoTire fabric fragment on his desk, then leaned against it "What are you doing here anyway?"

"Reporting for work," Smith said.

"I told you I have a plan, which you are going to ruin. Now—"

"Nobody saw me. I wore one of those stupid Guy Fawkes masks and pretended I was protesting whatever the people outside are protesting." He considered that for a moment. "What are they protesting?"

"Beats me," Zane said. "Factory conditions, low wages, my new haircut... But why did you come here? You had the run of the place with your boyfriend. I figured you'd spend a few weeks banging in all my parents' beds."

"Not gonna talk about it," Smith said.

"Yikes." Zane shot a few fake coughs into his hand to fill the gap in conversation. "Soooo—"

"I just want to get back to work," Smith said, "so tell me about 'The Afterlife.'"

Zane couldn't stay mad when asked to describe his pet projects. "It's exactly what it sounds like."

"You figured out how to bring people back from the dead?"

"What?" Zane said. "No."

"Then it's not exactly what it sounds like."

Zane rubbed at the inside corners of his eyes. "My team has figured out how to transfer a person's consciousness to a computer. From there, it's but a hop, skip, and a jump to giving them a virtual life to live."

"So you have to do it before they die," Smith said.

"Yes."

"It's not really an *after*life then..."

"Semantics," Zane said.

"But it works?" Smith asked.

Zane dragged out his one word response. "Well—"

"It doesn't work," Smith said.

"It works," Zane said, pacing. "There are just a few, let's say, bugs to work out."

Smith squinted. "Bugs?"

"We accidentally deleted a few people—"

"Oh, that's good."

"—and sometimes they end up trapped in some awful scenario for eternity."

Smith nodded, impressed. "So you invented hell."

"I mean, when you put it that way. Kind of. Yes." Zane ignored the implications and kept talking. "But the best part is this: when we get it working, the living will be able to communicate with the dead via a proprietary headset. Because the dead won't be dead, they'll be in the internet."

Smith tilted his head. "So they can tell their loved ones how much they're enjoying their eternity in hell."

Zane seated himself behind his desk. "I regret hiring you."

"I regret being me, if it's any consolation," said Smith.

"It is a little," Zane said, leaning back.

"What exactly do you want me to do, anyway?" Smith asked, taking the seat across from him. "I'm not a computer... developer... person. And it sounds like you already did the research."

"Well, we can't very well rely on people's own ideas of the afterlife or we get the whole people trapped in hell thing. Your job is to research people's thoughts on the afterlife so we can pre-program various scenarios into it. Figure out what people's ideas of heaven are and we can let them select from a list. It's gotta be all positive stuff to make money."

"You can't do that by yourself?"

"Could I? Sure. Would every scenario be based on 1980s music videos? Yes." Zane sighed. "I've tried. I keep getting stuck on heaven being a place..." He broke into song. "A place where nothing... nothing ever happens."

Smith pretended he didn't just hear Talking Heads lyrics. "You really want to leave this to me?"

"Yes?"

Smith's eyes lit up at the thought of filling Zane's product with nothing but obscene scenarios.

Zane seemed to read that thought. "If you want your name cleared, you'll do it right."

"If you want that building, you'll deal with whatever I do." Smith grinned. He had an elaborate blood orgy scenario brewing in his mind.

"If you and Brooks are broken up, I can just work with him and cut you out," said Zane.

Smith offered a harrumph, then said, "*Fiiiine.* No blood orgy."

"What the hell is a blood orgy?"

"It doesn't matter," Smith said. "Don't worry about it."

He was going to slip at least one fucked-up scenario in there.

23 / NO CREEP TIL BROOKLYN

Following the ferry incident, Patience and Lemon made their way back to Brooklyn, to an artisanal apricot restaurant that came highly recommended by Duke and Duchess. They sat at the worst table in the house—a narrow two-seater nestled between two restrooms—as it was the only one available without a reservation at 3:15PM on a Tuesday.

"Do you think it's best to hide these affairs from people?" Patience asked, prodding a stout-soaked apricot.

A bathroom door flung open with a THWAP.

Lemon glowered at the door. "No. Everyone's gonna find out about all this stuff eventually. I just don't think they're ready yet."

"You hail from the future. You're not surprised at anything that occurs," Patience noted.

"No," Lemon said. "I don't know everything that's ever happened. But I do know it's *not me* who reveals all this stuff to the world, so we should cover things up for now." Her jaw dropped as she remembered something. "Sweet Xenu."

A bathroom door flung open hard, punctuating her statement with a THWAP THWAP.

"We were supposed to look for Hudson," Lemon said. She'd gotten so caught up in the excitement of spray painting corpses and artisanal apricots that she'd forgotten. "We gotta go back to Staten Island after this. I guess we can take a cab."

There was another THWAP THWAP THWAP, and Lemon glared at the man who'd flung a bathroom door open with all his might.

"How can you afford all of this?" Patience asked. Their apri-tizer alone cost twenty-three dollars, and a cab ride to Staten Island would be beyond expensive.

"Tangelo left me some money to pay for college," Lemon

said. "Back when Eddie and Turo got fired. It's only like ten moon units in the future, but here it's worth a ton."

"I don't understand," Patience said.

"Me neither, but I'm not complaining."

Nobody truly understood the power of inflation.

Patience brought up an important point. "Mr. Marrow wasn't there last we heard."

"I know," Lemon said. "But there's like a ninety percent chance his ex-wife has seen him. The dude's pathetic."

Veronica Marrow had not, in fact, seen her ex-husband. That could probably be attributed to her having moved to Florida so she wouldn't see him. But the girls didn't know any better.

"What good will our investigation do?" Patience asked.

"What else are we supposed to do?" Lemon asked over a THWAP.

Patience frowned and looked down at her apricot skewers. She wasn't feeling hungry. If repeated whiffs of two bathrooms hadn't ruined her appetite, her nervousness would have.

Lemon, meanwhile, stared at the bar. There was a mirror behind it and, while there were six patrons seated, there were five reflections.

"Look at that," she said. "There's no reflection. That guy's a creepin' vampire!"

The reflectionless man was husky, bespectacled, and—sparkly heartthrobs aside—the last thing anyone would think of when they thought 'vampire.' He wore a red sweater vest, for crying out loud.

"Are you certain?" Patience asked. "Perhaps there are other creatures for whom reflection is—"

Lemon hopped up, full of porpoise. "Hey!"

"Can I help you?" the man asked.

"Yeah," Lemon said, raising a stake from her jacket pocket. "You can die." She jabbed him in the chest and smiled, proud of her quip.

Luckily for the man, he was not a vampire and did not explode into dust. Unluckily for the man, he had just been stabbed in the chest with a piece of wood. Luckily for the man, Lemon wasn't strong enough to plunge it all the way into his heart.

The bartender shrieked. "What are you doing!?"

"Thetans, no," Lemon said. "I thought you were a vampire!"

She pressed a cloth napkin at the man's chest while the bartender dialed 911. Lemon kept repeating "sorry," but it didn't make her stabbee feel any better, and he fainted. When she looked up for a moment, she noticed that the man actually did have a reflection. It just so happened that the mirror behind the bar was a funhouse mirror. For a moment, she resented Brooklyn.

As patrons poured out of the restaurant, Patience texted Burroughs:

Dearest Agent Burroughs,

There has been a troubling incident at Apricot & Sons, the address of which is 1117 Driggs Avenue, Brooklyn, New York. Lemon believed another patron to be a vampire, as he had no reflection in the mirror above the bar. However, (1/2) upon her stabbing the man with the stake you provided, it became clear that he is not a vampire but a human being. He is now bleeding on the floor. Your advice would be most appreciated.

Sincerely,

Patience S. Cloyce. (2/2)

Burroughs's response was neither as lengthy nor as polite:

You've got to be kidding me. I'm still cleaning up green bodies. Go home and stay there, don't take no for an answer, give the bartender my number.

EMTs arrived before the police, and Lemon let them take over. When she and Patience headed for the back door, there was a brief kerfuffle. Bargoers grabbed each girl by the arms to restrain them until the NYPD could show up. Shouts of "where do you think you're going?" and "don't let them leave!" came to a halt when the bartender dialed Agent Burroughs of the FBI. The girls didn't know what the woman on the other end of the line said, but it worked.

"I'm sorry," the bartender said. "Looks like we've had a misunderstanding."

Though they were freed, the incident had been too close for comfort. So the girls listened for a change and returned to Burroughs's home, shaken and ready to stay there.

24 / A COMPLETE SHITSHOW

Smith didn't do well with the phrase 'broken up.' He handled the concept only slightly better. Before he and Brooks moved in together, Smith had lived in near-total squalor. Since the brownstone was in Brooks's name and not his own, he grabbed the handful of things he felt he needed and moved them into a verminous studio apartment above a butcher shop in Koreatown. Nothing pressured him to do this but himself, so the pressure to leave was immense.

Something about lying on a half-inflated air mattress surrounded by ant traps seemed to clear Smith's head. The most striking thing was the quiet. No Trev Cracklin, no Brooks chastising Lemon about excessive Pop-Tart consumption, and no visits from that douchebag Duke. Granted, the couple next door engaged in screaming matches well into the night and the tenant below insisted on watching anime tentacle porn at an obscene volume, but none of that *involved* him. It was pure, blissful solitude.

He opened his laptop and, after a brief struggle connecting to the free café wi-fi across the street, navigated to the saddest place on the internet: the Craigslist Personals page.*

Smith was supposed to be researching the afterlife, but like anyone who has ever done research online, he found himself distracted. The next thing he knew, he was scrolling past thirty different iterations of "Where are all the nice guys?" seeking the saddest of the sad. Like many people who browsed the Craiglist personals, Smith's interest was not in

---

* A few years later, Congress would pass a law that forced Craigslist to remove its Personals page. They claimed this was to reduce human trafficking, but really Craigslist Personals had caused the demise of so many lecherous politicians that it simply had to go.

contacting any of the posters. Instead, he sought the satisfaction of knowing that other people's lives were worse than his own. As always, the site delivered:

BE MY SUGAR DADDY. 40F (Staten Island)
Lonly in Brooklyn 35M (Midtown)
LOOKING FOR MY PEE QUEEN. 57M (Queens)
Two guys (42/61) seeking middle bitch. (Staten Island)
let's go 2 Applebee's then smash (Crown Heights)
I'll have a tremendous time watching you pee 69M (Midtown)
Slave Leia looking 4 Jabba. Are you big enuf 4 me? 24F (Bronx)
MR. HERSHEY: CHOCOLATE TO LOVE 33M (Staten Island)

"Pathetic," Smith muttered to himself. He added "shit!" when some of his bourbon spilled onto his keyboard. He added "double shit!" when a spider skittered across the bed. He slammed his damp laptop shut and used it to strike the arachnid, bludgeoning his own left thumb in the process.

"Triple shit!" he shouted.

If that computer was broken, he owed Zane Industries a thousand dollars. Upon realizing that, he shouted, "Quadruple shit!" Then he asked himself, aloud, "What the fuck comes after quadruple?"

He didn't answer.

Yes, living a complete shitshow felt more right than having a happy family ever could.

25 / BIG MONEY

Zephyr was having a vision, and the other members of the Reticent board patiently waited for her to finish. Well, it began patiently. After twenty-seven minutes spent watching the psychic rub her temples and shake a miniature rain stick, Burroughs announced that she'd had enough.

"I thought there was going to be a point to this meeting," she said.

Zephyr shook the rain stick a little more. "The dictates of cognizance compel me to seek answers!"

"That's fine, but the rest of us have places to be."

Burroughs had no way of knowing whether that was true of the others in the room, but it was true for her. While Patience and Lemon were old enough to take care of themselves, they were also old enough to embark on another fruitless side quest and stab another accountant. Even if they stayed put, Burroughs didn't much like the idea of two teenagers rummaging through her things when they inevitably became bored. Her wires and cords were organized *just so*. Her pantry was organized *just so*. Her collection of Pez dispensers was organized *just so*. There was a good reason she never had any children of her own. The thought of them watering an already watered plant or failing to replace a roll of toilet paper was almost unbearable. She needed to get back and secure the perimeter.

Like most dead people, Travis Marsh was in no such hurry.

"This vision might be important," he said.

Wiles set his cuppa down and scowled. "When has it *ever* been important?"

Zephyr's last major vision claimed that a swarm of bees was coming for Nicholas Cage; after organizing a response that terrified the actor and resulted in three lawsuits, it was discovered that she had fallen asleep watching *The Wicker Man* the previous night.

"It never matters," said one of the Webers. Another Weber repeated the word "never" with a sort of echoey cadence.

Danny Guerrera, the organization's brand new CEO, President and Patsy, made a decision. "Zephyr, keep doing whatever it is you do in the corner. The rest of us are going to discuss an offer that's on the table."

Zephyr frowned, but dutifully moved herself to a corner where she could utter Latinesque words in peace, if not privacy. There was a gap in the tent's corner, and she shivered a little before securing it shut with an oversized brooch.

Nobody knew much about Guerrera. Before he became the organization's President and CEO, he had been a custodian. He was the eighty-fifth person asked to take charge, and the first to accept because the fates that met most Reticent leaders were well known. Having saved nothing for retirement, Guerrera had evaluated the risks and decided the potential windfall outweighed the danger. He didn't much look the part in a blue boilersuit with shaggy hair that reached his shoulders, but Guerrera had proven himself surprisingly competent. That was about to change, at least in the eyes of one board member.

"There's an offer on the table?" Knutsson asked.

Guerrera nodded. "As you know, there aren't many people willing to invest in this company right now, on account of the vampire incident and ongoing investigations."

"And all the death," Burroughs added.

Trebly perked up. "We try not to use that word. Remember: Demise is an opportunity in disguise!"

Nobody responded to that because nobody liked PR.

"An anonymous entity," Guerrera said, "has offered us three million dollars in exchange for a service."

Burroughs narrowed her eyes. "What kind of service?"

"They want us to reopen the portal," Guerrera said.

"What!?" Nobody else in the room seemed to see a problem with that, so Burroughs continued explaining the problem with that. "The same portal that ate thousands of people?"

Guerrera nodded. "Only for two minutes."

"Three million dollars, you say?" Wiles asked, with a hand to his chin, its pinkie out.

Guerrera nodded again.

"I dare say we should do it," Wiles said.

"We agree," said all three Webers at once. A lamp flickered.

This was outrageous, and Burroughs was outraged. "We're supposed to help people. Does nobody here want to do that anymore?"

"Sure we do," Knutsson said, "but how are we supposed to help anyone if we don't have any money?"

Burroughs sighed. "I don't know, literally anything other than 'make a tear in the universe and hope it doesn't kill everyone?' Why not just sell Monochrome the damn building site and we can rebuild elsewhere? He'd probably overpay for it."

"Somewhere else?" Trebly asked, aghast. "The Reticent has been headquartered at its current location for centuries!"

"I know we're positioned right over the ritual site," Burroughs said, "but still. Think of how much equipment and staff we could have if we relocated to Iowa or something."

"Iowa?" Knutsson raised a hand to his chest in horror.

"Maybe Kansas?" Burroughs offered. "They have Google Fiber."

High-speed internet didn't get her coworkers damp; the suggestion was ignored.

"A vote," Guerrera said. "In favor of taking the offer?"

Everyone but Burroughs and Zephyr raised their hands.

"Against?" Guerrera asked.

Burroughs raised her hand and waved it for emphasis.

"Zephyr?" Guerrera asked.

Her breath was visible in the chilly corner. "There is a grave menace on the horizon," she said.

"I'll mark that as a no, but that still makes it 7-2," Guerrera said. "Majority rules."

I hate this place, Burroughs thought.

26 / DROP THE MIKE

The existential crisis, unlike the nonexistential crisis, is a well-documented phenomenon.* The Foundation for Uncovering and Conquering Trauma (FUCT) defines three levels of existential crisis. Level 1 consists mostly of insomnia and general nervousness. Level 2 is a bit more severe. Sufferers spend an inordinate amount of time trying to figure out their purpose in life, often to the psychological detriment of those around them. Level 3, the most severe, indicates a shattered sense of reality. It is at Level 3 that many find new addictions, religions, or reasons to spend their life's savings on some fleeting joy or another.

Arturo Brooks was Level 2 FUCT. He was a bit young for the midlife crisis variant, but at ten months a cyborg, he was just the right age for the artificial-life crisis variant. Brooks wasn't sure what he was doing with his life and, given that he had nothing better to do than think about the fact that he wasn't sure what he was doing with his life, it was an issue.

A year ago, everything had been simple. Brooks knew he would be with Smith and the Reticent until he died and he knew when and how he would die. Simple. There was no worrying about the future; he knew he didn't have one. Now the amount of choice was paralyzing. He'd made one impulsive choice—breaking up with Smith—and he spent every other second since worrying about whether it had been the right call. He had no job, no partner, and no way out of Godwin Zane's idiotic mansion in Amagansett.

And idiotic it was. Brooks stood in the corner of the bedroom, eyeing a collection of miniature spoons. 'North

---

* The nonexistential crisis, in which a being laments having not been born, is only possible in Dimension Q.

Dakota' one read, like it was a normal thing to travel to North Dakota.

"I need to get out of here," Brooks said.

"You know I can't let you leave," Mike said. "I'm really sorry."

The terrorist-turned-security guard positioned a rolling chair in the doorway and seated himself. When Brooks went to the bathroom, Mike followed. When Brooks went to the kitchen, Mike followed. When Brooks violently shoved him out of the way and headed for the front door, Mike used a Zane Industries EMP generator to shut the cyborg down. Mike was only one man. He couldn't keep two grown men confined, as evidenced by Smith's escape, but he could get the job done with just one. There was still a chance, however small, that he would appear in *Look at Me! 7*.

He attempted to offer some consolation. "I saw a few puzzles downstairs. We could put one of those together to pass the time..."

Brooks had spent forty-eight hours with no human contact except for Mike, and he was about to lose it. He slammed his fist on the nightstand, sending the jazzy solo cup tumbling across the floor.

"*Vales verga. ¡Dale cabron!*" he shouted.

"Uh, *no hablos español*," said Mike. "Sorry." He reached into his pocket and presented a snack. "Fruit leather?"

Brooks shook his head.

Mike was a good-natured idiot, at least, and Brooks had an idea forming. He'd never been one for scheming—that was Smith's wheelhouse—but he'd worked for a secret organization long enough to know how to manipulate simple people.

Good-natured idiot, good-natured idiot... he thought. *Yes!*

He'd also worked for a secret organization long enough to have an underdeveloped sense of shame.

"At least you tried," Brooks said, raising the pitch of his voice ever so slightly. He bit his lip before continuing. "I can teach you a few phrases if you want."

"Uh, sure," Mike said, leaning his chair further back.

Brooks pulled another chair next to his, so close that the chairs were touching. He took a seat and leaned in. *"Me gustas mucho. ¿Tienes novio?"*

Mike leaned further back and rolled his chair a few inches away. "What does that mean?" This was basic stuff, and he had taken Spanish in college. If he weren't a good-natured idiot, he would have been ashamed of his capacity for language retention.

Brooks smiled as he translated. "It means 'I like you a lot. Do you have a boyfriend?'"

Mike's eyes widened and he let out a short, uncomfortable laugh. "I, uh, don't think I'll need that one."

Brooks rolled closer again and offered a new phrase. *"Quiero besarte."*

Mike sat with a quizzical look, awaiting a translation.

Brooks leaned in closer and whispered. "It means 'I want to kiss you.'"

Mike jolted up, nearly tripping on a wheel as his chair rolled out from under him. "I think you have the wrong idea."

"Do I?" Brooks asked, brushing a hand across Mike's cheek. "There's not a reason you keep *so close* to me?"

"Yes!" Gay panic had set in and Mike backed out of the doorway. "I have to. It's my job. Just my job! I want to be in *Look at Me! 7*!"

Mike didn't notice that Brooks had pickpocketed his EMP generator until the cyborg casually walked through the doorway toward the exit. That's when Mike reached into his pocket and found nothing but lint.

"Hey!" he said. "You're not allowed to leave!"

"Stop me," Brooks dared.

Mike didn't bother chasing after his fugitive. Instead, he slumped in defeat and kicked the empty solo cup. He attempted to sit back down in his rolling chair, but forgot that it had rolled away. Pain shot through him as he landed on his tailbone, but it didn't matter. He was never going to be in *Look at Me! 7*.

27 / REUNITED AND IT FEELS OKAY

It's never easy to watch a video of yourself. If the surprise of hearing how high-pitched your voice sounds doesn't get you, the realization of how unflattering your favorite outfit is does.

For Patience, the worst part wasn't her frock's frumpiness, but her sneaking suspicion that the camera had stolen a piece of her soul. No matter how many times she'd been assured that wasn't the case, it just didn't make sense that she could exist in both Erin Burroughs's living room and the television at the same time.

For Lemon, the worst part was the hokey crying. Zane's instructions had been perfectly clear: the girls were to appear as pathetic as possible in order to appease the public. Lemon sat between Patience and Burroughs, rolling her eyes at herself.

On screen, she sobbed. Her voice cracked as she said, "I just want my dads back."

In real life, she scoffed. "How is this supposed to help?"

"I guess if they're still alive this might encourage their kidnappers to let them go," Burroughs said. "I don't know. It wasn't my idea." The interview had been arranged after she received an email from PR@zaneindustries.biz.

Patience stopped nibbling popcorn long enough to comment, "Do you not believe they're alive?"

"I think if anyone can survive a kidnapping, it's Eddie and Arturo."

The TV screen flooded with red as the words 'BREAKING NEWS' appeared. An unfriendly chime coincided with the text. Before long, a newscaster spoke.

"We apologize for the interruption, but we have a breaking story out of Midtown where a local meat vendor discovered a grisly scene. Anna Apeldoorn is at 59th and 5th."

As is tradition, the story cut to a blonde woman standing in front of a generic brick wall, which offered nothing the crew in the studio couldn't, except proof that somebody was on the scene. In the United States alone, estimates place the cost of worthless field reporting at over sixteen billion dollars annually.

Anna Apeldoorn described the horrors that lay beyond the brick wall. "Over thirty people have been found dead on the third floor of a building that also houses an Italian market. Details are still emerging, but it looks as though residents were having a costume party when they were slaughtered. Detectives have yet to offer a clear description of the violence right now, but some witnesses are reporting stab wounds while others are saying a wild animal was involv—"

Lemon spoke over the news. "That's the AAVA office."

"Sure is," Burroughs said.

"We should determine whether harm has come to misters Frank and Alan," Patience said.

Lemon and Burroughs had already forgotten the names of the vampires they met earlier. They exchanged a confused glance before realizing who Patience was talking about.

"It *is* awfully suspicious," Burroughs said. "Someone murders a bunch of vampire wannabes right after they spot our kidnapper..."

"Or after they decided to make peace with Eddie and Turo," Lemon pointed out.

"That's a good point," Burroughs said. "Maybe someone was angry at them for—"

Her train of thought never pulled out of the station. A rapid knock at the door sent Burroughs away from the couch to greet their visitor. Because her peephole had been installed backwards by a less-than-diligent landlord, she couldn't make out much, just that it appeared to be one person. She cracked the door to peek, then threw it open to let a rain-drenched Brooks into her apartment. Most missing persons cases didn't end with the missing person standing in her doorway.

"Well hell," she said. "That was easy."

The girls turned to see what the fuss was about. Lemon exclaimed "Turo!" while Patience offered a more formal "Mr. Brooks!" They scurried to him, Patience abandoning her popcorn on the way.

"Hey," Brooks said at the center of a hug circle. "You two okay?"

"Yes, sir."

"Yeah."

"You're okay in the rain?" Burroughs asked.

"I'd be a pretty shitty cyborg if I couldn't handle rain," Brooks said. "None of my electronics are exposed except for..." He realized where that thought was going and shut himself up, for everyone's sake.

Burroughs stuck her head out into the hallway. "Where's Eddie?"

Brooks took a deep breath. "He's fine. He's not with me."

"What happened?" Lemon asked, scowling at Burroughs for her Smith-specific concern.

"Long story," Brooks said. "Basically Zane told us to lay low for a while so he could try and boost our reputation."

"Why does Godwin Zane want to help you out?" Burroughs asked. His involvement in the Brooks/Smith disappearance set off red flags, red lights, and other red alerts in her mind.

"Something about aesthetics, I don't know. Like I said, it's a long story." Brooks turned to the girls. "I'm just glad you're okay. I was worried you'd try to find us and get into trouble."

Lemon and Patience glanced at each other. A stern lip bite from Lemon told Patience not to say anything. Her face turned red as they looked back at Brooks.

"Did Mr. Smith not care to see us?" Patience asked.

"Yeah," Lemon said. "What gives?"

Burroughs read the despondent look on the cyborg's face and tried to steer the conversation in a different direction. "Look how tired he is. I'm sure Eddie's sleeping it off back home..."

"It's fine," Brooks said. They were going to find out one way or another. "We... aren't seeing each other anymore."

"What?" Lemon asked. "Why?" She reached a hasty conclusion. "He *was* cheating!"

Burroughs again tried to divert. "Girls..."

"Really," Brooks said. "It's fine."

"What will become of us?" Patience asked, her face growing redder.

Brooks attempted to answer both girls' questions at once. "No cheating. We just... disagreed on something that couples really can't disagree on. I don't know if that will change. But I do know that both of you live at 55 Decatur Street and that's not going to change. We'll figure out the rest."

The girls didn't press any further. Brooks sat with them and they chatted for a while about Godwin Zane's abomination of a family home, the AAVA, the time Lemon nearly decked a racist police sketch artist, the spray paint on the ferry, and so on. Conveniently left out was the time Lemon almost murdered a guy at an apricot bar.

Eventually, the girls went to the spare bedroom they'd been sharing (ostensibly to pack but actually to gossip). Brooks and Burroughs remained on the sofa.

"So what happened?" Burroughs asked. "If I can ask."

"You just did," said Brooks. "Yeah, it's fine."

The two weren't friends, but no two people are until they have a few sincere conversations. Their first broke out.

"It's so stupid," Brooks said.

"Maybe," Burroughs said. "Try me."

"I told Eddie he needed to see a therapist."

Burroughs tilted her head. "That's fair."

Brooks continued. "He won't because..."

She filled in what she thought he was too uncomfortable to say. "Because of the conversion therapy, sure."

"Wait, what?" Brooks blinked a few times, having trouble processing the information.*

"Oh, shit." Burroughs backpedaled. "That is deeply personal and I thought you knew and I am really, really stupid."

"I don't think you can backpedal now," Brooks said. "But I won't tell him you said anything."

She fiddled with her hands. "Sorry. I just assumed you would know. Now it's awkward—"

"It's fine," Brooks said, still processing. "I knew he lived with some real pieces of work... I just can't figure out why you would know that and I wouldn't. We've been... we *were* together for eight years. Like I wouldn't be sympathetic—"

"Well, you are a little judgy," she said. Before he could protest, she added, "You know he doesn't talk about personal stuff. It just happened to be one thing we had in common."

"Oh, shit," Brooks said, duplicating her hand-fiddling. "I'm sorry?"

"Ha! Now it's awkward for you too!" Burroughs shrugged it off. "For what it's worth, there was truth serum involved."

Brooks, completely unable to read her tone, chuckled for about half a second. Then he relayed his actions aloud as if it would help him accept them. "So I broke up with someone for rightfully having a problem with therapy."

"No," Burroughs said. "No. It runs deeper than that and you know it. It's a pattern of not talking to you, not listening to you... It's the 'I'm going to pretend I'm pretending to be an alcoholic to cover the fact that I'm actually an alcoholic' thing..."

Brooks nodded. "Yeah, he still does that."

---

* Not literally.

Burroughs, meanwhile, realized she had been talking about herself. "Sorry." But she couldn't shut herself up. "No. I'm not sorry. You sound like you're looking for a reason to change your mind and I don't know that you should."

Brooks let out a little half-snort. "Why? You want to move back in on that?"

"Fat chance," said Burroughs. "I just think you both have some things you need to work out on your own. Stop doubting yourself."

"I'm not," Brooks said. "I'm not. I just... don't know."

He had no idea what he was looking for, and his existential crisis was approaching Level 3 FUCT.

28 / VINDICATION

It was nearly two o'clock in the afternoon and Godwin Zane knew exactly what he was looking for. He'd been through a scandal or two hundred in his time, and he knew that public perception was everything. For the purpose of clearing Brooks and Smith of any involvement in Six Blocks, two sobbing teenage girls helped. His next step—releasing carefully edited footage of Brooks and Smith under duress during their kidnapping—helped even more. The public, always fascinated with celebrities losing their shit, ate it up. Every major news station placed the story in its rotation—between lurid tales about politicians using gloryholes and rumors that popstar Fergie engaged in cannibalism—and within just two hours of the news breaking, there were sixteen different Brooks/Smith hurt/comfort stories on FanficPalooza.

Smith did not enjoy the attention, and he barged into Zane's office to confront him.

"Why the hell did you do that?" Smith asked.

"Do what?" Zane asked from behind his desk. While he had a hunch what Smith was there to discuss, there were any number of things a person could be mad at him for and he didn't intend to incriminate himself. Feigning ignorance was one of his PR rules.

"This!" Smith said. He pulled out his phone and played a local news story discussing the embarrassing footage. On screen, he wept and thrashed his chains as Brooks tried to console him.

Zane barely glanced at it. "Ah, yep. That."

"*Why?*" Smith asked again.

"To make people feel bad for you?" Zane said. He was writing something by hand and didn't stop for the conversation. "Tough goal, I know."

"Now everyone in the world has footage of me whining about being cuffed to a wall!" Smith threw his phone to the ground, and a hairline crack that had been present for weeks transformed into dozens of cracks that rendered the screen almost unusable.

"Fuck," said Smith.

Zane didn't even look up from his work. "I don't see the problem."

"You think I want people to see me like that?"

"Like what, sympathetic? No, I don't imagine you do." Zane kept scribbling something.

"You have no right to—"

"It worked," Zane said, still refusing to look up. "A few days ago eighty-six percent of New Yorkers wanted you dead. Now it's only sixty-two percent."

Smith huffed. "And now one hundred percent of them think I'm a giant pussy."

"Eh," Zane said, still scribbling. "PR is looking great."

"You were supposed to make the Reticent look bad, not make me out to be a goddamn snowflake. I don't need your PR—"

Zane snapped, his passion for public relations evident. "Everyone needs PR."

"It has nothing to do with—"

"PR has everything to do with everything!" said Zane.

Smith yanked the billionaire's paper away. "What are you even doing?" Upon inspection, it was a page of paisleys from an adult coloring book. Zane had filled half the page with various grey tones. "Seriously?"

"It's *supposed* to be stress relieving," Zane said. "You know, the opposite of conversations with you." He stood and walked over to his window, gesturing for Smith to follow. "Look."

Smith didn't see anything unusual. "It's Manhattan."

"I still regret hiring you," Zane said.

"And I still regret being me," Smith said.

"Look," Zane repeated.

A cuckoo clock on the wall squawked two, and a beam of darkness shot into the sky above the scaffold-laden Reticent construction site. The beam spread to a funnel shape that blanketed several blocks, lasting a minute and thirty seconds before being sucked back toward the building. Zane looked at the stopwatch app on his phone with disgust at receiving only seventy-five percent of what he'd paid for.

"Was that what I think it was?" Smith asked.

"That depends. Did you think it was a miniature version of the rift that caused Six Blocks?"

Smith blinked. "Yes."

"Then yes."

Smith's face turned whiter than usual. "When you said you were going to discredit the Reticent, you didn't say you were going to open another goddamned rift."

"It's fine," Zane said, gesturing toward the ground. "See?"

"Yeah, that's the thing. It is *never* fine."

"I don't follow," Zane said.

Smith muttered to himself. "Of course you don't."

"They look bad now. You look good. They'll put you back in charge to make their bad look good and BAM I've got a good-looking building."

Smith sighed.

"What?" Zane asked.

Smith flopped into the seat opposite Zane's desk. "You're clearly new to this, so let me break it down for you."

"I'm not new to business," Zane complained.

"Not business, jackass. The paranormal. Listen."

Zane grabbed a water bucket from the corner, parked it next to his desk, and took his seat. "'Kay."

"Brooksy, er, *Arturo* and I spent months making the rounds to explain the rift away, telling people it was totally a coincidence that it opened up over Reticent headquarters and of course we weren't working on anything involving parallel universe generators."

"Yeah. So?"

Smith waited for Zane to follow along. When he didn't, he continued. "You just proved that we were lying. It takes more than a few weeks to build a portal generator, so obviously the Reticent were working on it when we were still in charge."

"Yikes," Zane said.

"So the natural conclusion," Smith said, "is that we were so incompetent at our jobs that it was happening under our noses. And there's no reason to hire back two people who were completely fucking incompetent."

"Yikes," Zane said again.

"Worse than that—"

"It gets worse than failing at the plan?" Zane wondered.

"It always gets worse," Smith said. "One of the reasons the first portal was a huge deal for us was that the Reticent tries to be... uh, reticent. You don't prance around telling the world you have a time machine or a portal generator unless you're confident you can stop someone from stealing it."

Zane's brow raised. "They have a time machine?"

Smith's face turned even whiter. "No. That's not the point."

"You don't think they can stop someone from stealing a portal generator?" Zane asked.

"They're down to under a hundred employees and they're working from tents," Smith said. "You just dared the assholes of the world to march in and take a device that can end all life on the planet."

"Shit," Zane said.

"You really suck at superheroing," Smith said.

"That's fair," Zane said, considering the ferry message.

"And also PR," Smith added.

Zane's hands began to glow. He stuffed them into the

bucket, which hissed and steamed.

Ninety seconds of rift was, as Zane predicted, enough for hundreds of people to capture cell phone footage of the incident. That footage was enough evidence to clear Brooks and Smith's names, as they no longer worked for the organization. It was also enough to mar their legacies with accusations of negligence and buffoonery. Still, ignorance was not the same as maleficence, and the next day the percentage of New Yorkers who wanted them dead plummeted to thirty-seven.

29 / TRUE DETECTIVES

Patience and Lemon weren't very good detectives, they decided. It wasn't a tough decision since the last time they tried detecting they vandalized a boatful of corpses and stabbed an average Joe. But given that their adoptive fathers were being, in Lemon's words, "total glorbdinks," they figured somebody ought to investigate the massacre at AAVA headquarters. Well, Lemon did the figuring. Patience tagged along.

They tucked into an alley and shuffled toward their ideal hiding place: a dumpster. They didn't make it far.

"What the hell are you kids doing here?" an officer demanded. "This is a crime scene not—"

"It's fine," said Burroughs, turning a corner in her best FBI Agent impression. "Those are our interns. First real scene for both of them." She turned to the girls and spoke with authority. "We're not paying you to hang around outside. Let's go!"

They had lucked out and been confronted by an officer who didn't watch their tearful tale on the news. He grumbled and let them past the barricade.

"What are you doing here?" Burroughs asked.

"What are *you* doing here?" Lemon repeated. "Aren't you a higher-up now?"

"We're almost entirely higher-ups," Burroughs admitted. "Everyone keeps quitting."

Lemon rolled her eyes. "Can't imagine why."

"We're all pulling multiple duties. At least I got this and not janitorial." Poor Guerrera, despite being the Reticent's CEO and President, was also a janitor again. Burroughs put herself back on topic as she gestured for them to follow her into the building. "Why are you here?"

"We're investigating," Patience said. "I am most anxious to determine whether Alan and Frank have been harmed."

"Uh huh." Burroughs kept them moving. "Just don't touch anything."

No sooner than they'd walked under some POLICE LINE DO NOT CROSS tape into the decimated AAVA headquarters, Lemon touched something. She didn't mean to, but her sandal became stuck in some gum and she tripped. Her newly unshod foot came down on one very sharp set of false vampire teeth, and the next thing she knew, Lemon was bleeding all over the bloody crime scene.

"Contamination!" Burroughs shouted, horrified. "What did I just—"

Lemon healed immediately.

"Huh," she said.

"That's curious," Patience said. Eyeing the bodies that filled the room, she frowned. "It appears Frank and Alan were not lucky."

"But *we* might be," Lemon said. She picked up the false teeth and pointed them at Patience.

"Contamination!" Burroughs shouted again. She wasn't shouting to anyone since 'the FBI' had been granted exclusive access to the room, so it wasn't clear what she was trying to accomplish. Her A-type brain just couldn't help itself.

Patience tried to back away from the fangs but Lemon was too quick for her and jabbed the back of her hand. The Puritan bled for a moment, but only a moment before she too healed.

"Our affliction has returned?" Patience wondered.

"Looks like," Lemon said, over it. She dropped the fangs and walked toward the bodies. "How come these guys weren't taken away last night?"

"I asked that they not disturb the scene." Burroughs pointed to her outfit. "I *am* a federal agent after all."

"You could have come in last night. They've been here a

while." Lemon pinched her nose.

"I needed sleep," Burroughs said. She left out the part where she'd been up until four in the morning helping Brooks through his personal crisis.

Lemon grumbled about the smell. Patience simply shook her head.

Burroughs asked a rhetorical question. "How screwed up have your lives been that you're not at all bothered by this?"

The 'this' was a massacre. Frank, Alan, and all the other members of the AAVA were strewn about like discarded toys. Pale and heaped atop one another, the bodies were peculiar because there was no blood. Yes, there was blood all over the floor, but there wasn't any coming from the wounds on the bodies. Those were completely drained.*

"My parents stood idle as I was sentenced to hang," Patience said.

"Mine died in a terrorist attack on the Moon," Lemon said.

"Last year, we discarded the decapitated heads of my town's elders in the streets," Patience added.

Years of working for the Reticent left Burroughs unsurprised by any of those statements.

The three moved in close to examine the bodies. Burroughs ran a gloved hand across two puncture wounds on Frank's neck. "Yep, these were real vampires."

"You think they were mad about the imposters?" Lemon asked.

"No," Burroughs said. Something in the corner of the room caught her eye and she walked toward it. In black Arial font on a white background—the universal sign for a generic product—an industrial sized bottle read 'Iron Supplement, 500mg.' She picked it up with both hands, anticipating some

---

* A later analysis of the blood on the floor would determine that it was stage blood and that—Lemon's aside—there was no genuine blood at the scene.

heft. Instead, three or four pills rattled around a mostly empty bottle. "No." When she repeated the word it was in a disbelieving tone.

"What's happened?" Patience asked.

"There *were* real vampires here," Burroughs said. "They were farming."

"Farming?" Lemon asked. "As in... people?

Burroughs nodded. "Get the cosplayers to go all in, pump them full of iron, then feast. I've seen liches do this before, but vampires normally hunt alone. It's a whole stalking thing and they sort of get off on it."

"*Twilight* wasn't lying," Lemon muttered.

Burroughs repeated her sentiment. "This is unusual."

"Perhaps they have changed their habits," Patience offered.

As a general rule, habits don't change. That's why the headpieces worn by Catholic nuns have been the same for eight hundred years. But it was possible.

30 / ONE SHADE OF GREY

Another day, another round of bullshit. That's what Smith thought as he again freed Godwin Zane's cape. In the past three days it had become stuck on a doorframe, in a grill, under an unnecessary prop anvil, and into itself. This time, it was stuck in a pool filter on the building's roof. The two men tugged at the cape, but it wouldn't budge.

"Why the hell do you swim in a cape?" Smith asked. "Have you considered *not doing that*?" He resented that he was in a pool and he resented that he'd basically become Zane's personal assistant. All because the billionaire did him one *tiny* favor in clearing his name and getting psychotic internet trolls to stop calling for his death.

"Have you tried not being an asshole?" Zane asked.

"Never," Smith said, giving the cape another tug and splashing his eyes with chlorinated water. "Ugh."

"This cape fits sixty-two ads," Zane said.

"You're in private," Smith noted. "Nobody knows whether you're wearing it or not."

"I signed an agreement," Zane said. "I follow my agreements. And you know the NosePhone™?"

Smith nodded. It was an invention that allowed people to smell what was on the other end of a call. Nobody used it except for late night talk show hosts, and they did so only as a punchline.

Zane took the product seriously. "Its development was paid for entirely through advertising. I make money being a jackass and Zane Industries gets to develop cool products."

"Your definition of cool is not the same as mine."

"No, it's likely not since I'm filled with magma."

Smith acknowledged the pun with a groan. But the cape wouldn't budge in the presence of the overbearing industrial pool filter, and he removed himself from the pool.

"Where are you going?" Zane asked.

"To shut the damn thing off."

Smith strolled over to the pool pump, realized he had no idea what he was doing, and shoved his hands in to remove pieces haphazardly. A bright yellow warning sticker ('Do not insert hands in pump') looked on in disgust.

"That seems important," Smith said, tossing aside a widget. He shoved his hands in deeper and pulled out some tubing. "That too." There was a grinding noise and some blood spattered out onto the pool's edge.

"That's disgusting," Zane said. "I hope you don't have any blood-borne diseases."

"Not that I'm aware of," Smith said, unfazed.

When six more pieces were removed, the pump shut off with a THUMP. Zane freed his cape and exited the pool to see that Smith's hands were mangled and bleeding profusely.

"Great idea," Zane said. "Shoving your hands into moving parts." He eyed the sticker. "I don't think you get worker's comp if you intentionally ignore a warning, so I hope you opted for the accidental D&D."

"Meh."

"Meh?" Zane watched as the gashes healed themselves. "Whoa now. Is *that* normal?"

"Yeah," Smith said. "Long story."

Already scheming, Zane put a hand to his chin. "How bad an injury can you heal from?"

"Anything, as far as I can tell, and believe me there's been *a lot* of trial and error. You could decapitate me and keep the head away from the body, I guess, but as soon as you put the pieces together I'd be fine."

Zane grabbed a nearby barbeque fork and jabbed it into Smith's side. "You can't die then?"

"Unfortunately," Smith grumbled, pressing the gap in his side back together. "My shirts don't heal, though. And that still fucking hurt."

A normal person might begin his next line of inquiry with "How did that happen?" or "Are you sure?" A normal person might inquire about Smith's real age. A normal person might question the definition of humanity given the existence of a person who contradicted one of its pillars. A normal person might show some sympathy to Smith's dire outlook.

Godwin Zane asked the question most important to him. "Can I have sex with you?"

Smith blinked a few times.

Zane did what he tended to do and kept talking. "Not in a sexual harassment way. Of course you can say no and the answer's no. I'm not even into dudes. I just can't—you know—on account of the magma, and I see an opportunity here."

"Did you just 'no homo' a request to fuck me?"

"I did. Yes." Zane paused. "So that's a no?"

Smith shrugged. "I mean..." On one hand, the thought was repulsive. On the other, there was the magma. He settled on his final answer, "I don't give a shit."

"So that's a yes?"

Smith offered a half-nod. "If there's even the slightest chance you magmatize my body, I'm in."

"Well, that's grim," Zane said. "And also not a word."

What followed was one of the least erotic sexual encounters in the Western canon. Its author debated how much to include, eventually settling on what follows. Nothing else happens in the rest of this chapter. Skipping it is encouraged and will only result in missing an offhanded reference or two later in the story.

"Soooo—" Zane said, drawing out the word.

Smith stared at him, wearing the facial expression equivalent of a question mark. "So..."

Zane reached toward Smith and was rebuffed.

"Ugh, don't touch me," Smith said. "This is business, not pleasure. I mean, technically... you know what I mean. This is a whore's kiss situation."

Zane was confused. "So I should pay you?"

"What? No. It's a metaphor."

"I don't think that's a metaphor."

"I'm pretty sure it is," Smith said.* As the discussion played out, he peeled his pool water-soaked boxers from his legs. They landed on the rooftop cement with a sloshy flop.

"Oh, wow," Zane said with a cringe. "It is incredibly difficult to make this seem arousing to me."

"I don't know what you expected, being straight and all."

"I just think if I were gay, I'd be into black guys."

Smith buried his head in his hands. "I swear to..."

"Nice dragon tattoo, by the way," Zane laughed. It was a reverse tramp stamp that also bore the words 'No Fear.'

"Oh, fuck off," Smith said. "Nobody makes good decisions when they're seventeen."

"You don't make good decisions *now*," said Zane.

Smith acknowledged that with a head tilt.

Zane reconsidered his offer. "The immortality doesn't happen to run in your family, does it?"

"You're the worst." Smith wasn't sure whether he was speaking to Zane or reminding himself.

"I'll take that as a no?"

The answer was yes—sort of—but Smith wasn't about to give a creepy grey billionaire the green light to pursue Lemon or Patience. Only one of those two would land Zane in jail, but the thought of either was disturbing, to say the least. He stood with his arms crossed, waiting for Zane to make a move.

"I can make this work," Zane said, turned off but desperate to lose his virginity. He grabbed his phone and pulled up

---

* In this instance, it is not.

a sext from one of his adoring fans—a busty brunette in grey lipstick. "Bend over."

Zane positioned the phone in his hand so that it blocked the entirety of Smith's body from his view as Smith lowered himself to his hands and knees.

Zane lowered his own body but before he could absorb himself in the sext, Smith shouted at him.

"Lube!"

Smith may have implored the cruel, unforgiving universe to melt him, but he didn't feel like experiencing any discomfort in his ass beforehand.

"Ugh." Zane excused himself for a moment and returned from a cabana with lube and a bluetooth speaker.

Smith glanced over his shoulder. "What in Carl Sagan's name is that for?"

Zane raised a finger to call for silence, then lowered that same finger to his phone. From the bluetooth speaker came the saxophone intro of George Michael's "Careless Whisper."

"Oh, for fuck's sake," Smith said.

"Exactly."

Zane got the silence he desired. Too much silence, considering sex was being had.

When all was unsaid and done*, Smith had a hole burnt through his torso, which didn't feel great. It began to heal almost instantly, but the emotional wound of the worst consensual sex of his life would linger for some time. He pushed the sides of the hole together, grabbed his waterlogged boxers, and wordlessly shuffled away.

---

* About two minutes later.

31 / A WALK IN THE PARK

On the subject of sex, Brooks could have been having plenty.* For reasons that weren't clear to him, he wasn't. Was it that he was growing old? He hoped not since he was going on thirty-three with factory-fresh cybernetics. Was it his lingering love for Smith? Maybe, since they'd only been broken up for a few weeks. Was it an overwhelming sense of responsibility for Patience and Lemon? Also maybe. Were the stars aligned in such a way that the influence of the Demogolans of Sector Four was being felt? Possibly. Was it because he was a Leo? No. Astrology is a sham.

Brooks stopped considering his own motivations long enough to check in with Patience.

"Are you enjoying yourself?" he asked. It was hard to tell.

"Hmm?" She looked up from her kettle corn. "Oh, yes. The colors are quite vibrant."

Though she'd been raised to wear only the most somber hues—black, dark black, grey, dark grey, brown, dark brown, brown-black, grey-brown, and the occasional russet—she'd come to appreciate the tones of the twenty-first century. And there was no place more colorful than New York Pride. When the parade ended, the group had made their way to Bryant Park to regroup.

"Stop!" Lemon shouted.

She was a bit too eager for their leisurely pace, and Brooks snipped, "What?"

Lemon made a rectangle with her fingers. "This is a perfect photo op! You two stand in front of that flower bed."

Brooks dutifully posed for her picture, extending his feather boa with, well, pride. Patience glanced up from her

---

* Transitions are hard.

kettle corn with apprehension, certain that still photographs, like videos, removed a piece of her soul. A smaller piece, but a piece nevertheless.

Lemon snapped a few quick shots, swiped through them and grinned, pleased with her work. The lighting was perfect, the framing was perfect, and she could fix Patience's facial expression in Photoshop. An old man on a nearby bench shot the group a look of disgust and Lemon soured.

"Did you see that?" she asked.

"What?" Brooks asked, distracted. He was busy considering whether every thought he had was his own or a piece of programming.

I'm not interested in what she's going to say, he thought. *But what if they made me not be interested? No, that would be stupid. But the Reticent did turn an intern into Nicholas Cage, so...*

Lemon gave his arm a tug and repeated herself. "Did you see the way he looked at us?"

Brooks shrugged. "You think he's up to something?" He didn't think so, but his detective instincts were admittedly off.

"What?" Lemon shook her head. "No. I think he's a homophobic jerk."

"Oh. Maybe."

"I'm gonna say something," Lemon announced.

"Why?" Brooks asked.

Her speechlessness gave way to mere confusion. "What do you mean 'why?'"

"Do you get worked up every time someone slights you even the..." He paused, but couldn't come up with a non-repetitive word. "...slightest?"

"I do when there's a mi—"

He curled his lip. "So help me, if you say the word 'microaggression'—"

Lemon crossed her arms in reply. "I was gonna say 'minvective.' Anyway, that doesn't bother you?" She uncrossed an arm and gestured at the old man, who seemed to view the entire world with disdain.

"Lots of things bother me," Brooks said. He rattled off a list to prove it. "Not being able to donate blood bothers me. That conversion therapy is a thing bothers me." He paused on that thought for a moment. "People running for office under the platform that I'm a threat to 'American Values' bothers me." That last one *really* bothered him, given how many times he had saved the world. "People telling me to speak English when they hear me talking to my tías bothers me. Hell, the existence of butter pecan ice cream bothers me more than some jackass shooting me a look. Besides, you don't even know it's the Pride thing. Maybe he thinks Patience is cosplaying, and he just really hates nerds."

"His bias may not be against Mr. Brooks but against your skin tone," Patience offered. She turned to admire some particularly vibrant tulips.

"Madre de Dios," Brooks muttered to himself.

Lemon ignored her sister's remark.

"See, you don't care when Patience says stuff like that," Brooks said.

"She's from the 1690s," Lemon said.

In the midst of the conversation, Patience yelped. She went ignored as Brooks tried to dull the influence of 'internet Millennials' on his other daughter.

He realized 'Millennial' really was a catchall for the annoying, and continued. "That guy's from the 1950s. When he was growing up, you would have had to use a different water fountain. You can't come to the 2010s and expect everyone to be as enlightened as you. He'll be dead soon, and assuming he's a 'homophobic jerk' that'll die with him..."

Patience yelped again.

"What?" asked Lemon and Brooks simultaneously.

"There's a dead man in this flowerbed."

32 / PAYMENT IN FULL

Hypocrisy has a long, storied tradition in many industries. Among them are the obvious like banking and politics, as well as less-considered fields like trash collection. It's not hard to find a garbage man who, while decrying those who leave insulin needles in the trash, brazenly discards his own smack needles in the same manner. He'll tell others that it's wrong to improperly dispose of batteries, but he'll be the first to throw his tablet into the trash after mainlining a bad batch.

The profession of superhero didn't exist yet, not really, but it was about to become the most hypocritical of all. Having paid three million dollars to reopen a dimensional rift that killed sixteen thousand people, Godwin Zane took to the media to decry the Reticent for doing what he paid them to do. A few dozen reporters met with him to get his fiery take.

"This is outrageous," Zane said, dropping a fist to the podium. "These people nearly killed us all once before and now they're doing it again."

A reporter raised her hand. "A few days ago, you cautioned against blaming Arturo Brooks and Edward Smith for the incident. Don't you think the same caution should apply now?"

Zane coughed a little. "Well, I think we have pretty definitive proof that those two had nothing to do with it, what with their being missing when the rift reopened."

He tugged at his cape to make sure the Moonoco ad on the side was visible to the camera. This spiel was partly about continuing to clear Brooks and Smith's names because he said he would, but it was mostly about how he'd been screwed out of thirty seconds of rift that he'd paid good money for. It was about revenge.

"You don't want to give the Reticent the benefit of the

doubt?" the reporter asked.

"I do not. I'm not saying any one person is responsible, but the organization is clearly flawed. If someone were popping open portals in my building, you can bet I would know about it." He continued rambling, which equated to passion in the eyes of the viewing public, and readied some air quotes. "Honestly, I think we need to take a long hard look at why a *'medical research company'* called *'the Reticent'* is opening portals in the first place. Why did their president know how to kill a vampire? What else are they doing and why?"

A reporter fact-checked him. "My understanding is that micro-rifts could have innumerable practical applications in surgery. It's believed they could send a tumor to a parallel universe, for example."

Several others nodded. They didn't want to find anything suspicious. They didn't want to do their due diligence. They just wanted to document the spat between Zane Industries and the Reticent because that was where the ratings were.

Zane blinked a few times and continued trying to ruin them. "Applications or not, they're dangerous. In my opinion, the entire organization needs to be shut down until there is some oversight." He did not add, "and so they go bankrupt and I can scoop up their property."

"And who do you imagine should provide such oversight?" Another reporter asked. "They've never been found to break FDA regulations, and recent FBI investigations have found no evidence of wrongdoing. Sources say it's likely the whole vampire thing was staged for publicity, whether by the Reticent or by Arturo Brooks and Edward Smith themselves."

God forbid these people ever have to deal with something more serious than a rift, Zane thought.

He tried to make them see the light. "How about the ferry incident? Was that staged?"

He was interrupted. "Some people think *you* staged that."

"You think I had a ferry worth of people murdered to show the city it needs me?" Zane asked.

"No," the reporter said. "I'm with Citizens for Ferry Massacre Truth and we can't find any proof that the so-called victims ever existed."

"Oh for—" Zane said. "How about the AAVA massacre? Was that staged? You people keep telling me I should be stopping crime, but you're not willing to look at what's happening... What crime do you actually want me to stop?"

After a brief silence, one reporter offered an answer. "Purse-snatching."

Several others nodded.

"Credit card fraud" was given as the next answer.

Another person offered "Insider trading."

Zane walked off the stage.

33 / THOSE MEDDLING KIDS

Hudson Marrow was not the dead man in the flowerbed because Hudson Marrow could not die. The dead man did, however, remind Patience and Lemon that the inventor of time travel had gone missing, something they'd overlooked (read: forgotten), first in their quest to find their adoptive fathers, then in their increasingly irrelevant and precarious side adventures.

Just under a year earlier, Hudson Marrow's estranged wife Veronica had sold many of his time-borrowed assets in an ill-advised yard sale. The man Patience found in a Bryant Park tulip bed had been one of the buyers. Eagan Cloudnik—the poor hippie—had only wanted Hudson's authentic 1960s lava lamp. What he got in addition was an authentic 2010s knife to the throat, at least as far as Brooks could discern. It was an ordinary enough murder and probably a coincidence, but Lemon couldn't shake the feeling that this was important. So she and Patience rifled through their brownstone's downstairs office, which had once been Smith's.

"Mr. Brooks doesn't believe there's a connection," Patience noted.

"I know."

"You are not a detective as he is," Patience added.

Lemon shuffled through some paperwork—a muddled mixture of dossiers, tax forms, and fast food receipts. "*I know.*"

"I witnessed many deaths in Salem, and though members of the same family may have perished at the same time it was not usually a matter of concern—"

Lemon cut in. "This seems important."

Unfortunately, Lunan public education had shunned Earth-centric history in favor of focusing on the Moon. Sure, she knew the basics like the 29th Amendment, but events that didn't involve the formation or dissolution of alt-rock bands were mostly foreign to her. Still, something rang a bell. She knew *something* about the year 2015 in history. Something important. Unable to put her finger on it, Lemon sighed and opened another desk drawer.

"Should we ask Mr. Tangelo?" Patience asked.

Lemon kept searching. "It's just Tangelo, and no. Time travel is a lazy way of solving problems. Since when are you into breaking rules anyway?"

"I am endeavoring to test God's will for punishment."

"Hoo boy." Lemon changed subjects. "Have you found anything?"

"No," Patience said.

It was Wednesday and, as usual, Brooks had gone to see his therapist, so the office was theirs to peruse. Unfortunately, its organization was a disaster. Not one file was labeled and not one label was filed. Patience removed and replaced books from their shelves, hoping to find the Hudson Marrow case file hidden among them. She had seen that happen on several detective shows, so she assumed it was where detectives put important things.

Having looked through the entire library, she changed her approach. "Where is the wall with string?"

"What?" Lemon asked.

"The wall with string and photographs. It's where detectives connect the facts of their cases."

"Oh, you mean a crazy wall." Lemon dismissed her. "That's just a TV thing."

Patience frowned in disappointment.

Lemon moved yet another empty bourbon bottle out of the way. What was under this one grabbed her attention: a selfie of Brooks and Smith taken during a beach vacation, a fact made apparent by the beach in the background.

Who prints a selfie? Lemon thought. Then she made a sad

sort of "aww" sound.

"Have you uncovered something?" Patience asked. She had the tendency to phrase statements in which she was confident as questions. It was a Puritan thing, or at least an immortal, time-traveling Puritan girl thing. It was, at the very least, a Patience thing.

"Nothing relevant," Lemon said. "Just..."

Lemon's sense of *déjà vu* quickly became *déjà au-dessus**. The time had come for them to deviate from the task at hand again. Hudson couldn't die, so he could wait. The dead vampires were already dead, so they could wait. Eagan Cloudnik could wait too. What couldn't wait was matchmaking. The Smithless brownstone was quiet—too quiet—and Lemon couldn't take it anymore.

"We're gonna get them back together," she declared.

"Are arranged marriages not frowned upon?" Patience asked, again making a statement.

"I'm not talking about marriage," Lemon said. "Just the way things were."

"Were Edward and Arthur—"

"—turo—"

"—not dissatisfied with the way things were?"

"Stop stating things as questions," Lemon scoffed. "Anyway... yeah, but not always. It's all the time travel and immortality and cyborg stuff."

"Are those not unalterable facts?" Patience stated.

The questatements were driving Lemon crazy. "Yeah. We can't change the past. We already know that. But we might be able to help them get over it."

"What do you propose?" Patience asked.

Lemon grinned. "How do matchmakers always do it in the movies?"

"I'm not sure," Patience said. She added, "Are you not

---

* Lunan-French for "already over it."

phrasing your statements as questions now, the very thing you've been chastising me for doing?"

Lemon pressed her lips together.

34 / BS

Brooks and Smith had already reunited, though not in the way Lemon had hoped. Instead of taking the A train home when his therapy session was finished, Brooks boarded the 1 and made his way to Smith's studio apartment. As the sounds of Fetal Fetish (a thrash metal band indistinguishable from Kitten Orgy) grew louder, he was sure he was in the right place. Several increasingly loud taps on the door later, Brooks confirmed that it was the right place when Smith silenced the noise and answered the door.

He looked... not great. It wasn't unusual for Smith to hang around shirtless in pajama pants, but it was unusual for them to be caked with...

"Yeah, that's sour cream," Smith said, noticing Brooks's judgment. "I tried to make tacos, but the kitchenette isn't big enough to turn around in."

"It's 10AM," Brooks said.

"I didn't say it happened this morning," Smith said.

Brooks offered a judgmental blink. "Can I come in?"

Smith stared at him. "Under one condition. You don't get to condemn anything. Not the drinking, not the clutter..."

"Can I condemn this building?" Brooks asked. "Someone should."

Smith glowered, then removed himself from the doorway, making room for Brooks to enter. "Decent pun," he said. "I'd offer you a seat but I don't have any."

It was apparent that Smith did everything from sleeping to eating to bug squashing on a sheetless air mattress. Everything but cooking, which was done on a two-burner stove and three feet of counter space across from it. Brooks stifled a strong urge to disparage the accommodations and took a seat at the cleanest part of the mattress, at its foot.

Always feeling responsible, Brooks made an offer. "I have some extra bedding if—"

Smith ignored the sentiment, instead seizing the opportunity to repay Brooks's pun. "Since when do you give a *sheet*?"

Brooks shook the pun off and tried again. "If you need money—"

"I can afford furniture," Smith said. "I just don't care. I didn't exactly expect any visitors."

"O... kay." Brooks noticed a different stain—what looked like dried blood at Smith's side—and inquired. "What happened th—"

"Don't worry about it," Smith said. "Immortality's back."

"If you need anything—"

"Actually," Smith said. "You might be able to help with something."

Brooks perked up.

"What comes after quadruple?" Smith asked.

Brooks stared at him. "What?"

Smith recited his tuples. "Double, triple, quadruple..."

"Oh," Brooks said. He'd been hoping for a more substantial problem. "Quintuple."

"Then what?"

"Sextuple."

Smith chortled. "Are you fucking kidding me?"

"No. Then it's septuple, octuple, and nonuple."

"Well, those aren't as funny."

"Shouldn't you be at work?" Brooks asked.

"Working remotely," Smith said, gesturing toward a laptop that sat atop a pizza box. "The last few days were... *not great*." He had no intention of explaining any further.

"You don't like working for the fabulous Monochrome?"

In the mood for neither small talk nor thoughts about Monochrome, Smith responded with a curt, "Why are you here?"

Brooks was there for any number of reasons, excepting his being a Leo. The most pressing was that he doubted his decision-making skills and needed reassurance that he'd done the right thing initiating the breakup. The pizza laptop and sour cream pants made a compelling case. On the other hand, Smith was still Smith. He still made terrible puns and kind gestures, like dusting crumbs off the mattress to give Brooks a little more room.

"I came to give you this," Brooks said.

As Smith took a seat next to him, Brooks handed him a small gift card. It was yellow with a perfectly wrapped purple cartoon present on the front. Above that it said 'Congratulations!' in jovial, rainbow-colored Comic Sans. He flipped it to the reverse side where it said, in a more subdued Garamond: 'Good for $500 in services at Washington Heights Psychiatric Associates.'

Smith handed it back immediately. "The cuckoo's nest sells gift cards?"

"They're good for everything but gambling addiction."

"Why—?"

"The state of New York prohibits gift cards from being used on gambling." And whether gambling addicts would come clean was certainly a gamble.

"I meant why the hell do they offer gift cards."

"Oh," Brooks said. "Well, it makes sense. See, I'll just set this card right here." He placed it on a shoebox next to the bed. "And, you know, if you ever feel like going... they welcome walk-ins."

"Walk-ins?" Smith scoffed. "Is it therapy or a manicure?"

Neither man was aware that the clinic also offered nail treatments.

"I'm not condemning," Brooks said.

"Telling someone they're crazy isn't condemning?"

"I'm not—"

"I know. I've heard this one." Smith held up a hand.

"Stop."

"You're asking me to stop caring about you and that's not going to happen," said Brooks.

Smith scrunched his face. "If I were capable of getting diabetes, you would have just given it to me."

"Actually, all the chocolate and Pop-Tarts would have," Brooks corrected.

Smith laughed. "Cute." Then his eyes shifted from side to side as he searched for his next remark. He tilted his head. "You do know *you* broke up with *me*, right?"

Brooks threw his hands in the air. "*¡Me da rabia que tenía que!*"

"It gave you rabies that had what?" Smith wondered. He was already getting a headache and trying to translate Spanish exacerbated it.

Brooks chuckled, then stared at his ex. "I adore you."

"I'm confused," Smith said, scooting closer. "I'm the mean, fat guy. Remember?"

"Your words, not mine." Brooks sighed. "You may be mean and... *chubby*, but you're also brave and funny and really good in bed. And you'd never admit it, but you can be sweet. You're better with the girls than I ever imagined." He enunciated the next words slowly: "You are everything to me."

"Diabetes," Smith said through a smile. "So you want to get back together or—?"

"Ugh," Brooks said. "No."

"I'm confused again," Smith said.

Brooks sighed. "Remember that time you tried to break up with me because you knew I was going to die and it was going to hurt you like hell?"

Smith did. It was in 2011.

"Vaguely," he said.

"I can't handle your problems and mine," Brooks said. "Maybe it's selfish, but I'm probably going to live forever and I have no idea what I'm going to do with that. For

Christ's sake, I'm turning thirty-three and I have no idea what I want to do with my life. That's not normal."

"I think it might be..."

"You didn't know me before Willowbrook," Brooks said. "That attack gave me a purpose and a clear endpoint and now I don't have either of those things." He continued. "I thought maybe I could help you and that would be *something* but I couldn't. And then I broke up with you because I didn't know what else to do, and I still don't. So that's great. It's just great. I don't..."

Brooks took a play from the Book of Bad Ideas. He leaned forward and pulled Smith into a kiss. Smith went along with it, for a bit. But when things got passionate enough that Brooks reached for the pajama pants, Smith pulled away.

"You're a disaster," Smith said.

"*Me?* You—"

Smith cut him off. "I didn't say I'm not."

Based on the intensity of Brooks's existential crisis (2.75 on the FUCT scale), Smith knew he could have convinced the vulnerable cyborg to stay—for the rest of the day, well into the night, or for the foreseeable future. But he didn't. Keeping Brooks preoccupied with him wouldn't do him any good. He took Brooks's hand in his own and stared into his eyes.

"You need to go," he said with conviction. "I've figured out my future, and you need to figure yours out for yourself."

He escorted Brooks to the door, and added, "Stop worrying. You're gonna be fine."

Brooks had no idea what Smith meant by that. He held the door for a moment like he wanted to say something, but he couldn't figure out what. They exchanged no more words, and the door shut.

On his way to the kitchenette to grab some more bourbon, Smith's foot struck an errant thumbtack. He jumped and shouted, "fuck!" then leaned against the wall and held his leg up so he could survey the damage. To his satisfaction, the puncture wound did not heal.

35 / HIGH JUMP CHAMPION

It didn't take long for Smith's dark place to morph into a darker place. Brooks's visit reinforced his belief that his ex would be way better off if he could never see him again. Working that out, though, was tricky. Sometimes Smith's healing worked and sometimes it didn't, and he knew he needed to die before *didn't* turned back into *did*. There was no other way to stop the endless parade of bullshit and allow Brooks to stop being hung up on him. It was not a logical thought process.

When he'd looked around his apartment, he'd found nothing that would do the job; his possessions could be summed up as a thumbtack, some plastic cutlery, a prop phaser, and a handful of ant traps. He'd considered shoving his head in the oven, but even if it had been in working condition he didn't reckon he could bring himself to put that much time and effort into this. There was the option of jumping out the window, but his apartment was on the third floor and there was a strong chance the fall would only injure him. Then the healing would come back and he'd look like an asshole. The Reticent had revoked his gun when they fired him, so he couldn't shoot himself without first making a black market deal that would take forever. The apartment had no bathtub, only a semi-functioning shower, so drowning would be a tough one. He definitely wasn't going to give Zane another go.

After considering all of that, along with some absurd notions like huffing spray cleaner, he had an idea, and it put him in a cab. An immobile, barely upholstered, patchouli-scented cab. As soon as the driver reached the Brooklyn Bridge, Smith asked to be let out of the car.

"I can't just stop on a bridge," the driver said.

Smith eyed the line of brake lights ahead of them. "You're

already stopped."

"No. If caught, I could have my license—"

"I'll give you an extra twenty bucks," Smith offered.

He was permitted to exit the car.

After a lengthy but surprisingly easy scaling of a bridge girder, Smith stood peering over the edge of the Brooklyn Bridge. Nobody seemed to notice (or, more likely, care) that he was up there. Below, dozens of cars sat bumper-to-bumper, their passengers filled with absurd hopes of reaching their destinations on time. Despite the time it took for a middle-aged man in mediocre shape to scale the bridge, Smith's cab was still among them.

He inspected his surroundings. There was no suicide net, and Smith wondered whether it was too expensive or too aesthetically displeasing, eventually settling on a darker thought. *There are nine million people in this city. Guess it can stand to lose a few.*

There was no doubt in his mind that jumping would be rude. The time it would take to file the police report alone could reduce a man to chills. But cops kind of had it coming, and it was less inconveniencing than hopping in front of a subway train or bus, with the added bonus that his body might drift out to sea and never be found. That would be good for his family. This was, at least, a very well-considered bad plan.

As Smith prepared to jump, he noticed a rusted sign affixed to the bridge:

Death isn't the only option.

If you're considering suicide, there is help.

Call 718-555-LIVE

Suicide Prevention Institute of Manhattan (SPIM)

Fine, Smith thought. *If they insist.*

There was no way the insisters would say anything he hadn't heard, but—feeling a twinge of guilt from not using his gift card—he decided he might as well give life one last-ditch effort. Someone did go through the trouble of putting a sign up, after all. He pulled out his phone and maneuvered around the cracked screen to get it to call SPIM. It rang once.

Smith looked down. Traffic was still stopped.

It rang again.

Nobody moved.

It rang again.

The cars began inching forward. His former cab's horn blared because the driver in front of it took 0.4 microseconds too long to get moving.

It rang again.

Smith became annoyed. For an organization dedicated to suicide prevention, they took an awfully long time to answer the damned phone.

It rang again.

Finally, a soft female voice spoke.

"Finally," Smith muttered.

"You have reached the Suicide Prevention Institute of Manhattan. Your call is important to us. You are currently the—" The voice changed to a deeper one for "—sixteenth—" then back to the original woman. "—caller in queue. Please hold and a suicide prevention specialist will be with you shortly."

"Yeah, I'm out of here," Smith said to the empty line.

He tossed his phone ahead of him and jumped.

36 / OPERATION: JEALOUSY

Almost everyone knows the *Guinness Book of World Records*. Created in 1955, it chronicles humankind's most impressive and outlandish feats. What most people don't know about the book is that its founders were compelled to create it. Far away, in the Aldebaran System in the constellation Taurus, lives an advanced species known as the Kibitzerons. These aliens collect records from throughout the known universe and, once a year, delegates from their planet come to Earth to collect the Guinness records. The most embarrassing thing ever documented by the Kibitzerons was a galactic oligarch sending a holographic image of its cloaca to hundreds of millions of residents, instead of an intended emergency alert. The second most embarrassing, though unrecorded, was Patience's attempt at making Brooks jealous.

It was part of what Lemon called Operation: Jealousy. In film, she argued, the best way to get two people together was to convince one that the other had moved on, so they would realize their feelings for each other. Hey, it worked in *Sgt. Bilko* and *The Thomas Crown Affair*.

While Lemon set out after Smith, Patience was given a photoshopped picture and vague instructions. She executed them to the letter.

"I believe you will find this most distressing," Patience said.

Brooks was in his office, filling out job applications on his laptop. He looked up, confused. "What?"

Patience shuffled over and handed him the printout. She nervously straightened her frock as she awaited his response.

Brooks scanned the image for a moment, then broke into laughter.

"I don't understand your mirth," Patience said. "This is

most serious."

"No, it's not." Brooks set the picture on his desk. It was intended to be a shot of Smith romancing a blonde woman on a beach, but was very clearly a paparazzi photo of Taylor Swift and some guy, with Smith's head pasted onto said guy.

"This image was taken just yesterday," Patience insisted.

Brooks's eyes narrowed. "What are you doing?"

"I am demonstrating that Mr. Smith has moved on so that the pangs of envy will strike," said Patience.

"Yeah," Brooks said. "You're not supposed to tell me the plan. And Lemon did some shoddy work on this one."

"Pardon?"

"She could have at least slapped a dragon tattoo on it."

Patience frowned. "You can tell it's a forgery?"

Brooks tilted his head. "Uh, yeah."

"Am I in trouble for lying?" Patience gulped.

"No," Brooks said. "Just sit down for a minute."

Patience moved to the seat across from the desk and obliged. She still felt like she was in trouble, and she lowered her head accordingly.

"I went to Eddie's apartment earlier," Brooks said.

Patience perked up, hopeful.

"We're not getting back together. At least not any time soon."

Patience nodded. Then she remembered Lemon telling her that her role was crucial. Then she panicked and forced herself to ask a question. "Why?"

"It's complicated," Brooks said.

"It seems less so than you insist."

He was taken aback. "What?"

"Several weeks ago, I watched a documentary about robots and artificial intelligence—"

Brooks pinched the top of his nose. "Oh, no."

"Yes, I did."

Brooks buried his face in his hands to muffle a loud sigh.

When he emerged, he said, "I wasn't disputing whether you watched it."

"Oh, good," Patience said. "I did watch it and the narrator indicated that robots can be programmed to do whatever humans wish them to do."

Brooks leaned back and stared at the ceiling. "I'm not a robot."

"Still, it seems you could be programmed to forget what troubles you."

That was a fair point, and Brooks began to wonder whether he could be programmed to forget that he was a cyborg at all. Then he thought about how he'd previously been programmed to forget Smith and become a Puritan death-bot and fell further into existential despair. What if he'd been programmed to do this very thing—to freak out to the point of uselessness?

He changed subjects to encourage Patience's exit. "You two don't have any other schemes in mind, do you?"

Patience shook her head. "No, sir."

"Good," Brooks said. "Why don't you go see if you can find Lemon for dinner."

"Of course," Patience agreed.

"I need a few minutes alone," Brooks said.

When she was gone, he grabbed his phone.

I can't do this alone, he thought.

But he would have to, as the number he dialed greeted him with: "Your call could not be connected at this time."

37 / RIVER TRASH GOLD MINE

Smith's senses made a slow return, one by one. The first was hearing, and he had the vaguest sense that someone was singing. A familiar, female voice...

River trash gold mine
A spoon for me, a fork for you
A bucket of paint, not shiny but new
River trash gold mine
There's nothing more free
Than a spoon for you and a fork for me

The singing switched to speaking. "What are you doing?"

After hearing came touch. The SPIM sign had been right: death wasn't the only option. It wasn't an option at all. Smith awoke on his side—having drifted ashore in Brooklyn—to the warm sensation of a stray dog peeing on his leg. He coughed up a salty bit of water, then a smoggy bit of air, then a bit more water as he shooed the creature away.

"Cough it up," the previously singing voice said.

"Decent pun," Smith groaned, rolling onto his back.

His sense of sight returned from a blurry haze, and soon the singer was visible.

"I thought so," Lemon said. "What are you doing here?"

Smith sat up and deflected through repetition. "What are *you* doing here?"

"I tried to stop by your apartment, but you weren't there so I went trashing," Lemon said.

"How the hell did you get here so fast?" Smith asked. "I left my place in a cab before you got there."

"Uh, I walked? Check it out."

One of Lemon's favorite things to do was stroll through

Brooklyn Bridge Park, hunting for garbage. She outstretched her reusable tote bag and Smith peered inside. It was trash, all right. So far, her best finds of the day were a jar of broken marbles and a sock that was patterned to look like a shoe.

"Oh, and this!" Lemon tossed the tote back over her shoulder and pulled a rusted multi-tool from her pocket. She presented it to him like a priceless artifact. "It has a half-scratched off skull on the side. I thought you might want it."

"Thanks?" Smith said, pocketing an item he did not want.

"Were you swimming in the East River?" she asked, certain that even a part-time immortal could catch something doing that.

"In a sense," Smith said.

Having taken her mind off of trash, Lemon noticed the search and rescue boats circling the deepest part of the river. "Sweet Xenu." She dropped her tote and gave Smith a chastising smack on the shoulder. "You jumped!"

He shrugged. "I'm fine."

"Obvs, but why?" She answered her own question. "This is because Turo dumped you."

"No," Smith said. "That would be pathetic. No."

"It is!" She folded her arms. "Honestly. I'm only eighteen and I didn't get this worked up about Duke."

Smith resisted the urge to complain about her comparing his relationship with a months-long teenage fling. He also resisted the urge to cheer.

"You and Duke broke up?" he asked.

Lemon nodded. "I'm seeing Zipplok now. It's cool." She resumed the previous topic. "I can't believe you'd jump over that."

Smith patted the ground next to himself, extending an invitation. Lemon took a seat and listened to his next words. "It wasn't that."

"Then... how come?" she asked.

"I'm tired," he said.

Lemon frowned. "So take a nap."

"You know that's not what I meant."

"No, I *don't* know what you mean," Lemon said. "I already know a bunch of stuff that's gonna happen and I'm still excited for the future. Even with 2020 coming up—"

He cut her off. "No spoilers."

"Seriously, though," she said.

"I've just... had enough. You don't know what it's like to do this for a hundred years," Smith said.

Lemon's face took on a look of disbelief. "Did you just tell me I'll understand suicidal urges when I'm older?"

"No..." He realized he did say that. "Yeah. I guess I did."

Lemon rested her head on a closed fist and stared at him. "This is D-grade parenting."

"Yeah. Sorry."

"Eddie," Lemon said. "You gotta go to therapy."

38 / MR. SMITH GOES TO WASHINGTON HEIGHTS PSYCHIATRIC ASSOCIATES

The Reticent never had therapists on site, but there was one office in New York where the organization sent its most troubled agents. Edward Smith was no longer one of those agents, but once he'd resigned himself to treatment, he knew where he needed to go: Washington Heights, specifically the office of Kendra Means. While others in the field tried to pretend that they hadn't seen someone stake a vampire on live television, Dr. Means was aware of the types of threats the Reticent faced and was the only licensed psychologist in New York who wouldn't recommend someone be locked away if they thought they were seeing monsters because they probably were. Plus, he had a gift card.

Smith sat in the waiting area, already annoyed. The degree on the wall was a PhD in Counseling Psychology from Fordham. He wasn't privy to all of the differences between psychology and psychiatry (he'd only recently figured out the difference between pilgrims and Puritans), but he knew the biggest: psychologists couldn't prescribe drugs. Certain that there was no point to this endeavor if he couldn't take a pill and be content, Smith stood up to leave. As he did, the counselor's door swung open and her previous client—Arturo Brooks—stepped out. It was a perfect example of why most clinics don't accept walk-ins.

"Do you need anything from me?" Brooks asked the office assistant, Ms. Brito.

"Not today," she said. "You'll be here next Wednesday?"

"Yep," Brooks said. When he noticed Smith, he let out a

little "hmp" in surprise before turning cordial. "Hey."

"It's not Wednesday," Smith said.

Brooks looked down. "Yeah, I had a cyborg thing so I just sort of... showed up."

"Huh."

"Can... Can I call you later?"

"I doubt the doctor recommended that," Smith said.

"She did not," Brooks said. "I just feel like we left things at a weird spot."

"Yeah, we did."

"So can I?" Brooks asked.

"You could if I had a working phone," Smith said.

There was an exchange of blinks. Then Brooks made an awkward motion toward the exit as he took the response to mean Smith was brushing him off.

"I have to go," he lied.

"Wait," Smith said. "That wasn't an excuse. You can stop by whenever. I'm pretty much planning on never going into the office again."

"O... kay. Nice seeing you," Brooks lied again. It was actually nerve-racking.

"You too," Smith replied, also with heavy emphasis on the lied. Seeing Brooks put him in an even worse mood heading into his session.

He walked into the room and dropped onto the first chaise sofa he encountered. Dr. Means was at the opposite end of the room, sipping tea from atop a purple high-back chair. She was a proper professional, with a face that said 'there's nothing I haven't seen before.'

"You're welcome to stay put," she said, "but there's a perfectly good sofa over here."

Smith leaned forward, patting the chaise. "Is this not where the lunatics go?"

Dr. Means didn't dignify that. Instead, she offered, "You're welcome to sit anywhere you want."

He took that to mean he should join her, so he hopped off the chaise and parked himself on the sofa across from her desk. He glanced down at its paisley pattern and scoffed. "What's with all the purple?"

"Some people think it's calming. Others think it promotes success."

"Yeah? Which are you?"

"I like purple," she said. "So how are you doing?"

"What?" Smith had expected an opening question prying into his past ('how was your childhood?' or some such nonsense), and he'd rehearsed an inelegant response. As usual, he was unprepared for niceties.

"Generally, how are you doing?" she asked.

He scratched his throbbing head. "Uh... shitty?"

"I'm sorry to hear that. How so?"

Smith tilted his head. "I'm sure you watch the news. You know who I am. You know my ex was just in here."

Dr. Means nodded. "Normally, I'd refuse to treat both of you, but—"

"Not a lot of therapists who talk about wraiths and shit, yeah. I get it." He added, "You probably shouldn't take walkins, though."

"So, is it the media attention that's bothering you?" she asked, ignoring his suggestion.

Lying didn't seem worth it in this case, so he shrugged. "Eh, not really."

"What's bothering you then?" asked the doctor.

"I can't die," Smith said.

"You don't want to die?" Dr. Means asked. It was a common fear among her clients, and among human beings in general. Entire belief systems had been created because of it.

Smith shook his head. "No, I *can't* die. It's a long story, but I'm like a hundred and ten years old."

"You look no older than fifty," she said, as if it were a compliment.

It wasn't. "I stopped aging at thirty-eight, so thanks for that."

"So... you're saying you *do* want to die?"

"Yes," Smith said, in the same way a person would answer whether they wanted to large-size a drink. "I guess."

"You guess?"

"Hell, some peril would be nice."

"Why is that?"

"Does it matter?" Smith asked. "Just write down that I'm fucked up or whatever and refer me to someone who can give me drugs."

That was the wrong approach.

"Do you have a history with drugs?" she asked.

"Oh, come on." To Smith, it felt like she was cheating, like Brooks had already told her everything about him. In reality, he rarely came up during Brooks's sessions, which mostly covered Staten Island and cyborg-induced anxieties. Smith just happened to look and behave like an addict, right down to blaming others. "I don't care what he told you—"

"You brought it up," she said. "You don't have to tell me, but I'm curious about your history with—"

"I like them," he said, glowering.

"Is there anything in particular you find yourself coming back to?" Dr. Means asked.

"Oh, come on," he said again. "Don't act like I'm a crackhead or something."

"We've never spoken before," she said. "Assume I know nothing about you because that's the perspective I'm going to take."

"*Fine.*" Smith thought about it. "Uh... I'll try just about anything once. I definitely won't do krokodil, though. That'll fuck you right up. I saw a guy once try to eat a live boar—" He decided she wouldn't want to hear that story. "Mostly I just drink."

"Have you ever been to any sort of rehab, or—?"

Smith snorted. "Oh yeah." He shook his head. "Worthless." After a moment's contemplation, he corrected that. "Actually, they gave me Valium to treat the alcoholism, so not entirely worthless because I found out I really, really like Valium."

"Do you think rehab would ever help you?"

"Not a chance," Smith said. "If I wanted to stop drinking, I would. I'm a stubborn asshole. I just don't want to."

"What does drinking make better?" asked Dr. Means.

"Everything."

"Everything?" She looked deep into his eyes. "If you want to die, it doesn't sound like it makes anything better."

Smith dodged the eye contact. "Well, like I said, I *can't* die so I'm working with what I have here."

"Then what does it make better?" she asked.

He leaned back into the sofa and ignored the directive that they start fresh. "You already have Turo as a patient, so you already know that my past, present, and future are all fucked." He scoffed. "I've gotta say... I've never hurt anyone because I was drinking, but I damn sure hurt a lot more when I'm not." The doctor almost got the chance to offer a response, but he continued. "And you know, it's not like I can give myself liver cancer, so I don't see how this is a problem. *Who am I hurting?*"

"Something brought you here," Dr. Means noted.

Smith groaned. "Just tell me what I need to do for your stamp of approval or whatever."

"That's not how this works," she said. "The goal is to help you figure out what's best for you."

"I know what's best for me!" Smith wasn't sure why he raised his voice. He repeated himself more softly. "*Danger* is what's best for me. There just isn't any. Look." He removed a rusted multi-tool from his pocket, opened the blade, and made a deep, professional cut down the length of his left forearm.

Kendra covered her mouth with her hand in horror.

"It's fine," Smith said, rolling his eyes and waiting for his arm to heal. Instead, his blood sprayed all over the relaxing purple sofa. "Oh, shit. This again. Sorry about the mess."

The psychologist looked around for something that could be used to wrap the wound. As she did, she shrieked for her assistant, "Ms. Burrito." Hilma Brito opened the door and once again chastised her boss for pronouncing her last name like a greasy food that wasn't even from her culture.

"Call 9-1-1," Dr. Means said. Her biggest client was cheap and the office was always cold, so she rifled through her drawers looking for the cardigan she kept handy.

Smith was unmoved. He made a rolling motion with his right hand. "It'll fix itself any minute now. Relax."

In the lobby, a man stood and pushed past Ms. Brito to get into the room.

"You can't come in here!" Dr. Means shouted. It was instinct when someone burst into a therapy session. She grabbed her cardigan and changed her mind as she rushed to apply it. "No, it's fine. I'm sorry." She wrapped the cardigan tight around Smith's arm.

"Why are you still here?" Smith asked, dizzy and not one hundred percent certain he was seeing what he was seeing.

"I wanted to make sure I got the chance to talk to you," Brooks said, taking over the task of keeping the cardigan tight. It was already soaked with blood. "Jesus, Eddie. What did you do?"

Smith glanced down and admired his handiwork. "A damn good job, apparently."

39 / PURGATORY

Someone once said that dreams are the windows to the soul. Unfortunately, Reticent scientists disproved the existence of the soul in 2014 when it was discovered that Jimmy Fallon had not actually surrendered his to Satan in order to receive *The Tonight Show*. It was but the evil of humankind alone.

Smith's dreams were not proper windows. They were a set of cracked, tiny block windows barely letting a glimmer of light into the basement that was his mind. He woke up trying to brush giant ants off himself. It took a moment's observation to realize the ants were a lie and that he was still in the hospital.

After he'd been patched up at the hospital next door to the clinic, Smith had been placed in the psychiatric care unit for observance. Given the nature of its patients, it was strange that the ward wasn't in better shape. Just looking at its mint green walls—their peeling paint obvious under flickering fluorescent lighting—made Smith want to die all over again. He rolled over in hopes there would be something more appealing than another wall.

"Eddie," Brooks said. He had been sitting next to the bed like the dutiful boyfriend he wasn't. He leaned in for an embrace and was rebuffed.

In his sleep—somewhere between fighting disgraced actor Shia LaBeouf and shooing the giant ants—Smith had put something together.

"It's you," he said. "When I cut myself with glass back at the house, you were there. When I broke my shoulder. When I stepped on a thumbtack. Every time I tried to kill myself you weren't there and it didn't work. I assumed it wouldn't work at the shrink's, but you were in the lobby. You're using robot powers on me."

Brooks ignored the robot powers bit. "Every time? No-body should have a big enough suicide sample size to draw that conclusion."

"You think I'm wrong?" Smith asked.

"Not necessarily," Brooks admitted.

"I'm sorry," Smith said. "If I knew you were there, I wouldn't have done it. I'd never want you to see—"

"No, you just want me to live with you being dead, like that's a hell of a lot better."

Smith glowered. "It has nothing to do with you."

Brooks startled himself with what he blurted next. "I hate you. I actually do."

"Yeah, well. Join the club."

"If you wanted to die, you should have done it a long time ago. You should have done it before I spent a decade of my life loving someone who doesn't give a damn about himself or me. You should have done it before we took in two girls who, by the way, miss you."

If there was anything Smith hated, it was being told what to do. "Yeah, well. I'm sorry I ever loved you," he sneered. "If it weren't for you and that goddamn time machine, I wouldn't want to die."

"You know what? This is..."

Brooks's voice became fainter and the entire room seemed to fade. As it did, a different voice called to Smith.

"Yikes. That's grim," it said.

His surroundings warped and transformed into Godwin Zane's office, where he found himself speaking to the man face-to-face.

Smith lowered his brow. "How the hell did I get here?"

"It works," Zane said. "I wasn't expecting the wacky dream-within-a-dream thing, but it works. And this... this is why we need to stick to the pre-programmed scenarios."

Smith immediately knew he was talking about The After-life™. The hospital argument was all in his head, and there was another problem.

"Shit," he said. "I'm dead."

Zane waved his left hand from side to side in a 'kind of' gesture.

"Kind of?" Smith asked. "How do you get *kind of* dead?" He could think of a few different scenarios, but this warranted clarification.

"You might want to sit down," Zane said.

"I don't exist," Smith said. "I don't think it matters."

Zane took a seat at his desk. "Well, something went wrong during surgery. You went into cardiac arrest and now you're in a coma."

"And you transferred my consciousness to... the cloud?"

Zane cringed. "I hate that word, but yes. Basically."

"And we're not really here," Smith said. "Where are you?"

"Sitting in my living room in my pajamas, jerking it. I'm basically Skyping your mind."

"But... if my mind is here and my body is in the hospital, they're going to run scans and think I'm brain dead."

"Obviously," Zane said. "That's the first thing I thought of. But you're not coming back from the coma, buddy. I've got some baaaad news."

There was no worse person to deliver bad news, except Andy Dick. Zane explained quickly and without courtesy that scans of Smith's brain had revealed a large tumor in the RAS area responsible for sleep-wake cycles. It was unlikely he would wake up, and even if he did, the tumor was malignant and not treatable. "So the plug's getting pulled any minute now. I basically saved you and you're welcome." He paused and tried to add something sympathetic. "Also, I'm sorry for your loss."

"How long have I been out?" Smith asked.

"A few weeks."

"I want to see," Smith said.

"I thought you might, what with the masochism. Don't

worry," Zane said. "I put a camera in your hospital room."

"Why? Why would you do that?"

"So I could keep tabs on the body, duh."

Smith breezed past why Zane needed to do that. "Bugging hospitals is a little fucked up, don't you think?"

"Yeah, well..." Zane worked some magic and transformed one wall of his virtual office into the live feed of Smith's hospital room. He then disappeared. "The pizza man just arrived, if you get my meaning, so let me know if you need anything in, like, two or three minutes. Give me five to be safe."

"You won't need five," Smith said under his breath.

"What?"

"*Nothing.*"

In the hospital room stood Brooks and two people Smith hadn't seen for a long time: Charles and Lucy O'Grady, his adoptive parents from Indiana. They were a lot older than he remembered, and it took a moment to register that it was them. His father helped his mother up from her seat.

Oh shit, Smith thought. If the O'Gradys were saying their goodbyes, he really was going to be dead any time now. *Oh shit, I'm getting It's a Wonderful Life'd. They're all gonna feel bad and it's gonna make me want to live again and it's gonna be gay as fuck.*

"Make sure you don't blame yourself, dear," Lucy said. "We never wanted to get this call, but we're not surprised."

Charles agreed. "He's been troubled for a long time."

They hugged Brooks one last time. When they left the room, Brooks stayed. He sank into the chair next to the hospital bed and stared at nothing. He wasn't angry like Smith had imagined. He scowled only at his arm, lifting it to his head and giving it a sniff. He scowled harder and muttered something in Spanish under his breath. If the near-black circles under his eyes hadn't made it apparent that he hadn't left the hospital in two days, the scent would have. As would the fact that Burroughs entered holding a pair of Quadrentasized coffees.

Brooks took a listless sip, then inquired, "Did you bring the girls?"

"They're outside talking to his parents now," Burroughs said. "Patience saw a doll in some kid's room down the hall and is theorizing that it stole Eddie's soul."

Brooks offered a slight, sad laugh. "He'd say you have to have a soul before someone can steal it."

Smith decided that—yes—that's exactly what he would have said.

"It's not your fault," Burroughs said.

"It's literally my fault," Brooks corrected. "I was supposed to die. The Reticent brought me back and now I suck the life out of people or something."

"I'm still looking into—"

"Oh, come on," Brooks said. "We both know it's me."

"You don't *know*."

He knew. It was a letter that traveled through Hudson Marrow's time machine that gave Patience her everlasting life. It was a similarly well-traveled Spirograph that gave Lemon hers. It was a skull-shaped cigarette lighter, stolen from Hudson's office, that gave Smith his.

On the other hand, a series of letters Smith scattered through time had added a few years to his appearance. All the objects that traveled through Hudson's time machine and came out granting immortality were also capable of taking it away, bit by bit. That's why the 2090 version of Smith had gone on a time-travelling spree: in hopes of aging himself to death.

Brooks was not a person anymore, but an object, and an innocent trip back to the set of *Star Trek* had granted him the worst superhuman ability of all time. The energy transference that worked with all those other objects worked with him. He knew.

"I look like a real asshole too." Brooks took a sip of his

drink. "Love of my life slips into a coma and I take off for a week."

"You thought he'd get better with you gone—"

"Now I show up in time to kill him and collect."

"Stop," Burroughs said. "He's already gone."

"Every time he was near me, that tumor grew. All the headaches I bitched at him about. I made everything worse—"

"Stop," Burroughs said.

"The drinking was probably to ease the pain! I—"

"It wasn't," she said. "Stop."

Brooks changed the subject, slightly. "I keep displaying his vitals, hoping something will change." His voice softened. "It's not going to change."

"No," Burroughs said. "It's not."

Smith complained out loud. "Put me back."

Zane appeared, in a huff. "You couldn't give me one more minute?"

Smith considered it strange how much time Zane needed alone versus with a partner, but this wasn't the time to sass him about it.

"Put me back," he repeated.

"For what? You can't do anything. Cyborg or not, he can't *see* your consciousness in there. They aren't scanning you again. If I did put you back, that body isn't going anywhere. You're screwed." Zane put a hand to his chin and pondered for a second. "Actually, maybe not screwed. I have an idea. Hang on."

Zane disappeared. Then Smith felt himself disappear into blackness. Then his point of view on the hospital room shifted. He was seated, looking directly at his own motionless body.

At the hospital, Brooks's eyes grew wide.

"What's wrong?" Burroughs asked.

"I think I'm hallucinating or having a stroke or something."

You're not, Smith's voice said.

"*Me vuelvo loco,*" Brooks complained. "*Estoy esquizofrénico.*"

You are not, Smith repeated. *Unless you just said that you're possessed by a dead person, in which case you are. I'm in your... brain? Hard drive? Whatever you have.*

Brooks was groggy. "Why? How?"

"You're talking to yourself," Burroughs said. "Are you okay?"

Just think at me, Smith said. *It should work.*

Brooks nodded at Burroughs, then spoke telepathically to Smith alone. *Okay.*

Perfect, Smith said. *So we have a bit of a problem.*

You think? Brooks asked. *What is happening, Eddie? How are you in my head?*

One of Zane's inventions, Smith said. *I could pop back into my body, but I'll probably never wake up and if I do and stay near you the tumor will kill me. Or—*

Brooks was hopeful. *There's an 'or?'*

Or I can just stay here.

In my head?

In 'the cloud,' Smith said, changing his voice so the cloud was an ominous one. A stratus cloud, if you will.

"This is horrible," Brooks said, accidentally out loud.

"I know," Burroughs said.

I know, Smith said. *It is. Look at me.*

Brooks eyed the body in the room.

Not that me. Me. Can we get visuals in here? he demanded.

I thought you tested this thing, Zane's voice said.

Why is he in my head? Brooks wondered.

Zane chastised him. *You shouldn't connect to public WiFi.* He switched on the visuals in Brooks's cloud. *There. I'm already bored with you two.*

In his mind, Brooks was now at the beach. Not a shitty New Jersey beach, but a nice Caribbean one. Smith lay in the reclining chair next to his own.

Oh, this is nice, Smith said.

The Afterlife™ comes preloaded with 72 basic scenarios, Zane said.

Yeah, I know. I fucking picked them, Smith said. *Go away.*

Finally, Zane scoffed.

Brooks was confused. *Did you just hijack my brain or...?*

I connected you to Second Life, more or less.

Eddie. This is insane.

I know.

I'm sorry—

Don't you dare go Canadian on me, Smith said. *You have nothing to apologize for.*

I did kill you, Brooks said.

I killed myself, Smith corrected. *I didn't actually mean to do it that time, but... this is okay.*

This is okay? Brooks asked. It sure as hell didn't seem okay.

It is, Smith said, scooting his chair closer and leaning in. *Way I see it, there were three possible outcomes for my life. The first was to live forever and never see you again. The second was to stay with you, slowly go crazy, then die. The third is this.*

I refuse to believe those were all the options.

Refuse it if you want, but I know you don't have any better ideas. He added, *I feel better.*

He meant it. Adventure was back. Peril was back. As it turns out, there's nothing like death (and shirking an eight ounce tumor) to improve a person's outlook.

Brooks was not as optimistic. *There were three possible outcomes for me*, he said with tears forming. *The first was to live forever and never see you again. The second was to live forever and watch you die. The third is this: to live forever and be haunted by your cyber-ghost.*

It doesn't sound great when you put it that way, Smith admitted.

Brooks leaned into his partner's chest and noticed how real his breathing felt. Everything seemed real: the crashing waves, the blistering sun, the squawking seagulls. Smith even smelled like *Acqua di Odio*, his signature sandalwood-heavy scent. They fell together and held on, neither saying a word.

In the real world, Brooks was aware enough of what was happening to go through the motions. He nodded when the doctor asked him if he was sure. He clasped Patience and Lemon's hands.

You're dying, he told Smith.

It's okay, Smith answered.

"He's gone," the doctor said.

"It's okay," Brooks answered.

40 / PALATE-CLEANSING ACTION SEQUENCE

"Holy shit," a man said.

Surrounding him were the sounds of public transit: the subway car scraping against its rails, some coughing, a panhandler rattling a can, the conductor's voice warning passengers not to give to panhandlers...

"I thought you said this was a comedy," the man said, shoving a book into his wife's hands.

"It is!" she insisted.

Ignoring conversation was standard subway procedure, but this bickering couple in particular stuck in Lemon's ear and she couldn't tune them out. They were loud. Really loud. Having just left Smith's funeral, she was sure their argument would make for a welcome distraction.

"I'm not laughing," he said.

"Well, it's a dark comedy," she said.

The man threw his hands up. "Everyone is miserable or dead!"

"Yeah, but there are puns and it has a happy ending."

"I don't see how since *everyone is miserable or dead.*"

"Just wait for the epilogue."

"I *hate* epilogues," he complained. "Tell the story in the story. You shouldn't need an epilogue."

Lemon's juicy gossip wasn't gossip after all. It was just two people who happened to be passionate about pulp. She looked down at Patience, who sat quietly reading a book of her own: *Practical Witchcraft* by Hermione T. Woodowl.

"Isn't that... not okay for you to read?" Lemon wondered.

Patience looked up. "Hmm. Well, I was falsely hanged for witchcraft once, so I've already suffered the appropriate punishment for reading this book."

Lemon found herself concerned that Patience's statement made complete sense. She continued her line of questioning. "Why are you reading that, anyway?"

"I'm considering all options," Patience said. "This book claims that witches can commune with the dead."

"Hoo boy," Lemon said.

"If it works, I may convert."

Lemon let go of the overhead strap to put her hand on her sister's shoulder. "I don't think that's a good idea. I know this creepin' situation sucks and you wanna stop hurting but—"

Before Lemon could finish, the car jerked to a stop and threw her to the floor. She tumbled into another passenger and landed with her hand firmly planted in a spot of gum. The man whose legs she'd battered grumbled something about "goddamned teenagers" and stepped away. Nobody was concerned for her and nobody was concerned that the train had come to a sudden and complete stop between stops.

Patience stopped reading. "Are you all right?"

"Ugh," Lemon groaned. "Yeah."

She peeled the gum from her hand and flicked it into a corner.

"Great," said the angry husband. "I bet someone jumped in front of a train again."

"You don't know that," said his wife.

"They were probably reading this damn book when they decided to end it," he added.

The wife stared at him and spoke, deadpan. "I'm cheating on you."

He didn't get it. "Is that supposed to be funny?"

"It is funny! See? You don't get it."

Lemon perked up to listen, then sank back to the floor as a tall figure loomed over her. It occurred to her that she should have asked Burroughs for more information about vampires because she was certain that this was a real vampire. Yes, she'd also been certain of that when she stabbed an accountant in Brooklyn, but the evidence here was incontrovertible. First, the man's pallor was at an extreme she could barely fathom. Second, his eighteenth century attire looked natural. This was not a bargain bin velour cloak, and he was not cosplaying. Third, he had sunken cheekbones and a horny stalker vibe. Her skin became cold in his presence and, though she wasn't one for cowering, she cowered a little when his voice boomed.

"You will stop pursuing my kind," he said, turning to Patience. "As will you."

The anonymous husband butted in. "Did you stop this train just to make a scene?"

He went unacknowledged by the vampire.

That wasn't good enough for the disgruntled reader. He stood up and poked the vampire on the shoulder. "Hey, buddy. I don't know what you think this is, but people have places to be. We—"

With a CRACK, the man's neck was snapped. The vampire tossed his body back toward his seat, causing panicked shrieks from his wife. Everyone else in the car backed away and shut up. A few tried to take pictures but soon found that vampires don't photograph, not even in Snapchat.

"We won't bother you, sir," Patience said.

Lemon agreed. "Nope. I've never even heard of vampires."

"Excellent," the vampire said.

He disappeared with a POOF as a small cloud of smoke concealed his method of escape. Did he turn into a bat? Did he turn into the smoke? Did he simply slip the door open and walk out? No one could say. They really weren't focused on it as much as the corpse on board. For a minute or so, the only sound in the car was the wife's anguished sobbing.

It was broken when Patience spoke to her. "Have you considered practical witchcraft?"

41 / THE AFTERLIFE™

Godwin Zane's press conferences were never ordinary. Sometimes there were dancers. Sometimes there were snakes. Once there were dancers wearing snakes around their necks, but that was soon found to be a mistake. The dancers' families received enormous settlements and Zane was legally barred from ever purchasing a reptile again.

The conference to announce The Afterlife™ was no exception to Zane's showmanship rule. A hundred or so reporters huddled in the largest pressroom on the first floor of Zane Tower. Behind them were a hundred Monochrome fans, there to add enthusiastic cheers from the back of the room. It was pitch black, and the reporters became agitated at having to use up their phones' batteries casting light.

A booming voice corrected them. "Phones. Off."

"How are we supposed to take notes?" one asked another.

A ceilingload of tiny notebooks fell from the ceiling, each with a different picture of Monochrome on its cover. The reporters attempted to dodge them, but three were knocked unconscious by notebooks falling at critical velocity.

"How are we supposed to see?" a reporter asked.

"Silence," the voice decreed.

Next, the room filled with fog and several reporters began coughing. Zane, backstage, wondered whether that had anything to do with his ordering unregulated fog from Oriental Trading Company, but decided that he didn't care. A few coughs were worth the bargain.

Then came the laser light show, set to a New Wave beat. Just as everyone started getting into it, a bevy of prop skeletons descended from the ceiling, suspended on ropes. Two reporters fainted in fright.

Finally, after two musical numbers—one from a recorder

quartet and the other from holographic Tupac—Zane took the stage to thunderous, exhausted applause from the reporters who'd remained conscious and the fans at the back of the room. The slide presentation behind him read 'The Afterlife™' in Comic Sans with little cartoon clouds and cherubs.

"You're probably wondering what any of that had to do with today's product," he said. "I'll tell you exactly what. This..." He outstretched his arms to gesture at women in panini costumes who filed onto the stage. "This is my idea of heaven."

Everyone mumbled in confusion. A few took notes.

"It's not really, you shmendriks." He clicked to the next slide: 'Heaven is a place on Earth.'

"Belinda Carlisle was right," Zane said. "Because no matter what kind of freaky afterlife you'd like to experience, you can. Even if it involves... t-shirt cannons!"

Two stagehands fired shirts into the crowd without warning. A veteran reporter fainted.

Next slide: '72 scenarios.'

"The Afterlife™ comes programmed with seventy-two basic scenarios. You and your loved ones can live forever for the low price of $16.99 per month. Forever."

Next slide: 'Upgrades.'

"With a premium subscription, you can have a custom scenario programmed. A custom scenario like..." The crowd braced itself. "...this one."

An elderly streaker ran through the crowd, pantsing two reporters at random. They were both relieved and underwhelmed that it wasn't something more severe. No one fainted.

"Nobody has to die ever again," Zane announced.

The reporters cheered. Zane fanboys and fangirls cheered. The internet lost its mind and crashed Twitter, Tumblr, Reddit, and (inexplicably) PornHub all at once.

Brooks sat in the brownstone's living room, watching the

press conference without cheer. He'd declined appearing as proof that The Afterlife™ worked. After the funeral, he'd declined appearing anywhere at all. He didn't even show up for his first day of work at Flaming Saddles.

This is getting depressing, Smith said.

"Getting?" Brooks asked.

You don't have to talk out loud.

Old habits, Brooks said, taking another swig of gin.

I'm not rubbing off on you, am I?

No, I think I'm allowed to have a few drinks when the love of my life dies and sets up shop in my robot head. Oh, and I broke up with him beforehand. Oh, and it was actually me who killed him.

Smith felt qualified to tackle one of those statements. *You're not a robot.*

Ayúdame Dios...

Before Smith could offer up a poor translation, a knock at the door distracted both Brooks and the man inside his head. While control of his body remained with Brooks entirely, Smith tapped into and borrowed his senses. If there was a sound, he heard it. If there was a sight, he saw it. If there was a smell, he smelled it. The last one was unfortunate, given Brooks's bathing habits over the last two weeks.

He made his way to the door and looked out the peephole. It was Burroughs again. Brooks sighed, unlocked the door, and retreated to his seat.

You're not even gonna open it? Smith asked.

She'll open it, Brooks said.

She did. On screen, a salsa band played. As the camera zoomed in, it became apparent that each member was adorned with a giant fake moustache.

"This guy," Brooks said. "He's the worst."

"He is," Burroughs agreed. "I know Zane has made some awful products in the past, but preying on people whose loved ones have died for fifteen dollars a month—

"$16.99," Brooks corrected.

"He's so full of it. It's obviously just a simulation."

In his head, Smith was busy enjoying the Starfleet scenario. When Brooks engaged in a private conversation, he felt it was his duty to try and stay out of it.

Smith gestured and shouted at the Tamarian Captain. *Darmok and Jalad at Tanagra!*

"Oh, I don't know about that," Brooks said, ignoring the sheer fucking nerdiness happening in his brain.

"How are you holding up?" Burroughs asked.

"Great," Brooks lied.

It didn't sound like a lie, so Burroughs accepted the statement as-is. "So when do you think you'll be ready to take the girls back?"

"Are they giving you trouble?"

"No." Patience and Lemon were pleasant, but the subway vampire incident had left them too terrified to leave the apartment and Burroughs wanted her space back.

On screen, Zane showed off a terminally ill child with a tangle of wires surrounding his head.

"There's no question," Zane said. "This kid is going to die." He took an unaffected stroll over to the boy's life support and pressed a few buttons. The child's head sank and, while his body lived, his mind had moved on. "On screen!" Zane shouted.

Projected behind him was the same child, now prancing around in a field of daisies with a golden retriever. The audience clapped.

"How are you doing in there, Aiden?" Zane asked.

The child gave two thumbs up.

Brooks stared at the screen with his mouth open like he wanted to say something.

"Maybe you shouldn't be watching this," Burroughs said.

Brooks took another swig of gin. "I'm just checking whether there are any features I don't know about."

"Excuse me?"

"Yeah. About The Afterlife™... I've sort of got the beta test in my head."

"What do you mean?" she asked.

"Eddie's in my head," said Brooks.

Burroughs thought back to two things: her Psych 102 class in college and the annual Reticent sensitivity training seminar. She offered sympathy. "I know it feels that way, but—"

"No, he's literally in my head."

She patted his shoulder. "No, he's not."

Brooks interrupted Smith's adventure. *Hey, back me up here.*

Smith looked up from the Captain's chair. *She's got a mole shaped like Africa on her left ass cheek.*

"You have a mole shaped like Africa," Brooks said.

On her left ass cheek. Say it.

"...On your left ass cheek."

That wording wasn't Brooks's and she knew it. "You're serious."

"As serious as that kid's terminal cancer," Brooks said, eyeing the TV.

Burroughs was taken aback. "Oh my God, he *is* inside you."

"No, that was me," Brooks said, a little bit ashamed. "That was rude. I'm drunk."

"It works, then?" Burroughs asked.

"Yeah, it works," Brooks said.

"For how long?"

"Since we pulled the plug," Brooks said.

"Are you o—"

He cut that question off. "Great."

Always possessing a keen sense of when to end a line of questioning, Burroughs pivoted. "So the girls..."

"I can't live with them," Brooks said.

"Do they know about this?" she asked.

Brooks shook his head. "No."

"You have to tell them, first of all. Then you have to bring them back here."

"I can't live with them," he repeated.

Her voice was laced with frustration. "Well you did adopt them and you're not dead, so..."

"I won't put them at risk," Brooks said.

"There's no risk," Burroughs said. "It's not like you gave Eddie cancer. They'll be fine. They just won't be immortal when you're around. You know, like normal teenagers."

Back me up, Brooks said.

Smith did not. *But she's right. You know that, right? I'm not dead because of you.*

Stop it.

It's not your fault.

Stop.

Burroughs waved a hand in front of Brooks's face. "Hello?"

"Sorry. Two conversations." He averted his eyes.

Burroughs knew that look. "He agreed with me."

"So what? I'm not getting anyone else killed."

You didn't get anyone killed, Smith said.

"You didn't get anyone killed," Burroughs said.

Brooks pressed at his temples in frustration. He stood up and freaked out at the echoing voices. "My mother died because I was born. My father and sister died because I had to go to some stupid concert to celebrate a stupid degree I didn't even end up getting. Eddie died because I'm a soul-sucking robot freakshow. It's not happening again. Lemon and Patience can live here if they want, but I have to go."

You're being ridiculous, Smith said.

"So help me, I will partition you," Brooks said.

"What?" Burroughs asked.

Brooks threw up his hands. "Two conversations!"

42 / HESITANT WITH THE PRESIDENT

Burroughs raised her voice to the highest level that could be seen as 'passionate' without reaching 'hysterical woman.' It was a delicate balance.

"We can *not* take another offer!" she said.

"This one is for six million dollars," Wiles said. He took a sip of tea.

Marsh agreed. "We're not going to brrrrrrrrrai—break anything."

Things were stressful enough for Burroughs without worrying about giant rifts. In addition to her daily commute from Queens, she was now making a daily commute to the Brooklyn brownstone where Patience and Lemon lived, just to check in on them. That was three hours of her day, every day, spent on or around subway trains. Her relief at their moving out wasn't nearly as relieving as she'd hoped.

"We are playing with fire here," Burroughs said. "Just because it was fine once—"

"Twice," Guerrera noted.

"I wouldn't call the first portal 'fine' when it consumed a six block radius of Manhattan."

"We could stand to lose a few more people," he said.

"Oh my God," she said. "What is it about this place that makes people evil?"

"Not evil," said two of the Webers at once.

"Evil!" the third laughed behind them. It seemed pretty evil.

Burroughs wasn't sure what she was doing anymore. If just one of the jobs she'd applied for would have called her, she'd have been gone in seconds; it didn't matter what. She would have been content with any respectable career: doorwoman, barista, door-to-door vacuum salesperson. She wasn't the only one. The few people who remained with the Reticent following the firing of Brooks and Smith had become the even fewer people who remained with the Reticent following the opening of yet another mysterious portal.

"We barely have an organization," Burroughs said. "What do we need another six million dollars for?"

"With six million dollars," Guerrera said, "we can rehire and retain talent."

"We could go into actual medical research," Burroughs said. "We'd make a lot of money *and* we wouldn't be making giant rifts in the universe..."

"That which we perceive to be a threat is rarely the true foe," Zephyr said.

Trebly interpreted that. "See? Even Zephyr is with us on this one. Elmo?"

A sign of how the organization was doing, Knut Knutsson had resigned his position to run a multi-level marketing shop. He and anyone else with an IQ above 80 knew that Fitsy Fitness Wraps, worn under a person's everyday clothing, did not have the ability to grant six-pack abs. Knutsson didn't care, though. He could earn a few dollars scamming his Facebook friends while he figured out what else to do with his life.

Nobody wanted his job. Research and Investigation, with its thirty-seven employees, was still the largest division within the Reticent. But bylaws were bylaws and the board had to have the correct number of voting members, so they lured in a Times Square Elmo with the promise of sixteen dollars and a bump of coke.

"Elmo no understand," said Elmo.

"Just shake your head yes if you want the coke, Elmo," Wiles said.

"Elmo love coke," said Elmo. His scraggly costume head

bobbed up and down.

"So it's decided," Guerrera said.

"Please don't do this," Burroughs begged. "Please."

"If you're worried about the organization," Marsh said, "don't be. Trebly came up with a brrrrrrr-illiant idea."

Trebly beamed. "I did!"

"And what's that?" Burroughs asked.

"No one will be able to tell we even opened it!"

Burroughs pressed for more details. "Because—"

"Because of my brilliant plan!"

Burroughs buried her head in her palms.

"Don't be sad," Elmo said. "Elmo no like sad."

With that, Elmo's stained head fell to the table and the muppet began to snore.

If she'd had a Thinkwayve shirt, Burroughs would have called up LL Cool J's "The Boomin' System" to ease her pain. Instead, she texted Brooks, shut her mouth and began thinking of how she could best update her resume.

43 / WRAITH TO THE TOP

As a disembodied mind, Smith didn't require sleep. Brooks, being at least part human, did. It wasn't a problem. When Brooks needed to sleep, he disconnected himself from The Afterlife™. Smith, meanwhile, put himself into it one hundred percent, tapping out of Brooks's senses. It was surprisingly intuitive for an off-label use of a technology neither man understood.

But, as detectives do, Smith became curious. Sleep was a microcosm of death, and he wondered where Brooks's mind went when he was asleep. So he intruded, expecting that he'd end up bored, listening to Brooks snore in total darkness.

He ended up outside a house he'd never seen before, peeked in the window, and realized that he had intruded on a dream. It wasn't hard to tell. In the real world, life was disastrous and imperfect. Streets smelled like homelessness and it was nigh impossible to walk ten blocks without being flipped off for one thing or another. In the real world, people sucked at communicating and jumped off bridges. In the real world, hordes of monsters massacred entire families.

Here, Brooks sat fireside, cozied up with the dream version of Smith. Smith noted that the dream version of himself was actually fatter than him and patted his stomach.

It was Christmastime, and Patience and Lemon unwrapped their gifts as the adults looked on. Besides the two of them, Smith recognized Norman and Tasha Brooks from photographs. Here they had not been mauled to death by wraiths, but were content to drink eggnog and hold what he could only assume were supposed to be Tasha's children. The scene was so perfect it made Smith want to gag. It became more so when an old woman entered with a plate of festive cookies.

Smith mumbled to himself. "Jesus Christ, Brooksy..."

He made his way into the house through an unlocked side door. From the kitchen, he could hear conversation that was as G-rated and dulcet as he imagined: chuckles and "thank yous" and sentiments of holiday cheer. Then, from nowhere, everyone went silent, and he glanced around the corner to see what had happened.

A shotgun pressed against his chest ended that notion.

"Whoa!" Smith said.

"Oh, it's you," Brooks said, lowering the weapon.

"Who else shares your damned mind?" Smith asked.

Brooks sighed. "What are you doing here?"

"I wanted to know what happened if I used your senses while you were sleeping."

"Charming," Brooks said.

Smith blurted what came to mind. "So you're a chubby chaser."

"I am not," Brooks insisted.

Smith eyed the dream version of himself with a face that said 'come on.'

Neither chubby Smith nor the others came over to interact with him. They didn't do much of anything, as they were figments of Brooks's imagination. Since he was in the kitchen, focused on Smith, he couldn't focus on giving them dialogue.

"Where are we, anyway?" Smith asked.

"My grandmother's house on Staten Island," Brooks said. "Tasha and I used to stay here when dad worked overnight."

"And the kids are?"

"Are you really going to make me describe my dream to you?" Brooks asked.

"I mean, you don't have to..."

"The twins are Maria and Brock. We adopted them."

One of those was Brooks's mother's name. The other was...

"Brock?" Smith asked, raising a brow. "You named one of

our imaginary children after the lead singer of Kitten Orgy?"

Brooks shrugged. "I didn't know how else you would name someone..."

"You actually looked up the members of Kitten Orgy."

"Yeah..."

"You are—"

"Pitiful. Yeah. I know."

"I was gonna go with something nicer." Smith gave up and gestured toward the living room. "So that's it. When you dream, it's grandma's cookies and a happy family."

"Basically," Brooks said, shuffling.

"Then why don't you look happy?" Smith asked.

"You made a noise in here. I thought—"

CLANG. Another sudden, loud noise jolted Brooks from that thought.

"Damn it," he said. "It *is* this one..."

"Huh? What one?" Smith asked.

Every window in the house shattered at once and a cacophony of growls and shrieks drowned out what Brooks said next.

"Wraiths."

He pumped his gun and bolted into the living room. Brooks skidded to the ground right in the middle of his family.

"Get down," he said, and they complied.

Smith was not imaginary, and he did not comply. "This is your dream. Just make them go away."

'They' were a group of eight wraiths, closing in on the family. Wraiths are similar to vampires in that they are undead creatures that consume human beings. Where they differ is that, while vampires take a classy approach to draining their victims' blood, wraiths tear their victims to shreds and consume anything that strikes them, be it skin, sinew, or bone.

Smith watched from the doorway, ignored by the monsters.

"Hey," he said. "Wake up."

Brooks couldn't force himself to do so.

He shot at one wraith and missed. It grabbed Tasha and began gnawing at her throat. She made a gurgling sound as he shot and missed again.

"Wake up!" Smith said.

She'd been holding Brock, and there was a horrific crunch as he became caught under the monster. Brooks had only three shots and all eight wraiths remained. He fired at one with success, but another took its place and grabbed Patience by her arms. Another shot missed as her limbs were torn off, sending a wave of blood over Brooks's face.

"Wake up!" Smith tried again.

Brooks's last shot was another failure, and the creatures closed in on the family that remained.

"*¡Despertarse!*" Smith said.

That jarred Brooks. "What?"

He awoke on a grimy hotel couch in a sweat, leaned forward, and ran his hands over his face, trying to pull himself together. A blinking red light on his phone told him he had a message, but he ignored it in favor of grabbing a nearby water bottle and squirting it at his face. It still didn't do anything but annoy.

Does it always end like that? Smith asked.

"No," Brooks said, still not used to thinking in place of speaking. "Sometimes it's nice. Everyone opens presents and goes to bed. Sometimes only a few people die. Sometimes everyone dies but me."

His matter-of-fact answer made an abrupt change into an uncontrollable sob.

Whoa. Hey. Come here.

Brooks had trouble processing his transition into The

Afterlife*.

That felt real, he said. *So does this.* The scenario was instantly recognizable. He sat in the exact same spot on a more familiar couch, with company. Smith reached over and pulled him close.

Brooks, having just moved into a virtual copy of their brownstone, was at a loss. He sobbed into Smith's shoulder. *Estoy perdiendo mi mente.*

Smith stroked his back. *You're not going crazy. One of the scenarios is our house.*

I am going crazy. You spoke Spanish at me.

Smith sighed. *Tuve mucho tiempo libre en setenta años. I wanted to figure out if there was anything I'd missed all those years. Anything that could bring you back. I kept replaying all our conversations in my mind so I figured... I had nothing better to do and I couldn't die...*

You've understood everything I've said since you came back?

Yeah.

Brooks blushed. Nearly everything he'd ever said to Smith in Spanish had been an insult. That's why he'd said them in Spanish. *Why didn't you tell me?*

Smith shrugged. *You like having your thing and laughing at me being inept. I like entertaining you with my ineptness. After I pretended to have no idea what you said the first time, I just... kept doing it.*

You are...

Pitiful? Smith offered.

Something nicer, Brooks said. If he'd had a Thinkwayve shirt, he would have called up "Por Qué" by Banda de Queso. He didn't, though, so the smile he gave went without a score.

---

* Literally.

44 / EVERYONE IS MISERABLE OR DEAD

Lemon did have a Thinkwayve shirt, and it was about to come in handy. She couldn't get the guy on the subway out of her head. It wasn't the casual neck snap that did it. It was one sentence he said shortly before he perished.

"Everyone is miserable or dead," Lemon said. She'd been sitting on the floor of Smith's old office, trying to think of an answer for why the phrase seemed so familiar. Saying it out loud, she thought, might help.

Patience had been with Lemon for hours, but hadn't spoken a word. She sat at the desk, still reading about practical witchcraft. When Lemon spoke, Patience looked up from her book and bumped her glass of milk, sending it off the table and spilling the drink all over Lemon's Arcade Fire tee.

"I'm sorry," Patience peeped, dropping down and blotting the spill with her apron.

"Don't worry about it," Lemon said. "They're old news anyway."

Lemon hadn't done her laundry in weeks, so she went to her room and pulled out the Thinkwayve shirt she'd been saving for a special occasion. She slid it on over her head as she re-entered the room. She sat down and muttered the phrase again. "Everyone is miserable or dead."

She didn't need or expect a response from her sister, but Patience looked up and nodded. Everyone was indeed miserable or dead.

Lemon's Thinkwayve shirt began playing a song.

Everyone is miserable or dead
Everyone is miserable or dead

The corpse on the subway was right when he said
Everyone is miserable or dead

"Wait," Lemon said to herself. She knew this. Before she'd gone on to form Pop Tart & the Activation Energy, her namesake Lemon played lead fiddle for a band called Temporal Anomaly. Almost no one had heard their music because it wasn't very good, but Lemon had downloaded and listened to every PT&TAE-related rarity in existence. Her shirt remembered.

"L. Ron Hubbard!" she exclaimed.

Patience asked what was going on.

Lemon, unable to form an elegant response, shouted her own name. "I'm Lemon!"

"I'm Patience," Patience said. "We are already acquainted."

Lemon jumped up and down. "I'm Lemon!"

"Should I leap as well?" Patience asked.

"No, I'm *the* Lemon." Suddenly it made sense why so many PT&TAE songs were applicable to her life since she'd arrived in the past... she had written them! The prescience of "Bridge Jumper," "Duke and Duchess," "My Two Dads," "River Trash Gold Mine," and "Staten Island Dumpster" was no coincidence; they were *her* songs. More importantly, "Immortality Rally" was her song, and she realized exactly what was going on with the vampires and the dead guy in Bryant Park.

"We need to move," she said, grabbing her reusable tote.

Patience didn't move. "Why?"

The house rule was "no spoilers," but there were no rulemakers in the house, so Lemon grabbed her sister's arm and pulled her along.

"We've got a crime to stop!" she said.

45 / CYBORG SECURITY

Being a cyborg wasn't all it was cracked up to be. A robot would have a single, functional purpose. An android would be aware of and accept its androidhood. Cyborgs, on the other hand, were once human. Was he still human? Brooks wasn't sure. Humans definitely wouldn't be able to rip metal chains from their anchors, and they definitely wouldn't be able to hold their exes in their brains. But scientists were always going on about how the human brain is just an advanced computer when you get down to it. Plus, there was The Afterlife™. Human beings living forever inside computers added another layer of trickiness.

Brooks inflicted his existential crisis (2.9 FUCT) on Smith. *What am I?* he asked.

Are you still doing this? Smith asked in turn. He was as exhausted as a disembodied mind could be. *You can't change what happened.*

Brooks was snippy, and he wasn't having a 'move on' from someone who could not do the same. *Oh, I'm sorry. Does it bother you that I'd rather talk through my problems than kill myself?*

No, Smith said. *It bothers me that you're upset.*

And you say I'm going to give you diabetes.

In the outside world, Brooks was taking the subway to Zane Tower. He had a few strong words for the billionaire regarding a dimensional rift, as well as a few questions about what to do with Smith. In the world of The Afterlife™, meanwhile, Brooks and Smith floated on inner tubes atop a pool of green jello. It was the sixteenth scenario they'd explored together and the stupidest so far. Smith's bias against pools showed, as it wasn't even a nice one. It was a Motel 6 pool. The green didn't convey whimsy as much as it did mold and grime.

Listen, Smith said. *We'll make this work.*

How!?

I'm sure Zane can hook me up with a cyborg body of my own and then BAM. I can share your existential crisis.

Brooks took an ominous tone. *You don't want this.*

I don't know... there's a little bit of danger there with EMPs, the ability to be hacked, and that one exposed circuit. Plus, I could turn myself off sometimes and boot back up a few months later. Seems sort of ideal.

Ideal? Brooks scooped up a handful of the gelatin and threw it at Smith. It hit his chest with a SPLORP. *Remember when I had evil Puritan programming in my head? Remember when Mike shut me down with a gadget? What part of that seems ideal to you?*

Who the fuck is Mike? Smith asked, brushing the jello away.

The fake jihadist. You know, Mike.

Whatever. I already told you which part would be ideal: the shutdowns. Plus, you and I could stand to have the cyborg thing in common.

Why? We don't have enough Reticent-induced trauma in common?

No, so you wouldn't have to deal with it alone.

When he finally arrived at Zane Tower, Brooks encountered two problems. The first was that Depeche Mode's "Just Can't Get Enough" played on a loop. The second, more important problem was that he was denied entry beyond the lobby.

"We can't let you in," said the woman at the front desk.

"I work here," Brooks said.

Take the laundry chute, Smith insisted for the third time.

I'm not taking the laundry chute.

The receptionist stood firm. "I'm sorry, but without proof that a Zane Industries employee resides inside your brain, I can't let you in."

Brooks folded his arms. "How the hell would someone prove that?"

"Entry is permitted only with three-factor authentication," she said.

"I can hook up to The Afterlife™ if—"

The woman spoke slowly. "Entry is permitted *only* with three-factor authentication."

"Okay, so..."

"ID badge, password, and iris scan."

Brooks handed over Smith's badge. "The password is..." He sighed. "Handies4Hammies."

Handies4Hammies? Really? Brooks wondered.

Are you going to tell me you wouldn't give someone a handy for Hamilton tickets?

I would not. Because I have some dignity. Also, they don't require special characters?

The woman at the desk was not impressed. "First of all, you're supposed to scan the badge and type the password, not hand it to me and say the password out loud. Second, you don't have his eyes, I promise you. Remember: it's three-fact—"

"Three-factor authentication, yeah. I know."

You can do this, Smith said. *Your eyes are all cyborgy*. Just make them look like mine.*

"Can you just call Mr. Zane and tell him I need to see him?" Brooks asked. "Please?"

Zane was busy testing out the MouthPhone™, a phone that allowed people to taste what was on the other end of a call. She stared at Brooks. "No."

Come on. Zoom and enhance, Smith said.

Brooks rejoined Smith at the jello pool. *What?*

Look at my eyes.

Brooks obliged, but hoped he couldn't do what Smith

---

* This is not the correct scientific nomenclature.

thought he could. He squinted his right eye a few times, focusing on Smith in his mind.

Green, green, green, Brooks thought aloud. He smiled a little.

What? Smith asked.

I've always liked your eyes.

You're such a creep.

Shut up.

The nanomaterial that comprised Brooks's iris shifted, and his right eye became identical to Smith's. Brooks sighed. This didn't do anything to soothe his existential crisis.

"I like the look," the woman said.

Brooks glared. "Can I try the door now?"

She nodded, and Brooks approached the employee entrance with Smith's badge, password, and right eye. All three factors were factored, and the doors slid open with a friendly chime. He made his way through two mazes and up the rock-climbing wall with ease, but it was mentally taxing.

Why didn't you tell me about the mazes?

Oh, you think that's bad? Smith asked. *Just wait. You haven't even gotten to the laser puzzle.*

Seriously, why didn't you mention this? You love schtick.

Smith tapped at some jello. *Well, you did break up with me before I started working here.*

How many times are you going to bring that up? Brooks asked.

Smith grinned from his tube. *Until you change your mind.*

You're dead, Brooks said.

Really? I hadn't noticed.

You know what I meant, Brooks said.

No, I don't, Smith said. He made a few jumping motions in his tube to get it next to Brooks's, then extended a hand. *Here.*

What? Brooks asked.

Take my hand.

Brooks obliged. *Okay?*

Feels real, doesn't it?

Brooks nodded.

So does this, Smith said. He intended to lean in and kiss Brooks. Instead, he fell out of his raft, where the jello collapsed under his weight. He lay on his side, half-submerged. *Fuck.*

Back in reality, Brooks aligned a series of seven mirrors to reflect laser beams onto a switch that activated Zane's office door. Though it was a regular wood door, the sound effect of a stone gate coming together blared from the speaker system.

How often do the puzzles change? Brooks asked.

Every day, said Smith.

No wonder you wanted to work from home.

You have no idea.

Brooks barged into the room. "Zane!"

"Hmm?" Zane wondered, distracted. He was seated behind his desk and appeared to be working on his laptop. He bit his lip as he concentrated on the screen.

This is weird, Smith said. *He can't be working. Every time I come in here, he's doing something stupid.*

"What are you doing?" Brooks asked.

"Placing a bet on the National Spelling Bee," Zane said.

"...What?"

Zane stared intently at the screen. "Well, I look at all the kids and pick whichever one looks the most Indian."

"Oh my God," Brooks said.

There it is, Smith said.

"You have to spend money to make money," Zane said.

Brooks approached the desk. "I don't think that's what that saying means."

Zane shrugged, and looked up. "What do you wan—AAAAGH. What the hell happened to your eye?"

"Three-factor authentication," Brooks said.

"Change it back. It's aesthetically displeasing."

"You're grey," Brooks said. "Do you really want to go

there?" He lowered his head in shame. "And I can't fix it. I can't remember what my eye is supposed to look like. I need to go find a picture later..."

"Well, don't look at me then," Zane said.

"Not a problem." Brooks walked over to the window and looked out that instead.

"What do you want?" Zane asked.

"You can't open another portal," Brooks said.

"What are you talking about?"

Brooks tilted his head. "You shouldn't have opened it the first time, but you already cleared our names. Eddie's dead. I don't want to go back to the Reticent. There's no reason to do it again."

Zane fidgeted with his cape. "I seriously have no idea what you're talking about."

Liar, Smith said.

"Oh, come on. Eddie's in my head. He was there. You paid them to open it. Burroughs told me they got another offer. Six million dollars."

"Yeah, but I wouldn't pay them to do it again. They ripped me off last time." He thought about being shorted thirty seconds of portal time and his hands began to glow.

"Then who is?" Brooks asked.

"How would I know?" Zane stepped across the room and shoved his hands into a bucket of ice water.

This is probably not good, Smith said.

"Not at all," Brooks said.

"What?" Zane asked.

Brooks frowned. "I'm having two conversations at once, okay?"

He then texted Burroughs:

Not Zane who paid 6 mill

Normally, she responded to texts within thirty seconds, but this time there was no reply. He waited in silence for a minute.

Zane was annoyed that he was still there. "Is that all?"

"No," Brooks said. "I need your help with Eddie."

Brooks and Smith had moved on from the jello pool scenario. They were now seated in a movie theater—the only two people in a room built for an audience of two hundred. Their seats were the best in the house, right behind the railing that Smith used as a footrest. On the IMAX screen, the film's title appeared: *Superman IV: the Quest for Peace.*

Why? Brooks asked, bashing his head against the railing.

I told them to put a movie theater scenario in here, Smith said. *But there were some problems getting the rights to decent movies, so here we are.*

No, why is this happening? Why?

Is it really that bad? Smith asked, referring to his brain occupation. He reached over and tried to rub the tension out of Brooks's shoulders.

Yes, Brooks said. *Thank you, but yes.*

Outside the theater, Zane refused to be of any use.

"What about another cyborg body?" Brooks asked.

He was trying to figure out how they were going to remove Smith from his head. Yes, the virtual shoulder rubs were nice and sharing personal space was to be expected, but sharing headspace was a bit *too* personal.

"I told you. I don't build cyborgs. We can shove him in The Afterlife™ like everyone else if you want to pay $16.99 a month."

Brooks did not want to pay $16.99 per month. More than that, he didn't trust Zane not to discontinue The Afterlife™ after just a month or two. Yes, it was revolutionary and extremely popular, but so was his line of self-driving cars. Those were discontinued because Zane just didn't like the way they looked anymore. His engineers told him they could redesign them, but his fleeting interest had moved on. Smith was much safer inside Brooks's head than anywhere in Zane's care.

"It can't be that hard to build a cyborg," Brooks said.

"You do it then," Zane said.

Brooks blinked. "It can't be that hard with billions of dollars and a team of engineers."

"First of all, we've never made one before. Second, the Reticent got your corpse fresh. You want me to dig your boyfriend up and give him the Frankenstein treatment? It probably won't be pretty."

Brooks pondered in desperation. "What about a robot?"

"You want me to put him in a Roomba? We don't build robots either," Zane said.

Brooks's lip curled. "You build whatever you want. You're going to tell me you have time for the NosePhone™ but not robotic bodies?"

"Yes."

"But—"

"Your idea bores me," Zane said.

Brooks snapped. "Your movies bore me!"

Zane's hands began to glow again.

"Sorry," Brooks said.

"Look," Zane responded.

"At what?"

Zane pre-emptively dunked his hands again. "You know I meant 'listen.'" He sighed. "I might look into some solutions..."

"Thank you," Brooks said.

"If—"

There was always an 'if.'

Zane sauntered over to his desk and handed over a paper list of errands. "These are all things your dead boyfriend was supposed to do. Get them done and I'll think about it."

"Okay." Brooks glanced down at the list. It was weird, but

not outside his weirdness comfort zone. "Fine. We'll continue this later tonight."

Zane laughed. "I doubt it. The maze changes over at six o'clock and it's going to be a doozy."

46 / PRIVATE EYES

Lemon gathered her investigative team, which—because Brooks was still being a glorbdink—consisted of herself, Patience, and Burroughs. She relayed the lyrics of "Immortality Rally" as they boarded an Uber.

"The song says they're at 39th and 11," she said. Then she sang a little.

39th and 11 looks nothing like heaven
Where the vampires dwell
It's just like hell
And no one can save us from Kevin

Burroughs wanted to note how terrible the lyrics were, but she didn't want to rile Lemon up. Instead, she offered an objective fact. "That's not what the AAVA website said."

"But that website was for recruiting humans who wanted to be vampires," Lemon said. "I'm talking about the actual AAVA. For actual vampires. The song says it's at 39th and 11."

"The vampire on the subway warned us not to intervene," Patience said.

"If there's a nest, we need to destroy it," Burroughs said, hoping to do something good for a change. She'd brought all the appropriate supplies: wooden stakes, wooden crosses, and wooden clogs. Fictional accounts of vampires generally leave that last one out because it seems ridiculous, but roundhouse-kicking a vampire in the chest while wearing traditional Dutch footwear is extremely effective.

"Are you sure you two want to come?" Burroughs asked. "I've already asked all eight people in my chain of command to come back me up."

"No," Patience said. Lemon nudged her. "Yes. I am brave and wish to fight the creatures of the night."

Lemon smiled. "Don't worry. I've got your back."

"Brooks would kill me if he knew you were here," Burroughs said.

"I don't think he cares what we do," Lemon said. "He sent us away after the funeral and never looked back."

"Don't say that," Burroughs said. "He just... has issues."

"I have issues as well!" Patience said, hoping it would get her out of chasing vampires.

Burroughs was not moved. "Everybody does."

Some people have more issues than others. At their annual symposium, the Association for the Advancement of Vampire Americans had twenty-three issues on the table. These ranged from marketing plastic stakes in hopes vampire hunters would buy them and fail at staking creatures of the night, to campaigning for a secret vampire Congressman in order to assert their influence in Washington, D.C. They also had a bountiful sales floor—full of false teeth, stage blood, and velour cloaks—to attract vampire wannabes to the convention center. Iron supplements were free, of course.

The conference was in its final hours when the three detectives arrived, and the sales floor was empty of products and full of drained corpses. Twenty-one of the twenty-three issues had been resolved, and leaving two up in the air for next year would give the vampires something to discuss on their message board for the next twelve months. All in all, it had been a successful weekend, and the vampires celebrated with blood cocktails in conference room 24B.

"Hi," Burroughs said, standing in the doorway. Lemon and Patience flanked her at either side, and her eight backup agents stood beside them.

The subway vampire was there, and he was agitated. "I told you to keep out of this."

"You had to know we wouldn't," Lemon said.

"I would like to state that I wished to stay out of it," Patience said.

"Oh, well," another vampire said. "Our plans aren't ruined."

"Your plans?" Burroughs wondered.

He made a whistling noise and six of his fellow vampires pulled out wooden stakes and began staking the others. The subway vampire let out an inhuman shriek as he dissipated into nothing. One by one, other vampires turned to dust as they shouted lines comparable to "*et tu, brute*"*, "curse your sudden but inevitable betrayal"† and "for fuck's sake, Jimmy, you should have seen this shit coming."‡

The vampires fought back, of course, but vampires don't commonly carry weapons, so they were unarmed. On the rare occasion that a vampire managed to snap its attacker's neck, the attacker recovered and staked him to death.

"What are you doing!?" Burroughs asked, unsure whether to be pleased or horrified.

One of the offending vampires finished staking his victim and turned toward the group. Patience stood still for a moment, taking in his features. The glasses, goatee, and overall frumpiness were familiar. Then it hit her.

"That man purchased a shield at Mr. Marrow's yard sale," she said.

"How do you remember all these faces?" Burroughs asked. "There are nine million people in New York."

Patience hadn't an answer.

---

* *Julius Caesar.*
† *Firefly.*
‡ *Titanic 2.*

"Those aren't vampires," Lemon said.

The yard sale vampire broke into a slow, deliberate clap. Soon the others joined him in mocking the young detectives.

"The ones we just staked were," the lead vampire said.

"Who are you?" Burroughs asked.

"My name is—"

"That's Kevin," Lemon said.

"What?" the man asked. "No. My name is Tim."

"It can't be. The song says it's Kevin."

"It's Tim, I assure you. Tim Buchtu."

Lemon turned to Burroughs and stared through her, as if the older woman were a camera and they were trapped in a reality TV series. "You can't be serious."

"It's spelled with a c-h," Tim said.

"Still," Lemon said.

"I know," Tim said. "Believe me, I know."

It wasn't the most unfortunate name in the world. That honor belonged to Catheter Blood, a schoolteacher in Maine whose parents used the hospital surroundings of her birth for inspiration. But Tim Buchtu was still a top-tier bad name.

"I guess I changed the name for the rhyme," Lemon said.

No one paid her any attention.

"What the hell are you doing, Tim?" Burroughs asked.

"Did you know nearly every vampire in the world comes to this conference?" He thought on that. "Well, they did until we killed them."

"But why did you kill them?" Burroughs asked. "Not that I'm complaining."

"Do you know what it's like to be immortal?" Tim asked.

Burroughs groaned. "Oh, here we go again."

"Hoo boy," Lemon said. "Do we ever."

"Yes," Patience agreed.

"No you don't!" Tim shouted. "You're young and optimistic. I'm a fifty-three-year-old optometrist. You don't know what it's like to have an eternity of optometry to look forward to."

"So the time machine made you immortal too," Lemon guessed.

Tim stared at her. "The what?"

Time travel was supposed to remain a secret, and Burroughs nudged Lemon as she corrected her. "The items at Veronica Marrow's yard sale. They were exposed to a temporal anomaly that Lemon mischaracterizes as a time machine."

"Oh," Tim said. "Yes, then. All of us." He gestured with an arm at his companions. "We are all immortal now, and we suffer for it."

"My God," Burroughs said. "If I have to listen to one more grown man complain about being invincible, I will go back to school to get a PhD in Immortality Studies and spend the next decade of my life researching a cure." She exhaled. "Get over it."

Tim, never in any sort of danger, took a seat. The other immortals seated themselves around him.

"We *are* getting over it," Tim explained.

"What do you mean?" Burroughs asked.

"It took us a while to figure out what we needed to do," he said. "What happened to us, what the point of being immortal was..."

"This seems ominous," Burroughs said, tucking her stake away and taking a seat of her own.

Lemon knew the lyrics. "Yup."

"You know how many people purchased stuff from that yard sale?" Tim asked.

"Fifty-four," Patience said.

Tim was taken aback. "That's... correct."

"I studied the sales ledger," she said.

"Anyway... of those, twenty-two ended up being immortal."

Burroughs recalled Eagan Cloudnik, the poor deceased

hippie the girls had found in a flower bed. "You killed the others."

"It was nothing against them," Tim said. "It's just... to figure out who became immortal and who didn't, we had to tell them our plan... and once they knew about our plan, we kind of had to kill them. You know how it is."

"We do not," Burroughs said.

Lemon, already familiar with the lyrics, tried to speed this along. "They want to be the only immortal beings on the planet, so they killed the vampires."

Tim cleared his throat and corrected her. "We want to be the only *beings* on the planet, immortal or not. We'll form our own society and—"

"Oh, great. They're anarchists too," Burroughs muttered.

Lemon didn't understand. "That wasn't in the song."

"What song?" Tim asked.

"Never mind," Lemon said. "You wouldn't get it anyway."

"Is there something about immortality that makes people crazy?" Burroughs wondered. "First it's making the entire world Puritan, then it's exterminating everyone..."

"We are superior," Tim said.

"No we're not," Lemon said. "We're an accident."

"I do appreciate it when the bad guys tell me their plan, though," Burroughs said. "It makes it a lot easier to stop them."

"We cannot be stopped."

Burroughs knew better than that.

47 / LEVEL 3 FUCT

Brooks didn't think he would ever set foot in Smith's shitty apartment again, but he found himself there to collect Smith's work laptop before Zane Industries charged a thousand dollars for it.* It was among the last of his errands, after 'collect exactly three hundred aluminum cans' and 'acquire the hair of a homeless person.' Brooks figured it was best not to ask questions.

What if I die in here? Smith asked.

What!? Brooks said. It was the last thing he wanted to think about.

I mean... say I'm doing the Firefly Season Two scenario and reavers kill me. Do I wake up in the base scenario? Do I die? What happens?

You worked on it! Brooks said. *You tell me.*

Correction: I was supposed to test it at one point, but I kept skipping work. All I did was describe the scenarios.

Brooks looked around. *Yeah, about that—*

Inside The Afterlife™, the two men were at a summer camp. But there was a problem.

Did you have to—

It's not my fault, Smith insisted. *Zane said to research people's ideas of heaven, so I googled and it turns out... there's a lot of Nazis out there.*

You are just white enough to be surprised by that.

Smith gestured toward a row of olive tents teeming with activity. *I kept the swastikas out, at least.*

Everyone here looks like a Wehrmacht officer.

Or Macklemore, Smith offered. *It could be a Macklemore camp.*

In the distance, a dozen blond-haired, blue-eyed men began doing push-ups.

---

* It was worth two hundred dollars.

You're sure this one wasn't your idea? Brooks asked.

No, Smith said, offended. *I tried killing Hitler, remember?*

I'm not saying you're racist. I'm saying I wouldn't put it past you to put some fucked up scenario in here for the laughs.

Smith gave that statement an accepting shrug.

Plus, those guys are kind of hot.

Smith cut in. *Here lies Arturo Brooks: beloved friend and father, lover of hot Nazis...*

I'm just saying... you could have made them ugly old Hitlers. Anyway... Brooks made a quick transition back to the original topic, offering a few words of caution. *Don't do Firefly Season Two. I really can't take you dying again.*

Well, that's why I haven't picked it yet.

Good. Don't.

I kind of feel like you're gonna hold the white supremacist scenario against me, though...

Can you just be quiet for a few minutes? Brooks asked. It wasn't the all-white summer camp that was bothering him, though he could come up with a litany of reasons the 'just doing my job' excuse was a bad one in this instance. What was bothering him was, again, the entire ex-in-the-head situation. Before Smith took up residence in his brain, getting time alone to think had been a lot easier. Now it had to be explicitly requested, and each time he worried about what Smith's response would be.

Smith fucked off, certain that he could find something to do aside from Firefly Season Two. Assuming things had been programmed according to his research (and they had been so far), there should have been a laser light show scenario. He asked for the channel listing. When a holographic interface appeared in front of him, he prodded it and—sure enough— Laser Light Show (on Pot) was an option.

"Ugh," Brooks said to himself as he stomped a roach. He made a quick lap around the room, searching for anything else he'd want to collect and bring home, but there was hardly anything worthwhile. In the kitchenette, he saw the type-3 phaser he'd given Smith for their anniversary lying on the counter and freaked out a little bit. That stupid thing was the reason he traveled back in time, and it was why he was able to kill Smith. He had rolled the time travel dice and came up whatever is a bad result in dice. He backed away, determined to grab only what he came for.

The laptop was still on the pizza box, and Brooks scooped it into a laptop bag. He looked around the room and thought about Smith's last few weeks alive. They were spent here, in filth and misery. He sat down on the edge of the bed one last time, taking it all in: the acrid sour cream smell, the ants, the shouting neighbors. This, he reflected, was his fault, and he soon regretted taking time for his own thoughts.

He noticed the shoebox where he'd previously set a gift card, and decided to look inside. It was a mistake, not because the contents were private, but because their existence worsened his fragile state. There was a photo of the two men enjoying themselves at a Reticent holiday party. There was a copy of *To Kill a Mockingbird*, Brooks's favorite book. There was a note Smith had written to himself as a reminder of all the reasons he loved Brooks. Just the realization that Smith had taken nothing from their home but items that reminded him of their relationship made Brooks's eyes water. He moved a carnival prize out of the way to reveal a ring box.

What is that? Brooks asked.

Smith didn't want to intrude, and he didn't want to stop watching the laser light show. *Are you actually asking me or are you trying to talk to yourself?*

I'm actually asking you. What is that?

Smith removed himself from The Afterlife™ and tapped into Brooks's senses to observe the ring. *Oh shit*, he thought. As a non-corporeal being, he was his thoughts, and thus it was said aloud.

Oh shit? Brooks asked.

Smith tried to calm his ex. *Don't worry about it.*
Eddie...
It's nothing.
It's not nothing. Did you change your mind on—
No. Not necessarily.
Brooks's voice faltered. *How—*
Listen. It was just something I'd been thinking about because it meant something to you. Shit, don't say it like that. That's going to sound like accusing, and he's all fucked up right now...

You have no inner monologue, Brooks said, letting himself fall backwards onto the grimy mattress.

Seriously. Don't worry about it, Smith said. *I do all sorts of spur-of-the-moment things that don't make any sense.* He paused a moment, then added, *I jumped off a bridge.*

It was too late to backtrack. Brooks would never forgive himself. Just as he hit Level 3 FUCT, his phone rang.

It was Burroughs, requesting a small favor.

48 / IMMORTAL COMBAT

After explaining his evil plan, Tim had invited Lemon and Patience to dinner so they could get to know him and his immortal companions better. Burroughs sent her agents away, but insisted on tagging along herself. They returned to 2045, and Nitish Mitra—embarrassed at having kicked the teenagers out of his restaurant due to false rumors before—made sure they got the best seats in the house. The reserved dining room was two hundred and fifty square feet and offered privacy for what needed to be a private conversation.

"Here's what I don't get," Lemon said. "How did you get the actual vampires to think you guys were vampires too?"

"Easy enough," Tim said. "All we had to do was drink human blood and not die."

Patience frowned at her plate of spaghetti.

"Why did you send one of them after us on the subway?" Lemon asked.

Tim sighed. "You're like us," he said. "I'd hoped our plan would be finished by the time we met and I knew if you kept investigating the vampire angle you'd end up finding out about the murders and you'd get the wrong idea."

"Yeah, wouldn't want them to get the wrong idea about you committing mass murder," Burroughs said.

"What's the right idea?" Lemon asked.

"You two are *like us*," Tim said again. "We need to be at peace for the new world order."

"What kind of order?" Burroughs asked.

Tim snapped at the only mortal in the room. "None of your business."

A voice interrupted the meal.

"Am I late?" Brooks asked, joining the party. He tried to say it nonchalantly, but his voice wavered against his will.

Lemon didn't let that soften her response. She crossed her arms and glowered. "You do exist."

He mouthed an "I'm sorry."

"No," Burroughs said. "Tim Buchtu here was just telling us about how he wants to kill everyone who isn't immortal so he can start some sort of cult."

"Paradise," Tim corrected. "And we need to do it quickly... before that idiot Zane grants immortality to the teeming masses."

Brooks eyed the man. "Tim Buchtu?"

Jesus Christ. Smith broke into laughter.

Your middle name is Lock, Brooks snipped.

"I know. I know," Tim said. He tilted to look around Brooks. "Where's the other one?"

"Excuse me?" Brooks asked.

"Your husband is immortal, right?"

Brooks went on the defensive. "Why does everyone think we're married?" Before he could receive an answer, he added, "He died."

"Are you no longer distressed?" Patience asked.

Tim put up a finger. "Wait a minute. He died?"

"Yeah," Brooks said.

"Bu—"

Brooks interrupted with a long string of words. "But not before I broke up with him for refusing to see a therapist..."

"Bu—"

"...which," Brooks continued, "was part of an overall strategy I had to help him accept the immortal thing and maybe be comfortable with himself so maybe we could live a normal, somewhat happy life. Maybe we'd get married, I thought."

"Bu—"

Brooks wouldn't let Tim get a word in. "*Turns out,* he was actually thinking about proposing to me, and he did go see the therapist, but I was so wrapped up in having a pity party over being made a cyborg against my will that I had no idea until it was too late and *he died*."

"Mr. Brooks is still distressed," Patience said to Lemon.

"He did die, though?" Tim asked. "Really?"

"Yep!" Brooks said, strained.

Burroughs slid a steak knife away from her plate and hid it behind her back. She stood up and straightened her skirt as though she was heading to the restroom.

"Excuse me," she said.

"But he was immortal," Tim said, uneasy.

"Yeah, about that..."

Tim was seated right next to the door. As Burroughs passed, she thrust the knife into the side of his throat, sending blood everywhere.

The Lannisters send their regards, Smith said, suggesting another alienating pop culture reference. *Say it.*

Brooks declined.

Tim's followers stood and Lemon and Patience readied their own steak knives.

"Wait," Brooks said. The sight of the knife-wielding teens, for a moment, jarred him from his own bullshit. "You two don't need to murder anyone."

Lemon rolled her eyes. "*Now* you want to parent us."

"Tim was leading this, right?" Brooks asked.

One follower nodded. "Yes."

"Do the rest of you really want to continue with his plan?"

"Not really," another immortal said. "I thought we were actually going to become vampires, not start a doomsday cult."

Another chimed in. "I thought we were going to create our own nation on a tropical island somewhere. A nudist one. I didn't think we were going to hurt anyone."

It soon became apparent that no one knew what they were doing. Nobody but Burroughs, who began sawing at Tim's neck to decapitate him, just to be safe.

"So it's settled then," Brooks said. "You all go on your way. If you ever want to die, let me know and I can help you out."

"Okay!"

"We will!"

One of the immortals opened the door to exit just as Nitish came to check on the party. The restaurant manager's jaw dropped. At the head of the table, Burroughs was prying a corpse's head from its torso. On the floor, an already enormous bloodstain spread farther and farther. He glanced from one to the other, then at the guilty parties.

"I'm afraid I'm going to have to ask you to leave."

Outside, Brooks apologized to the girls.

"I'm sorry," he said. "You're out running around trying to kill people. I shouldn't have left you to yourselves."

"Hey, I think I did okay," Burroughs said.

"I'm sorry," Brooks repeated.

It wasn't good enough, and Lemon let him know it with a side eye and a huff.

"Will you return home?" Patience asked.

"I... can't," Brooks said.

Yes, Smith said.

What? Brooks said. *I can't, Eddie.*

Yes you can because I'm sick of you sitting around being miserable.

That's rich coming from you.

"Please," Patience said.

Brooks looked into her pleading eyes.

I know you can't say no to that, Smith said.

"Fine. I'll come home," Brooks said.

"Something's bothering me," Burroughs said, interrupting the moment.

"What?" Brooks asked.

"They kept saying they had plans to destroy all mortals. How?"

"What?" Brooks repeated.

"How were they going to destr—" She realized how. "Oh my God."

"What?" Brooks asked for the third time. He'd missed a lot, apparently.

"Remember when I told you Godwin Zane was paying us six million dollars to reopen the portal and you found out he didn't make the offer?"

"Yeah?" Brooks asked. Then he realized. "Oh. Oh no."

I know what to do, Smith said. *Come here.*

Brooks popped back into The Afterlife ™ to find Smith at the summer camp again.

You sure are using this scenario an awful lot, Brooks said.

Yeah, but I have a reason to.

Brooks ignored that. *What's your idea?*

Marry me, Smith said, dropping to one knee. He'd had plenty of time to think during the laser light show and while he was ignoring *Superman IV: the Quest for Peace.* Communication and men can go together like peanut butter and battery acid, but he'd thought about the root of Brooks's problems and he'd narrowed it down to 'not feeling human.' It helped that Brooks had articulated that exact problem on several occasions.

Brooks didn't follow. *What? How does that help? ...What?*

I don't have a ring because I'm dead and all, but...

And this is the place you chose? Brooks asked.

There is no better 'fuck you' to Nazis, Smith said. Then he repeated himself. *Marry me?*

We have bigger issues right now. Plus, we're not even dating anymore.

Yeah, but I mean... come on. We kind of are. Smith winked.

I really don't think this is the time.

It's always the time, Smith said. *Two conversations at once.*

49 / EXTENDED ACTION SEQUENCE

Brooks, Burroughs, Patience, and Lemon rushed to the tents that constituted Reticent headquarters, but the board was not present. Most of it, anyway. Zephyr sat alone in the chilly corner of the conference tent, handling a reflective resin ball that stood in for crystal.

While Patience and Lemon scouted for the portal generator, Brooks and Burroughs confronted the psychic.

"There's so much power," Zephyr said.

"In a plastic ball?" Burroughs asked. "I doubt it."

"Where's the generator?" Brooks asked.

Zephyr rolled the ball from one hand to the other and stared off into space. "Where intent is not clear, no answer can be found."

"What?" Brooks asked. "Are we serious with this?"

Burroughs attempted to reason with the unreasonable. "Our intent is to stop it. The client is evil," she said. "Well, he was evil before I killed him. But we have no idea what he set to happen when that thing opens up. He wanted to kill *everyone*."

"The moment of awakening is—"

Brooks took her ball away. "You can have this back when you tell us where the portal generator is."

Zephyr harrumphed. "It's not here."

"What do you mean it's not here?" Brooks asked.

"There's nothing here," Lemon said, bursting into the tent.

"You checked everywhere?" Burroughs asked.

"There are literally three tents," Lemon said. "We checked everywhere."

Patience nodded. "There was, however, another corpse."

"Who was it?" Burroughs asked.

"We were unsure," Patience said, "so we brought her here."

Patience stepped out of the tent, grabbed a corpse by the legs, and dragged it into the room.

"You have issues," Brooks said.

Patience nodded in satisfaction. It was about time someone took her seriously.

Burroughs identified the head of HR's body immediately. "Trebly! I wonder if they picked off the other board members..."

"*Trebly's* on the board now?" Brooks asked in disbelief. Next someone was going to tell him the Webers were on it.

"Well, not anymore," Burroughs said.

Hey hey hey, Smith said.

Brooks shook his head. *Not now.*

I figured it out, Smith said. *I solved the mystery.*

They're picking off Reticent agents, right?

No. Zephyr and Burroughs are fine. Trebly was public relations.

"Are you okay?" Burroughs asked. "You're staring at nothing again."

"Hang on," Brooks said. "Eddie's thinking."

"Oh," Lemon said. "Wait, what?"

"Do you mean to say that Mr. Smith lives?" Patience asked.

"Yeah. He's in The Afterlife™ in my head."

"Did you intend to discuss this with us?" Patience asked.

"Hang on. Like I said... Eddie's thinking."

"That's a first," Lemon jeered.

Hey, I can still hear her, Smith complained.

"He can still hear you," Brooks said.

"Good!" Lemon said, folding her arms. "Eddie, you're a glorbdink."

Brooks continued in his thoughts. *So... what does PR have to do with this?*

Smith echoed Zane's words to him: *PR has everything to do*

with everything! I'm thinking the immortals hired Trebly to work the PR angle then killed her once she gave them a good idea.

That makes zero sense.

Your face makes zero sense, Smith said.

He was just trying to be an ass, but Smith felt terrible when he realized Brooks's mismatched eyes could have made that a literal statement. *Oh, shit. I'm sorry. Anyway, I just have a hunch and if they did what I think they did, they won't have put the portal here. They'll have gone for maximum visibility and someone the Reticent wouldn't mind slandering...*

Godwin Zane, Brooks said. *He called them out.*

As he finished that thought, another dimensional rift opened over lower Manhattan. A giant beam of emptiness shot into the air, its epicenter just above Zane Tower.

"How long did they pay for?" Brooks asked.

"Six minutes," Burroughs said.

That wasn't enough time to get over there, but they started running anyway.

Godwin Zane was reconfiguring his maze when the phone rang. He ignored the first two calls, opting to continue moving virtual walls on his tablet as workers followed his lead and moved actual walls downstairs. He wanted nothing to do with the man on the other end of the line, but the third time the phone rang, he answered.

"I told you," he said. "I won't even consider building a robot until you finish the list."

"You haven't looked outside in the last minute, have you?" Brooks asked.

"Why would I?" Zane asked, walking toward the window. "What, do I just spend my entire day staring wistfully out the windo—oh hell." He paused. Across the street, dozens of office workers' faces were pressed against glass. At street level, hundreds of New Yorkers looked up. "Why is everyone staring at my building?"

"Look up."

"How am I supposed to look *up*? I'm indoors."

"Check your roof!"

Zane switched his tablet to roof cam. Sure enough, there was a growing spire of emptiness.

"What is that?" Zane asked.

"What does it look like?" Brooks said.

"Another rift."

"Yeah, it's another rift."

"Over my building!?"

"Yeah, can you shut it down?" Brooks asked. Attempting to maintain his composure, he added, "Please."

"Assuming I get there in time, what do I know about shutting down portals?"

"If it's anything like the last one, there should be an off switch," Brooks said.

"Of course. I bet it was red and clearly labeled too."

"Actually..." Brooks thought about that. "Yes." Prior to Six Blocks, the Reticent had been very good about building things up to code.

Instead of sighing, Zane said, "Sigh." With a dramatic motion, he threw back his cape and ran toward his private staircase. It was the only one in the building that afforded roof access, and he had no idea how someone could have gotten a portal generator on top of the building. Sure enough, though, there it was.

About six feet tall, the device hummed and whirred and occasionally made a noise that sounded like SPLOINK as it shot a dimensional rift straight up into the air. The device was cylindrical and grey, which Zane appreciated, but there didn't seem to be an off switch.

"There aren't any buttons at all," he said.

"None?" Brooks asked.

"None."

"The immortals must have sabotaged it," Brooks said.

Burroughs mumbled something about "budget cuts" in the background.

The rift, having reached its maximum height, began to stretch outward. This one was big, and soon it hovered over the entirety of New York City as well as parts of New Jersey.

"Hello?" Zane spoke at silence. "What am I supposed to do?"

"Hang on," Brooks said.

Zane tapped his fingers against the device, waiting. In the background of the call, Burroughs harassed Zephyr for details but came up empty.

"We don't know," Brooks said.

"Can I melt it?" Zane asked.

"Hang on," Brooks said.

There was a muffled "can he melt it?" and some arguing before Brooks returned to the line.

"We don't know," Brooks said.

The rift grew and grew.

"Come on," Zane said. "This thing is hovering over Ohio by now. Can I melt it?"

"I don't want to say yes, but..."

"I'm going to melt it."

Zane pressed his hands against the tube and thought about melting things. Nothing happened.

"Sigh," he said.

"What?" Brooks asked.

"I can't do it."

"Why not?"

"I can't control my powers," Zane said. "I just... melt stuff when I'm emotional."

"The prospect of the world ending isn't enough to make you feel emotional?" Brooks wondered.

"No?"

Brooks thought for a moment, then unleashed a tirade. "Your movies suck. Your building is ugly. The scenarios in The Afterlife™ are dumb—"

I put most of those in there, Smith said, offended.

"—Your mazes aren't even challenging. You're probably bad in bed."

Definitely, Smith said.

Hmm? Brooks wondered.

"Well, this is working," Zane said, his hands aglow. "Also, screw you. I'm definitely not building a cyborg now."

"Robot," Brooks corrected.

With that, Zane gave the portal generator a bear hug and soon there was an orange glow at the base of immense blackness. The metal began to warp and the SPLOINK sounds became more and more frequent, like the machine was popping metallic popcorn.

"I think it's working," he said.

Soon, the whole thing began to melt. But even as the generator collapsed into itself, the rift did not disappear.

"Um," Zane said. "The generator's gone but—"

"I can see," Brooks said. "Shit."

"Wait."

"Is that—"

The glow began reaching upward into the emptiness. Within moments, orange really was the new black as the entire eastern seaboard became blanketed in the glow of Zane's magma powers.

"Hello?" Brooks asked.

"I don't know what's happening," Zane said. "I'm not even touching it anymore."

Hey, you want to marry me before the world ends?

Jesus, Eddie.

"Can you... take it back?" Brooks asked.

Zane responded in a huff. "What part of 'I can't control

my powers' don't you understand?"

He heard Brooks mutter something in Spanish as the glow dissipated and fell to Earth.

50 / SOMETHING DRAMATIC

Nobody died, for a change. When the group of detectives arrived at Zane Tower, it was intact. Everything that had been hit by the glowing wave was intact. It made no sense, and there was no one around who could make sense of it.*

"Let us bypass the maze," Brooks said into his phone.

"Nobody bypasses the maze," Zane said.

Use the laundry chute, Smith said.

Two hours later, Brooks broke into Zane's office. Burroughs, Lemon, and Patience followed.

"What happened?" Brooks asked.

"Hell if I know." Zane chugged from a gallon jug of kombucha. "I'm ruined, though."

"How do you figure?" Burroughs asked.

Like any good person experiencing a personal crisis, Zane was simultaneously watching television and browsing Craigslist on his tablet. He gestured at the TV screen, where a trio of talking heads—each in a framed square in front of an American flag—engaged in a shouting match.

"It was Zane the whole time!" one shouted.

"I'm inclined to agree," another said.

"I do think it looks bad," the last one said. "But we don't know. He did invent The Afterlife™ so I'm not sure we can declare him a bad guy just yet."

"I'm calling it now. He did it out of guilt! This guy goes on a huge crusade about figuring out who was responsible for Six Blocks. It seems like a pretty clear frame job to me. We

---

* Two months later, scientists would determine that the rift possessed heat absorption abilities. What fell to Earth were heatless bits of magma dust, and so nobody was burned. Scientists would then determine that they were sick and tired of being scientists in a world where the science of things clearly didn't matter.

know Zane was trying to acquire the property underneath the Reticent—"

An announcer interrupted and the three squares moved aside. "—Breaking information. I'm told we have a receipt of a business transaction between Godwin Zane and the Reticent that appears to show him paying that organization to open a rift over Manhattan."

"Oh, fuck me," Zane said.

Don't do it, Smith warned.

Hmm?

At the bottom of the screen, Zane Industries stock (NASDAQ: ZAN) dropped one hundred points. The squares retook the screen and the pundits resumed shouting at each other.

"I'm ruined," Zane repeated.

"Would it help if I told you your business survives?" Lemon asked.

Brooks chastised her. "No spoilers!"

"What?" Zane asked.

"She's from the future," Brooks said. "Don't worry about it."

Zane could practically hear a record scratch in his head. "Waitaminute. You're a cyborg."

"Mmhmm."

"Your boyfriend was immortal until he wasn't."

"Yeah."

"Your daughter is from the future."

"Yes."

"And that one?" Zane asked, gesturing at Patience.

"From the past," Brooks said.

Patience blushed. "Nice to meet you, sir."

"Of course," Zane said. It explained the frock.

Zane wallowed in his pity for a few minutes as the group watched more and more talking heads eviscerate him on camera. Then came another BREAKING NEWS flash.

"—Reports coming in from all over the east coast of the United States. It appears that some people who were exposed to the particulate released from Zane Tower are exhibiting strange behavior."

"Oh no," Zane said.

On screen, cell phone footage of a young girl in a suburban back yard appeared. One moment she was swinging on a swing set, the next she was shooting laser beams from her eyes. That scene was followed by more cell phone footage: a utility worker growing antlers and becoming stuck in a power line. At the bottom of the screen, ZAN dropped another fifty points.

"I'm ruined," Zane repeated.

No one had anything comforting to offer, nor did they want to walk out on the billionaire and draw attention to themselves in the middle of his emotional breakdown. The result was ten minutes of five people just sitting around, occasionally clearing a throat or scratching a nose as the news played in the background.

Eventually, Zane's keen capacity for distraction overcame his grief. He stood up with flair, giving everyone the impression he had a light bulb illuminating over his head. "I have to do something to get my approval rating back up," he said.

"Something like...?" Burroughs asked.

"Something dramatic." Zane put his hand to his chin, pondering. He removed it and pointed at Brooks. "You."

"You're not doing me," Brooks said.

Good call, Smith said.

"No. I need your help," Zane said.

Brooks sighed. "With what?"

"How crazy is your cyborg strength?"

"Above average?" Brooks guessed. "I don't have a handbook. Why?"

"People keep telling me I should help," Zane said.

"Because you call yourself a superhero?" Burroughs asked.

"...Yes."

"You actually want to be a superhero?" Brooks asked.

"No," Zane said. "I can't control my powers. I want to form a superhero team of people who can. This lot is all the proof I need that there's a bunch of weird shit out there."

"You're not using us as proof," Brooks warned. There was no way he would allow Patience and Lemon to be thrust into that kind of spotlight.

"No. Not what I meant."

Zane's proposal was a classic *quid pro quo*. If Brooks would join his superhero team and work hard to save lives and improve Zane's PR, Zane would, in return, develop a Robotic Body Solution™ to contain Smith's mind.

"Does it pay?" Brooks asked.

"No," Zane said. "But your boyfriend can keep his job."

I don't want it, Smith said.

Brooks thought about it for a moment. "Deal."

Hey! Smith complained.

I love you, but you have got to get out of here at some point.

Smith observed his surroundings—he was re-enacting *Space Jam*—and shrugged. *Yeah, that's fair.*

"What are you going to call the team?" Burroughs asked.

The Mon-stars, Smith suggested.

No, Brooks warned.

"The Bedazzlers," Zane said.

Patience thought it was a perfectly nice name. Everyone not named Patience broke into raucous laughter.

"Why?" Brooks asked between gasps.

"After *Bedazzled*," Zane said. "It's my favorite movie."

Said no one ever, Smith said.

"Said no one ever," Brooks said aloud at the same time.

Get out of my head, they thought simultaneously.

"The original or the remake?" Burroughs asked.

Zane mocked her with an exaggerated, stupid voice. "'The original or the remake?'" His hands began to glow. "Get out."

"Let's go," Lemon said. "He obviously needs some time to *cool off*."

Solid pun, Smith said. *Tell her I'm proud.*

"Eddie said he's proud of you," Brooks said.

"Whatever," Lemon offered.

51 / POP TART & THE ACTIVATION ENERGY

At 55 Decatur Street, a family was putting itself back together. Lemon sat at the kitchen table with dozens of sheets of paper scattered around her. Each had the lyrics to a PT&TAE song scribbled down the best she could remember. She crossed out a few words and corrected them as Patience helped her by googling the other band members' contact information.

"Is this not Ms. Burroughs's job?" Patience asked.

"No," Lemon said. "The band manager finds gigs, not the band itself."

"Well, It says Mr. Jaxx Watkins is an attorney in Rhode Island," Patience said.

"That can't be right," Lemon said. "Jaxx was about the same age as Lemon." She believed that was the case, anyway. Following the Portland Craft Beer Wars of the twenty-second century, there were no surviving photos of Pop Tart & the Activation Energy.

"Please don't refer to yourself in the third person," Brooks said. "It's ridiculous." He stood at the refrigerator, staring at a selfie of himself and Smith at the beach that was pinned to it with a souvenir magnet.

"Please stop printing selfies," Lemon said. "It's ridiculous."

Brown, brown, brown, Brooks said.

It's not that bad, Smith said.

I look like a damned Weber.

"Are my eyes normal yet?" Brooks asked.

Lemon glanced over. "No."

Ugh. I'm a freak.

Yeah, it's the bicolored eyes that make you a freak, Smith mocked. *Not the cyborg thing or the fiancé in your head.*

Ugh.

Babe. It's fine.

"So?" Lemon asked, staring at Patience.

"Hmm?"

"Did you find another Jaxx?"

"Oh. Hmm." It was clear she had not.

Lemon reached across the table for her sister's laptop. "Are you even looking for—"

With the screen turned her way, Lemon saw what Patience was actually doing: writing fan mail to Godwin Zane.

"Are you serious?" she asked.

"Quite," Patience said. "It cannot be coincidence that a man whose shortened name is God has provided us with the afterlife and performed miracles."

"Hoo boy," Lemon said.

"I am starting a group for his worship."

"That's a cult," Brooks said.

"It's my new religion," Patience said.

"It's a cult," Brooks and Lemon said simultaneously.

"Either way, it's what I wish to do."

Brooks sighed. "Just don't go overboard with it."

"Oh, I shan't," Patience said. "I have heard far too many horrors of seafaring."

Brooks let his head crash into the freezer door. "*Híjole.*"

Está bien, Smith said.

I will never get used to that.

Seriously, Smith said. *You're going to be a superhero and save the world and shit. Maybe the eye thing can be your signature. They'll start calling you One Eye or...*

That's a cyclops.

Well, that name's taken.

I have two eyes! Brooks said.

You can be Heterochromia Man.

You know, for the only forty-year-old I know who still reads comic books, you are terrible at coming up with superhero names.

Hispandroid was a great name.

No it wasn't.

Ask Lemon.

"What do you think of 'Hispandroid?'" Brooks asked.

"Oh, they're awesome," she said. Hispandroid was a Lunan proto-punk folkwave band.

Hipster band, Brooks said. *I knew it.*

In their virtual world, Brooks and Smith visited Disney-world for the first time. Specifically, they were in line for Space Mountain. They had been for an hour. They shuffled a few inches ahead and tried to tune out the screaming virtual baby behind them.

Why did they program the lines in? Brooks asked.

Authentic experience? Smith put a hand on his shoulder. *Stop worrying.*

Who said I was worrying? I'm just asking about the line.

When you're worried you go on and on about shit that you don't care about. Smith took his partner's hand. *Listen. Saving people is the purpose you wanted and you're gonna be great at it.*

Yeah?

And I'll be there with you.

Until you get your very own robot body and leave me for a Roomba, Brooks said.

I do go wild when they spin.

52 / ONE WEDDING AND NO FUNERALS

The Afterlife™ base model headset was solid white and resembled a futuristic motorcycle helmet. There were, of course, upgrades available. For just $299.99 more, grieving relatives could interact with the deceased using a sleek chrome headset. For just $399.99 more than that, there was an officially licensed *Star Wars* rogue leader helmet. Charger not included.

"Put this on," Zane said, still annoyed that he was facilitating this. There was an instruction manual, if anyone would bother reading it.

"Must I?" Patience asked.

"It's the only way for you to interface with The Afterlife™."

"Must I?" Patience repeated.

"You have to be there," Lemon said, slipping on her own headset.

Patience knew her sister was right. She ran her fingers across the headset and eyed it for a moment. Eventually, she slipped it partway on, then back off again. She stared at Lemon, who was already bravely logged in, sighed, and placed the headset all the way on. In an instant, the Puritan was at the beach for her first non-Puritan wedding.

Attendance was excellent, all things considered. All things including that it was a virtual event featuring one dead and one cyborg groom, neither of whom had very many friends on account of their working as undercover paranormal investigators their entire lives. Forty people showed up, most of whom were irrelevant to this story.

Patience seated herself in the front row, next to Lemon.

242 \\ MARTINA FETZER

"Do you know any of these people?"

Lemon shrugged. "Burroughs," she said, eyeing her new band manager from across the aisle. She gave her a wave, and Burroughs raised her own hand in acknowledgement.

"Is it not odd that we've never met any of them?"

Lemon shrugged. The only thing she found odd was that the O'Gradys weren't invited, but Brooks and Smith had determined that an elderly couple already near death didn't need the shock of finding out that their dead son wasn't actually dead but was living inside a cyborg.

The faux beach's weather was perfect, of course. Sunny, no chance of rain. The tide would never come in and force everyone's feet into sludgy sand. The wind would never swell and knock over the altar. A seagull would never fly by and poop on someone's head. It was a little too perfect. Luckily, everything Smith touched turned into a dumpster fire.

Brooks knocked at a door in the virtual cabana just down the beach from the ceremony site. "What are you doing in there?" he asked. "I'm pretty sure you can change clothes just by thinking about it in here."

"Not the issue," Smith said from the other side.

"Then what?"

Smith cracked the door. "I'm not done."

Brooks opened it all the way. "Done what?" He looked at Smith, standing there in a tan linen suit, and smiled.

"I think I'm too white for this color," Smith complained.

"You look great." Brooks gave him a peck on the cheek. "What aren't you done with?"

Smith cracked his knuckles in the air and looked away. "I, uh…" He continued his fake stretching routine, avoiding eye contact. "I haven't written any vows."

"What!?"

"I know."

"You've had a month."

"I know."

"You have *nothing* better to do."

"I know."

"Literally nothing."

"I know."

"Because you're dead."

"Yeah."

"People are waiting."

"I know."

"This was your idea in the first place."

"Help?" Smith asked, for the first time in a long time.

Brooks sighed. "What do you have so far?"

Smith's eyes shot around for a moment as he tried to find a good answer. He didn't. "Nothing."

"I have to say I'm not really feeling the love," Brooks said.

"I'm not a writer," Smith said. "You have to be feely and shit and I keep trying but I can't come up with anything." He paused for sincerity. "Please don't think that means I don't love you."

Brooks chuckled. "I know you do. Here." He handed over a slip of paper. "Use mine."

"What are you gonna do then?"

"I'll figure something out," Brooks said.

"I can't read words about me about you. It'll make you look bad when you make something up on the spot."

"No it won't and yes you can. Just change the relevant bits."

Smith scanned the paper. "This is... If I weren't an asshole I'd be tearing up right now. Do you mean all of this?"

"Yeah," Brooks said.

Smith teared up. Just a little.

"See? You're not an asshole," Brooks said. "Come on."

Outside, everything was still too damn perfect. At Smith's request, a seagull had been programmed to fly by and poop on someone. Its victim was Mike, who still hung around Godwin Zane in hopes of making the cut for *Look 8 Me!*.

With a SPLORT, the shoulder of his black suit was ruined.

"Damn it," Mike said.

As he and Smith walked together, Brooks asked, "Who invited Mike?"

"I have no idea," Smith said, "but I'm glad the seagull picked him."

At the altar, Zane prepared to officiate. In her seat, Patience muttered a little prayer for him. In her seat, Burroughs muttered something about Brooks and Smith's terrible decision-making skills. No longer in her seat, Lemon played a violin cover of Pop Tart & the Activation Energy's "My Two Dads." No one could identify the tune, but they nevertheless found it to be lovely. It was, in all honesty, much better without Lemon's lyrics.

"Okay, let's do this," Zane said.

Smith whispered to Brooks. "We couldn't find anyone else to run this thing?"

"He's ordained," Brooks said. "Somehow. Plus, he was free."

"What? How?"

"Paid in publicity," Brooks said.

Half the audience scowled at New York's newest and biggest enemy. The other half patiently waited for digital hors d'oeuvres. Weddings are traditionally boring for guests, and this one was no exception.

Smith read his plagiarized vows first:

"E—Arturo... the day we met was one of the hardest days of my life. In a lot of ways, I'm still not over the things that happened that day. But when I look back on that, on all of the terrible things I have endured, there is a bright spot. It's you. Out of bad things can come good, and E—Turo, you are the good. You might not think so. I know you'd argue with me on that, but you are. You always are. You always have been. You always will be. I love you, and I'm going to keep you."

Brooks hadn't come prepared with a second set of vows, so when his turn came, he recited his original creation—the exact words Smith had just spoken—in Spanish. His two tías from Flatbush beamed, and most everyone else was left confused.

Zane waved his hand. "I now pronounce you gay married."

For a moment, the pair ignored that as they shared a kiss.

Then Smith turned to Zane. "You don't have to specify *gay* married."

"What am I, an expert at this?"

"Obviously not."

"This photo had better be on *Entrepreneurity Hour*," Zane said. That show, following a brief hiatus, had returned with a new, human host.

Brooks took Smith's hand. "Come on."

They walked, as the crowd cheered, into a perfect sunset.

While they carried on, another seagull flew by and made its mark.

"Damn it," Mike said.

EPILOGUE

Godwin Zane readied himself for his press conference by drinking three glasses of kombucha and using a head massager on himself. It wasn't that he was nervous. He'd held plenty of press conferences, and plenty of them had taken place when the public wasn't happy with him. What he was concerned about was making an ass of himself. Yes, he always made an ass of himself, but that was the thing. He *couldn't* make an ass of himself. PR was everything, and the announcement of his superpowers and the formation of The Bedazzlers had to be handled *just so*. He needed to come across as mature and subdued. He turned on the TV in hopes of clearing his mind.

On screen, he'd been beaten to the punch on at least one account. The headline read 'THE IMMORTAL MAN' and a man who looked like a fatter version of Edward Smith spoke.

It wasn't Smith, of course. He was dead and on a virtual honeymoon in Sweden with Brooks. The man on screen was Hudson Marrow, the man whose disappearance everyone had forgotten to investigate. He wasn't dead, but he had left the Reticent in hopes of making a fortune doing something else. That something else unfolded as Zane watched.

"Watch," Hudson said.

The immortal man took a gun and—to everyone's horror—shot himself in the face. The screen cut to black with a loud BEEEEEEEEP as the station censored the scene. A short moment later, the footage returned. Hudson stood, unscathed. He took questions.

"When did you first find out about your superpower?" a reporter asked.

"When I was just a few years old," Hudson explained.

"Given recent events, do you plan on using this ability for good?"

"Of course," Hudson said. "I can't sit idly by anymore. Not with everything that's been happening. I've called you all here to announce that I'm forming a team of people with abilities..."

"Damn it," Zane said.

APPENDIX I / APPLICATION

Zane Industries Personality Profile for Job Applicants

Please fill in the following form to the best of your ability.

Name (Last, First, M): _____

Birthdate (YYYY/DD-MM): _____

Address: _____

Zip Code: _____

City: _____ State: _____

Phone Number: _____

E-Mail Address: _____

Blood Type: _____

MBTI: _____ Favorite Food: _____

Height: __'___" Weight: _____ kgs Eye Color: _____

Grey Skin? Y N

Your idea of heaven is:

_____

Measurements: Chest ____ in   Waist ____ in   Hips ____ in

Inseam ____ in   Arms ____ in   Thighs ____ in

Are you afraid of bees? Y   N

Are you afraid of magma? Y   N

Are you familiar with the *Look at Me!* film series? Y   N

If not, why?

_____

What is your favorite thing about the *Look at Me!* film series?

_____

Have you ever been arrested? Y   N

Was it for hilarious reasons? Y   N

What is your favorite Pokémon? _____

Would you eat a Pokémon? Y   N

In a thirteen-page essay, explain how Depeche Mode has personally impacted your life. Use the reverse of this page and attach additional sheets of paper.

APPENDIX II / PT&TAE GREATEST HITS*

Track Listing:
1. "Duke and Duchess"
2. "Bridge Jumper"
3. "The Spectacular Failure of Elon Musk"
4. "Staten Island Dumpster"
5. "Puritans and Pilgrims Aren't the Same"
6. "Ant Trap"
7. "My Two Dads"
8. "Vamp Ire"
9. "Immortality Rally"
10. "River Trash Gold Mine"
11. "I Liked the Moon Before It Was Cool"
12. "Life of an Olympic Curling Champion"
13. "Ballad of the Glorbdinks"
14. "Two-Eyed Cyborg"
15. "I Miss the Future"
16. "I Don't Miss the Future"
17. "29th Amendment"
18. "The Questatement"

---

* Never released due to lack of demand.

APPENDIX III / THE AFTERLIFE™
BASE SCENARIOS

1. Beach Relaxation
2. Running with a Dog
3. Darmok and Jalad at Tanagra
4. Movie Theater
5. Pool Filled with Jello
6. Christmas Morning
7. Road Trip
8. Cabin in the Woods
9. Clouds and Angels and Shit
10. Disneyworld
11. Baking Cookies
12. Massage Parlor
13. Straight-up Hell (Heaven for Satanists)
14. Gone Fishin'
15. Kittens and More Kittens
16. Hot Tub Time Machine
17. Blood Orgy
18. Elysium
19. Gladiator Fight
20. Becoming POTUS
21. Nothing Ever Happens
22. Labyrinthine Mansion
23. Seafaring
24. Simple Farm Life
25. Fame and Fortune
26. Sherlock Holmes Holodeck Adventure
27. Floating through Space
28. Jew Heaven
29. Train Robbery

30. Narnia
31. Good Mormon Heaven
32. Mediocre Mormon Heaven
33. Shit-tier Mormon Heaven
34. Athletics
35. Swimming with Dolphins
36. Freeing Willy
37. Coney Island without Syringes
38. Super Mario Bros. 3
39. Snowball Fight
40. The Price Is Right
41. Cozy Sweater
42. Titanic Before It Sank
43. Santa Claus
44. Ski Lodge with Fireplace
45. Nothing But Shrimp
46. Horseback Riding
47. Ewok Target Practice
48. Total Darkness and Silence
49. Laser Light Show (on Pot)
50. Grand Theft Auto
51. Desert Oasis
52. Aurora Borealis
53. Sea-ciety
54. Regular Orgy
55. Sweden
56. Taco Bar
57. Video Game Night
58. Carpentry
59. Revel as Assholes You Hate Are Tortured
60. Biker Bar
61. Rainforest Adventure (No Snakes)
62. Space Jam
63. Firefly Season Two
64. Mountain Climb

ACKNOWLEDGEMENTS

This is my second book. All of the thanks from my first book apply to this one, but I'm aiming to fill an entire paragraph here, so... Ellen Campbell came through again and reminded me that people cannot, in fact, put their head in their heads. Thanks to Josh, Erinn, and Amanda for forcing me to show myself in public, where books are sold. Thanks to Lianna-bob, Defne, Adam, and Katherine for beta-testing this story.

Finally, thanks to everyone who came back for a second book. You are the real MVPs. If you enjoyed yourself, I'd love a review on Amazon or Goodreads. If you didn't enjoy yourself, I'm sorry.

Brooks and Smith return in:
A Genie Ruins Everything (Book 3)
Fun Times in a Dystopic Hellscape (Book 4)

Monochrome returns in:
The Bedazzlers

For announcements about new projects,
sign up for the mailing list at martina-fetzer.com, or
scan this little QR code...